PRAISE FOR AB

"Abby Brooks is a wizard with Beyond Us—entertaining and pure enjoyment!"

ADRIANA LOCKE—USA TODAY AND WASHINGTON POST BESTSELLING AUTHOR

"A masterful blend of joy and angst.

PRAISE FOR *ABBY BROOKS*

"As a voracious reader it is not unusual for me to read 5-7 books per week. What is unusual is for me to be thinking about the writing and characters long after I've finished the book. With just the perfect amount of angst and remarkable character development, Abby Brooks has crafted a masterpiece..."

PRAISE FOR *BEYOND WORDS*

"Once again Abby Brooks creates a world filled with beautifully written characters that you cannot help but fall in love with."

PRAISE FOR *BEYOND LOVE*

"A lovely story of growing beyond your past, taking control of your life, and allowing yourself to be loved for the person you are."

MELANIE MORELAND—NEW YORK TIMES BESTSELLING AUTHOR, IN PRAISE OF *WOUNDED*

"Abby Brooks writes books that draw readers right into the story. When you read about her characters, you want them to be your friends."

PRAISE FOR ABBY BROOKS

FATE

A HUTTON FAMILY ROMANCE

ABBY BROOKS

Copyright © 2022 by Abby Brooks

All rights reserved.

No part of this book may be reproduced in any form or by any electronic or mechanical means, including information storage and retrieval systems, without written permission from the author, except for the use of brief quotations in a book review.

Cover image copyright © 2022 by WANDER AGUIAR PHOTOGRAPHY LLC

Cover design by Abby Brooks

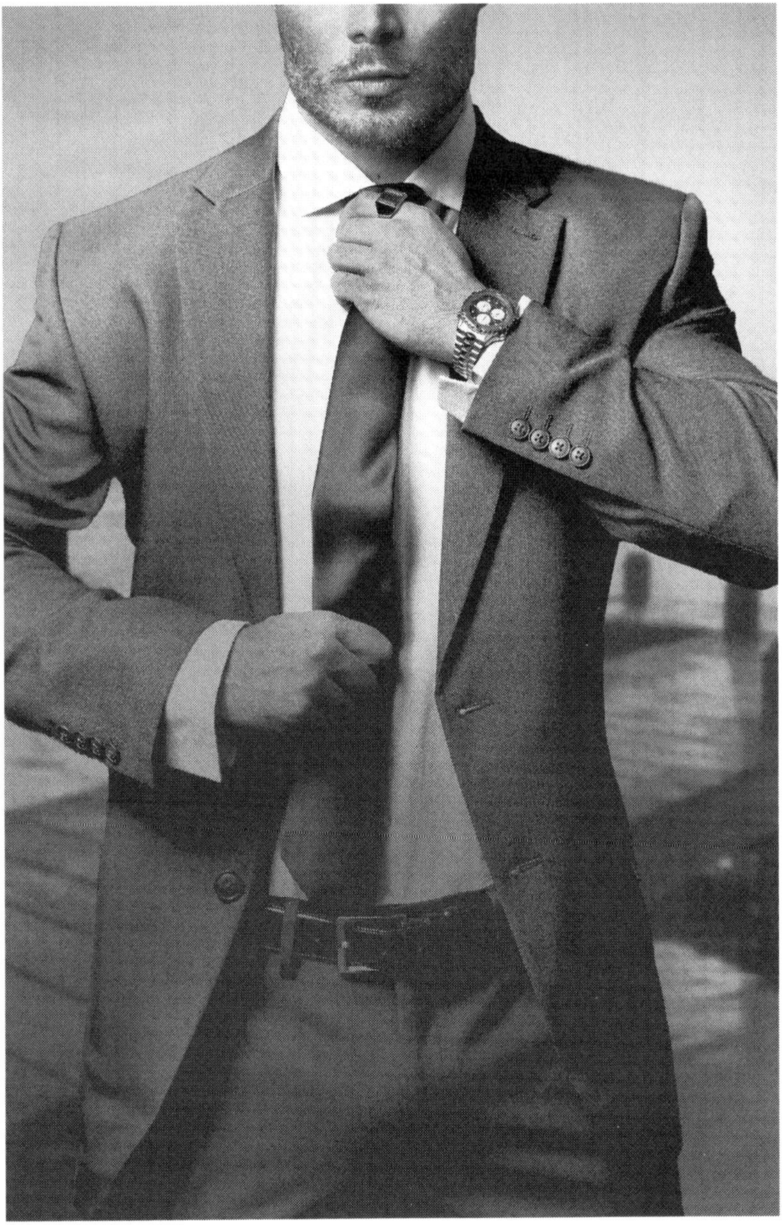

CONNECT WITH ABBY BROOKS

Abby Brooks writes contemporary romance about real people in relatable situations. With equal parts humor and heat, her books provide an emotional smorgasbord readers love. You'll laugh, cry, and cheer her characters on as they chase down their happily ever after.

Abby lives in Ohio with an amazing husband, three fabulous kids, and a stinker of a cat. In her spare time you'll find her messing around outside, dancing in the kitchen when she should be paying attention to cooking, and enjoying the company of her family.

For more books and updates:
abbybrooksfiction.com

facebook.com/abbybrooksauthor
instagram.com/xo_abbybrooks
tiktok.com/@abbybrooksauthor

Books by

ABBY BROOKS

THE HUTTON FAMILY SECOND GENERATION

Fate

WILDROSE LANDING

Fearless

Shameless

Reckless

THE HUTTON FAMILY

Beyond Words

Beyond Love

Beyond Now

Beyond Us

Beyond Dreams

It's Definitely Not You

The Hutton Family Series - Part 1

The Hutton Family Series - Part 2

A BROOKSIDE ROMANCE

Wounded

Inevitably You

This Is Why

Along Comes Trouble

Come Home To Me

A Brookside Romance - the Complete Series

WILDE BOYS WITH WILL WRIGHT

Taking What Is Mine

Claiming What Is Mine

Protecting What Is Mine

Defending What Is Mine

Wilde

THE MOORE FAMILY

Finding Bliss

Faking Bliss

Instant Bliss

Enemies-to-Bliss

THE LONDON SISTERS

Love Is Crazy (Dakota & Dominic)

Love Is Beautiful (Chelsea & Max)

Love Is Everything (Maya & Hudson)

The London Sisters - the Complete Series

IMMORTAL MEMORIES

Immortal Memories Part 1

Immortal Memories Part 2

AS WREN WILLIAMS

Bad, Bad Prince

Woodsman

Fate

ABBY BROOKS

CHAPTER ONE

Angela

I ruined everything.

Shattered my father's dream.

Obliterated the family legacy.

I'm supposed to be the one who drives us forward, into our future, but with one hastily scrawled signature, I delivered a killing blow to The Hutton Hotel.

The knowledge keeps me awake at night and waits for me each morning. Taunting me. Teasing me. Tugging at my heart the way a child tugs at his mother's hand.

Needy. Insistent. Incessant.

You ruined everything, Angel. Nothing will be the same and it's all because of you.

I'll do whatever it takes to solve the problem I

created. I'll sacrifice my time, my energy, my entire life if that's what it takes, but I will not let the hotel go down without a fight.

I'm a Hutton. That's what we do.

"Angela." Dad's frown says he's called my name more than once.

Sitting across from him at his desk, I shuffle through a stack of papers—projections, estimates, the financial future of our hotel laid out in black and white. I've spent the last week going over them. Tweaking them. Looking at the numbers from different angles.

No matter what I do, it's not good.

"Yeah. Sorry." I blink, tap the papers on my father's desk to straighten them, then lay them flat. "I'm listening."

Lucas Hutton is an intimidating man. A Marine, injured in the line of duty, he approaches everything with a "take the hill or die trying" attitude. Fatherhood. The hotel.

Fixing the mistake I created while reminding me he still trusts me.

"You've got the lead in tomorrow's meeting with Garrett Cooper. Wyatt and I will be in the room with you, but you're in charge."

So, basically my worst nightmare.

I sigh. Pinch the corners of the papers, straightening them even though they're already straight. "Dad, I—"

The slow lift of his brow stops my rebuttal in its tracks. "You're taking the lead."

So much swims in the undercurrent of his words. Dad wants me to know he still has faith in me. He still believes in me. He wants me back on the horse before fear stops me from believing in myself.

Too late for that.

A few months ago, I thought I had everything under control. I thought my education meant I was infallible. That my dream of expanding our hotel into other markets couldn't fail.

Overconfidence joined hands with naivete and blinded me to the truth. Now I second-guess every idea I come up with. Like this meeting with Garrett Cooper from Vision Enterprise.

Another company, so much like the one that set this disaster in motion. I researched the hell out of them before reaching out and found nothing but positives, but I'm still nervous. What if I'm making another mistake?

Dad steeples his fingers under his chin, staring me down as if I was a Marine under his command rather than his daughter. As a kid, his intensity overwhelmed me. As I got older, I understood that under his stern face hid a heart that adored his only child and a mind so full of deep thoughts, he couldn't always find the words to let them out. "Let's go over the plan of attack one more time. Lay it out for me step by step."

I square my shoulders. Back straight. Chin up. Don't let him see the doubt. I will fake it 'til I make it and The Hutton Hotel is safe. "Lesson one. Assume Garrett Cooper is the enemy, from the start."

Pleased, Dad nods. "He'll promise us the stars and the moon, but at the end of the day, he's here to make money for *his* company. We can profit off that if we're smart, but these investment guys are—"

"All about themselves. I know that now." I cross my legs and fold my hands in my lap, painting a picture of calm. Of confidence. "A wise man once told me, 'Lessons learned the hard way are lessons that stick.'"

Dad smiles as I repeat the advice he gave me every time I ran into trouble as a kid. The crinkles in the corners of his eyes reassure me. No matter what happens, he will always love me.

"What else?"

"Everything Mr. Cooper says, everything he puts into writing, it's designed to make me think he's on our side, but he's not. Verify everything until he proves himself trustworthy." It's a shitty way of operating in the world, but one I'm going to have to get used to.

"I know that's not natural for you, Angel. You trust

everyone to be exactly who and what they say they are. And sometimes they are..."

"Just not in business. I know that now."

And I should have known it then. If I hadn't been so trusting, so overconfident, so stupidly naïve...

"What else?" Dad's voice is gentler now, like he knows what's going through my mind and wants to soften the blow.

I hang my head. This is so remedial, so humiliating. I know this stuff. I do. It's all so basic. And yet, I trusted everything the man from the last investment company said, saw him as a friend just like he wanted me to, then failed to vet a contract change and here we are. Staring at the end of a legacy instead of the beginning of our future, in a private meeting with my dad, brushing up on the basics before the most important meeting of my life. "All contracts, all revisions, everything, it all goes through the lawyers before a signature hits the line."

Dad sits back in his chair, threading his hands behind his head. "Exactly."

And just like that, my mask of professionalism falls and I'm a little girl talking to her father, mortified to have let her family down. "I'm so sorry I messed up and I hate that this conversation is necessary. I know you wouldn't even meet with this new guy if I hadn't put us in a position to need the money—"

I feel physically sick, swiping at the tears forming in my eyes. For the hundredth time that hour, I inwardly promise to devote all my energy into turning the ship around. I'll sacrifice everything if I have to.

"Angel." Dad leans forward to take my hand. "Mistakes are part of life. You aren't perfect, and no one in this family expects you to be…except yourself."

"I just feel like such an idiot."

"Good."

"Good?" The word bounces into the conversation on a laugh. That was not the response I expected.

"You're an intelligent woman and you know that. But that feeling? The one that keeps you awake at night, reminding you that you're better than the situation you're in?"

I nod. I haven't told anyone I'm having trouble sleeping. Somehow, Dad knowing brings me comfort.

"Rocket fuel, Angel." Sunlight cascades through the window behind him, like a smile from the universe. "That's what that feeling is. You have a choice in how it affects you. You can wallow in it, let it eat you up from the inside out, then let it destroy you when it finally explodes. Because it *will* explode. Or you can harness that power. Let it propel you forward, boosting your momentum while you put one foot in front of the other, until you bring your dream to fruition. It's your choice, but you have to make it. Nothing happens without action."

Fear whispers that the last choice I made put us in this situation, but I brush it away. After all, I'm the daughter of Cat and Lucas Hutton, people who don't understand the meaning of the word quit.

"I'm gonna harness it." Pride surges through me. I can do this. I can fix the things I've broken. Every time I look at this Garrett Cooper from Vision Enterprise, I'll remember he's not a friend. I won't even see him as a person. I'll imagine him as the vulture he is, ready to profit off someone else's blood, sweat, and tears.

He's not here to help.

He's here to make money off us.

Sure, we might arrive at a mutually beneficial deal, but only if I remain vigilant.

And I *will* remain vigilant.

I refuse to be the Hutton who ruins the family.

"Good." Dad's smile says he knew that'd be my answer. "Now, walk me through the pitch and projections one more time."

CHAPTER TWO

Garrett

"I think Melinda's cheating on me." I pinch my phone between my ear and my shoulder while adjusting the strap on my carry-on bag. Despite an uneventful trip to the Keys, I'm ready to collect my luggage and get the hell out of the airport.

Too many people.

Too much recycled air.

Not enough decency to go around.

The world's going to hell in a handbasket. Don't believe me? Fly commercial.

My sister Charlie snorts in my ear. "I hate to say I saw it coming..."

"But you'll find a way, because you love being right?"

She scoffs. "Not as much as you, Bear. Not as much as you."

Shaking my head at the name I will never live down—a shortening of Gare Bear, a nickname I hate even more than Bear itself—I step onto an escalator on my way to baggage claim.

"Rubbing my constant rightness in your face wouldn't be very sisterly of me," Charlie continues, "especially when I'm right about something as despicable as infidelity. But I definitely saw this coming." She pauses, then whispers, "I hate it for you, though. I really do. You know. After Elizabeth..."

Anticipating Charlie's train of thought, I shift my phone to the other ear. Anything to avoid hearing that name and the onslaught of pain it brings. "It's not a big deal. The Melinda thing."

"Why do you keep choosing these awful women? You have to know they're only in it for your money."

Of course they're only in it for the money. Everyone's only in it for the money, I think but don't say. Charlie already believes I'm a jaded fuck. No need to fuel that fire.

I step off the escalator and pause until I find a sign directing me to baggage claim. "Work's my priority, Charlie. It's what I'm good at."

Sarcasm drips from Charlie's deep, sad, slow sigh.

"And to think, I actually thought this one would last forever."

When I first told my sister I was seeing someone, she confiscated my phone and changed Melinda's contact name to "The Future Mrs. Cooper." It was a joke, because of how quickly I cycle through women after…well…after *Elizabeth*. Charlie thought it was hilarious, and honestly, I did too. Our brother Connor never understood what was so funny about the whole thing, but he's a serial monogamist. In his opinion, my dating style is "something to address," not joke about.

"I *have* found my forever." This one's going to piss Charlie off, but that's what she gets for using that fucking nickname even though I'm a grown ass man.

"I swear to God, Bear. If you say work's your forever, I'll fly to the Keys and beat you up for being a moron."

My jaw clenches. I've built myself from nothing. Amassed a fortune after growing up in a small town in the middle of nowhere. Morons don't end up where I am. I'd eviscerate anyone else for calling me one, but Charlie's "little sister pass" means I'll keep my mouth shut.

For now.

I arrive at baggage claim alongside a frazzled mother cradling an infant while clutching the hand of a travel-crazed toddler. The little guy looks me straight in the eye and shoves a finger into his nose. Nice.

Charlie clears her throat. "You're in Florida for what? A week?"

"Give or take. The initial meeting with the Huttons is tomorrow. If things go well, I might be here a little longer. If not..." I shrug as the cranky toddler yanks free of his mother's grasp. "I'll be back in Wildrose Landing before you know it."

God help me. I promised my family I'd take some time off after I'm done with this deal. They swear it'll be good for me, and my therapist agrees, but I don't see how. Not working makes me antsy. Restless. Somehow, they talked me into it anyway. I agreed to not only come home to my house in WRL before I head back to my apartment in the city, but that I'd "relax" while I'm there. Whatever that means. I haven't told my boss yet. Branson Masters already hates that I split my time between Wildrose and the city, but he deals with it because I'm the guy who put Vision Enterprise on the map.

"I can't believe the Hutton Hotel is in financial trouble." Charlie sounds so deflated you'd think it was *our* business about to go down the shitter.

Clenching my jaw, I glance at the time. When I called her to check in, I wasn't looking for a full-blown conversation. Not only am I in the middle of a crowded airport, but there are emails to check, messages to reply to. This little chat is costing me money. I clear my throat, prepared to end the call.

"I have such great memories of that place," Charlie continues, "and if your boss has his way, everything good about it will die as he squeezes the last dollar out of the name."

"Which is why I'm here. I won't let that happen. I have great memories too and will do everything in my power to make the deal fair for everyone. If Branson had given the job to Jordan Clement—" His name clamps my jaw shut as a ball of rage chases it up my throat. Fucking Clement. Fucking *Elizabeth*. I swallow hard and try again. "If that asshole got the job, the Hutton Hotel would be a soulless franchise faster than you can say I told you so."

"And we all know how fast I can say that."

I shake my head, chuckling at my little sister. "Exactly. Look. I gotta go. I just wanted you to know I landed. I'm here. I'm safe."

I pull the phone away to check how many messages are waiting for me as Charlie huffs in exasperation.

"But we didn't even talk about the Melinda thing! You're gonna drop a bomb like that and hang up?"

"Calling it a bomb makes it a bigger deal than it is. The relationship had come to its natural conclusion."

"Natural conclusion?" Charlie sighs dramatically.

"I don't know how you grew up in the same household as me and Connor and came out so…so cold."

"Wow. Thanks for that." I recoil, shaking my head like she landed a right hook. "That feels really fucking good, coming from my little sister."

"Hey, don't shoot the messenger. And you know I love you anyway."

We say our goodbyes and I end the call in time to catch the toddler climbing onto his mother's luggage. She's distracted, strapping her baby into a stroller, and the glint in her little boy's eyes says he's about to get into some trouble and knows it. Holding on to the extended handle for support, he pulls himself to stand on top of the suitcase.

The thing wobbles precariously.

"Hey now." I take an involuntary step forward and the little shit rocks back and forth, whooping in excitement. All he needs is some ketchup and mustard warpaint and he would look like Connor when he was little, playing his favorite game—and that never ended well. For anyone.

The suitcase hitches onto the wheels, then clatters onto the opposite edge and the kid tumbles backwards with a shriek. I lurch for him, my phone catapulting from my hands while I catch the little guy seconds before his head slams into the tile floor. His mother whirls when the suitcase topples over, clobbering the thousand-dollar extension of my brain.

"Jesse!" She rushes to me, swooping him out of my arms. "Oh my God! Are you okay?" She peers into his face, swiping his hair back from his forehead before crushing him to her chest. "Thank you so much for catching him," she says, breathless, her chest heaving and her eyes watering.

"Anyone would have done it." Though no one would have needed to if she was paying better attention. I rake a hand through my hair then stand the suitcase up and retrieve my phone.

Shit.

The screen isn't just cracked, it's fucking obliterated.

"Oh, no." The mother swallows hard as she follows my frowning gaze to the carnage. "Is it ruined?"

Ruined? It's decimated.

The screen won't recognize my touch and rewards the effort by sinking glass into my finger. I pinch the bridge of my nose and close my eyes. So much for checking in on work before I head for the hotel.

"It's fine," I growl.

"It doesn't look fine." She releases her little boy and stands.

The woman's baby is starting to wail, and her kid is

staring at the suitcase like he wants to go for another ride.

I'm done with this conversation. Time to disengage.

Over her shoulder, I spy my luggage coming down the belt. Perfect.

"Gonna wanna keep an eye on that one," I say, pointing to her son as he toddles off, then claim my bag and make my way to pick up my rental car.

After I sign the paperwork, the clerk—a twenty-something who hasn't once met my eyes—hands me the keys. "There you go, Mr. Hooper."

"Cooper. My last name's Cooper." I dangle the fob for inspection. "You sure this is supposed to go to me?"

"Sorry. Yeah. Cooper." The jerk dismisses me with a wave of his hand.

I stare, daring him to acknowledge me. To look at me. To offer a hint of customer service. I guaran-fuck-ing-tee the second he thinks he might weasel a tip out of me, his entire personality will change. It's the way it always goes. You're not even supposed to tip guys like this, but you better believe they expect it anyway.

"Is there anything else I can do for you?" The sarcastic lilt to his question solidifies my opinion of the man. He's part of the entitled, self-important, "I'm more important than anyone else" problem that's ruining the world.

"I need directions to somewhere that can take care of this." I place my phone on the counter and the man sneers.

"That's seen better days." He folds his arms over his chest and stares at the cracks spider webbing across the screen. "I don't think it's fixable."

"I'll buy a new one."

"Just like that, huh." He waves his hand. "Plonk down a grand like it's no big thing."

"It's not a big thing." I watch my statement land.

He's gauging who I am now. Asking himself if I'm lying. Wondering what he can get out of me if he treats me differently.

"Must be nice."

"It is. Directions?" I arch an eyebrow.

The asshole finally looks at me like I exist. "Of course, Mr. Cooper. I'm happy to be of assistance." He quickly prints out directions to several stores nearby and hands them over.

And that right there is why I put all my energy into my job. Two things are broken in my life: my phone and my relationship with Melinda.

I can use money to buy a new phone.

But I can't fix other people, not with all the money in the world.

I reach into my pocket, pull out my wallet and rifle through the bills like I'm deciding which one to hand over, then put the thing away with a smirk. The man gapes after me, but I refuse to feed the greed. I'm tired of being decent to assholes only for them to hold out their hand and expect more.

I scan the list of stores and pick the one at the top: Seaside Mobile. Time to replace my phone and get this shitshow back on track. Anything to ensure my meeting with the Huttons goes better than my arrival in the Keys.

CHAPTER THREE

Angela

"Sweet Jesus, that's a long line." My cousin Nick stops inside the door of Seaside Mobile and stares.

I pause beside him as the door swings closed. "I wonder what the maximum occupancy is here."

"Why?"

"I'd bet good money they're exceeding it."

The place crawls with customers and the single clerk behind the counter doesn't instill confidence. He moves at a snail's pace, bored—annoyed even—gaping at a young woman as she explains a problem with her tablet for the third time. The man standing behind her catches my attention. He's easily as tall as Nick's six-foot-three, with dark hair and a rugged jawline that hints at the kind of bone structure I love. Strong jaw.

Straight, angular nose. Full lips. Black dress slacks hug a fantastic ass and a white button-down drapes perfectly off broad shoulders. Everything about the guy screams "disgustingly rich with romance hero sex appeal."

"Let's get out of here." I give Nick's hand a tug. "I'll come back after I drop you at the airport."

"We're here. There's time. Let's get this taken care of." He throws an arm around my shoulders. "A brilliant businesswoman needs the right tool for the job and a five-year-old phone is not gonna cut it."

I laugh off his compliment and roll my eyes. "I have the education of a brilliant businesswoman, but a track record that belongs to someone more like him." I lower my voice, jerking my chin toward the clerk. Maybe the guy's having a bad moment. Maybe he kicks Seaside Mobile's ass every other day of the month. But something tells me we're looking at the best he has to offer.

"Angel—"

I lift a hand before Nick can continue. "Here's the thing though, having a crappy track record gives me something to overcome. And I'm good at overcoming things. Some might say I'm a master at overcoming things. The more I overcome, the better I get." I run a hand through my hair because come on now, how many times can one woman say 'overcome?' If only my mouth didn't have a mind of its own most days. "What

I'm trying to say is that I'm going to harness the rocket fuel of this mistake and let it launch me to success."

Nick's eyebrows hit his hairline. "You're going to do what now?"

"See, this feeling of having something to overcome…it's rocket fuel. I can let it destroy me or…" I trail off as my cousin looks more and more incredulous. "Or I can ride the rocket," I finish lamely. "To success."

"You want to ride the rocket to success." Nick can't hide his laughter now and I smooth my hands over my stomach before punching him in the arm.

"It sounded cooler when Dad said it."

"Obviously. Your dad's much cooler than you." Nick gives me a squeeze. "You're gonna have to come to terms with that, Angel."

Growing up, I loved that nickname. Angel, short for Angela, after my mom's mom, who passed away a few years before I was born. To my little ears, being called an angel made me feel like I could take care of the whole world if I wanted to—and oh man, did I want to. Still do. But one of my college professors suggested the name sounded "unprofessional," so with much reluctance, I switched back to Angela.

"Believe me. I'm fully aware I'm not living up to my dad. He would never be in the position I'm in."

Nick runs a hand over his freshly cropped hair, a clear sign he's frustrated. We were born one day apart.

Raised more like siblings than cousins. Our fathers are brothers, Lucas and Wyatt Hutton, both blond haired and blue eyed. Nick and I got the Hutton eyes and our mothers' hair, which means I have copper locks while he sports this full head of chocolate hair that shines with a light of its own. It's a cryin' shame the Marines require him to keep it short—though, with him in his dress blues right now, he's drawing a lot of attention from the women in the store, even without the help of his hair. There's something about a man in uniform that gets the imagination flowing.

Though personally, I'm more of a fantastic bone structure, white button down, and black slacks kind of woman. I let myself enjoy the view in front of me while Nick brushes a fleck of lint off his chest.

"Even if your dad did pass all his coolness down to you, it couldn't have prepared you for a company to go under and leave you with the bill." Nick shakes his head like he still can't believe what happened.

I get that.

I still can't believe it, either.

"I got excited and overconfident and now our family's livelihood is at risk." I square my shoulders and lift my chin. "You're being very sweet, but I'm owning my mistake. It's the first step to harnessing that rocket fuel."

Despite my outward confidence, the spinning ball

of nerves in my stomach speeds up. My grandparents started the Hutton Hotel—mostly called The Hut within the family—by turning their oceanside home into a bed and breakfast, then expanding into a full-blown wellness resort as the years progressed. After my grandpa passed, Dad and Uncle Wyatt took over, leading the Hut through an era of unprecedented success. I spent my entire life preparing to continue what they started, and what do I do? Put the entire thing at risk the first chance I get.

"I never did understand why you want to expand, anyway."

Tearing my attention away from the man in front of us, I glance at my cousin. "You've seen the way our guests look when they check in. They're tired. Life is hard and it's heavy and they're wearing it all on their shoulders. You just see the weight of the world on 'em. But when they check out?" I grin as I watch him understand.

"It's gone."

And there it is. The reason I want to expand our hotel into other markets.

"It feels like we've made an impact. They're smiling and hopeful and excited to get back into the world and what if...what if we could do that for more people? You know? We're booked to capacity every day, but if we had other facilities, we could help more people."

"That's a beautiful dream, Angel."

"It's more than a dream. It's our future. I know we hit this bump in the road..." I laugh and hold out my hands. "Okay, okay, I know I drove us headfirst into this bump, but this is right. This is real. Everything will be better after tomorrow's meeting with this new guy. I'll make sure of that."

Step one, assume everything that comes out of Garrett Cooper's mouth is a lie.

Step two, remember he is not my friend, no matter what he says.

Step three, trust nothing, verify everything.

"That's the kind of attitude that makes a great Marine."

"I don't understand why you couldn't be something a little less...murdery?" I shift my weight, worrying about his upcoming flight. We should have left as soon as we saw the store was this busy.

"Can you imagine how I'd handle the situation you're in right now?" Nick whispers. "A shady investment company adding The Hut as collateral to a loan they knew could fall through, squeezing as much money as they could out of things before they filed bankruptcy and disappeared? I'd..." He huffs a laugh, shaking his head as his fists clench. "It wouldn't be pretty."

"I can see it now. You'd roll into the meetings like an oversized ape with extensive training in combat and weaponry."

"Speaking of combat and weaponry..." He glances at the time. "If we don't get some help soon, I'm gonna miss my flight."

"I told you we should have left." I grab his arm and start for the exit, but a second clerk comes out of the back and gestures us forward.

"What can I do for you today?" he asks as I approach.

Beside me, the sexy stranger leans on the counter, watching intently as the first clerk brings out his new phone. He meets my eyes and frowns, his gaze strong. Intense. It sends my stomach into a tizzy, and I blink as I give my attention to anything else, but damn. There's something in the way he looked at me. Something that feels like he saw right through all the bullshit to my most secret hopes and dreams. It makes me feel equal parts alive and uncomfortable.

"I'm here for an upgrade." I smile at the clerk and place my phone on the counter, rattling off the specs for my new one.

"Solid choice," the frowny man says in a deep

voice. He taps a phone sitting next to one with a shattered screen. "Picked the same model."

"Good to know I'm not making a mistake." My eyes lock with his, an unbelievable shade of blue with flecks of green dancing through them. I could stare into them forever...assuming I had time to waste by staring into the eyes of beautiful men.

Beside me, Nick casually checks the time, then rubs his hand through his hair again.

"It's not too late to leave," I say, bumping my shoulder against his.

"It'll be fine. You're almost done and as long as we get out of here in the next ten minutes, we're good to go." He glances at my clerk, a short man with greasy hair and a name tag that reads JJ. "What do you think? She'll be done in ten minutes, right?"

"Totally." JJ nods, smiling confidently as he meets his colleague's eyes like they're sharing an inside joke.

"Great. I'm gonna get the car and pull it up front." Nick holds out his hand for my keys. I pass them over and he taps me on the top of the head before heading for the exit.

Only, JJ starts up a conversation with the clerk helping the man beside me. Apparently, our new phones are exciting enough to warrant an eight-minute discussion about the upgrades from the previous year's model. The stranger glowers at the duo, watching the whole thing play out with complete and utter dissatisfaction.

"In a hurry too?" I ask, hoping to distract myself with a little conversation. "Whenever I'm in a situation I can't control, I remind myself everything always works out the way it's supposed to, given enough time. Setbacks are often opportunities, you know? This little delay could be serendipity…or, you know, fate…" I trail off before I mention anything about rocket fuel and the stranger's jaw muscle starts pulsing. "…or something…"

The man turns his intense stare my way and I regret ever opening my mouth. "Because having my time wasted definitely means things are working out."

His tone makes me recoil. The condescending curl of his lip. The arch to his brow.

I flinch.

Okay, then. Message received.

I turn and lean my back on the counter without another word. I won't waste my energy on him again. So much for romance hero sex appeal. You can't be that ugly on the inside and still pass for pretty on the outside. I mentally rescind all thoughts and comments about his beautiful eyes and perfect bone structure. Jerks are jerks. The end.

On the other side of the store windows, Nick sits in my car, drumming his fingers against the steering wheel. If he misses his flight, I'll never forgive myself.

"Are we good?" I ask JJ, interrupting him as he picks up both phones to continue his conversation with his colleague. "Because our ten minutes are up, and I need to go."

"Yeah. Sure. I just need to turn this bad boy on and check that everything's ported over."

"I'm sure you've done an excellent job and if there's a problem, I know where to find you." I hold out my hand because we need to be on the road pronto.

JJ stares at the phones like he's rebooting. For shit's sake. Why is this so hard?

"I'm sorry," I say, lifting my brows, extending my hand further, "but I've gotta go."

Reluctantly, he gives me my device and I hightail it out of there.

"I'm so sorry," I say to Nick as I slide into the passenger seat. "They were going on and on about how amazing these phones are. You know how guys like that get when they're talking tech."

"Relax, Angel. It's all good."

I slide my phone out of the box to power it on, but he puts a hand on mine.

"Don't. Not yet." His eyes dart away as he shifts the car into gear. "I sent you a goodbye text and I'll feel stupid if you read it with me here."

"Right. Who would want to express how they're feeling to someone so they could respond in real time?"

Despite my response, I put the phone back in its box and close the lid. Nick hates goodbyes. He says it makes leaving feel too permanent and I get that.

I do.

Every time he ships out, I worry he won't come back. Or that if he does, he won't be the same. He's been my best friend since the day he was born—one measly day after me. I'm close with a lot of my cousins, but Nick? He's an extension of my heart.

"Right?" My cousin grins as he shakes his head. "All those emotions, just out there? In the open? Nobody wants that."

"Nobody indeed." My smile is as bright as possible to hide the lump in my throat. The day he enlisted, I cried myself to sleep. I put on a brave face when he's around. We all do. But Dad was a Marine and he almost lost his life in Afghanistan. Technically he did lose his life. Clinically dead for several minutes, but some miracle brought him back. I don't know what I'd do if something like that happened to Nick.

When we arrive at the airport, I hop out of the car as he grabs his bags from the trunk. "Have fun playing Army," I say, rising up on tiptoes to wrap him in a hug.

"As a Marine, I resent your implication, but something tells me that's why you said it."

"Of course that's why I said it."

He shakes his head as he squeezes me tight. "Why are you such a pain in my ass?"

"Just keeping that ego in check."

Nick draws himself up to his full height, lifting his chin as he throws a bag over his shoulder. With a quick smile, he thumps a fist on his heart, smiles softly, then turns and heads for the doors, threading into the crowd and disappearing from sight.

I stare after him, a breeze whispering through my hair as I let out the breath I've been holding.

You better come home, I think as I cross in front of the car and lower myself into the driver's seat. *Because I don't know what I'd do without you.*

CHAPTER FOUR

Garrett

"What flew up her butt?" JJ, the clerk who was helping the overly peppy redhead, mutters as she hightails it out of the store and climbs into a waiting car. He rolls his eyes and gives me a conspiratorial smile. "Bitches be crazy, am I right?"

"Crazy. Sure." I don't return the smile as I look the guy dead in the eyes. "Especially when their time is wasted by two unprofessional twat-waffles who can't handle a menial job."

The idiots laugh. Then frown. Then the guy helping me—a mouth-breather named Chuck—hands me my phone while JJ disappears into the back for another break, despite the waiting customers crowding the store. These guys aren't helping my view on humanity.

"Here you go, Mr. Cooper." Chuck plasters on a massive smile after the dressing down I gave him. "If you could just power that bad boy on and make sure everything looks okay, we'll be good to go here."

I turn on the device and stare at the loading screen, wondering if the lackadaisical attitude comes hand in hand with being a native of the Keys. Never in my life has buying a phone been this unprofessional—and that's saying something. From the packed store with one clerk hiding in the back, to the ten-minute conversation these morons had about my phone, to them being offended when the woman beside me left in a hurry. The Marine she was with—boyfriend maybe? They looked awfully close—even told them he only had ten minutes and they still fucked around.

I skip the security setup because I am so done with Seaside Mobile that I wish I'd chosen any other store on the list. The stock lock screen blinks to life and I swipe it open. The phone buzzes almost instantly with a text from...Nick the Wonderful? Who the hell is that? And why is there a middle finger emoji next to his name? Did Charlie mess with my phone again?

Confused, I tap on the message.

> **NICK THE WONDERFUL** 👆
>
> Just wanted you to know you're an amazing woman and I'm proud of you every day. You'll get through this rough spot. You know it. I know it. That's just what you do. But if things get hard, I'm here to hold your hand through it all. Even when I'm on another continent. Love you pretty damn big, silly angel

My brows furrow as I read. This isn't Charlie messing with me. This is...this text was meant for someone else. Fuck me. What the hell is going on?

Chuck's grinning face comes into view. "Loving it already, right?"

"This isn't my phone." Irritation sets my teeth on edge. As if it wasn't bad enough that they wasted my time, I don't even have what I came here for.

"Well, no." Chuck folds his arms over his chest. "Not yet. You still have to set everything up the way you want it, security, home screen, or, you know, you could restore from a backup—"

"No." I place the device on the counter and slide it his way. "This is not my phone."

Baffled, he picks it up and turns it over in his hands. "I don't understand, sir. Isn't this the make and model you asked for?"

"It *is* the make and model I asked for. It's also the make and model the woman standing next to me asked for." I point at the device. "When you two were messing around, you mixed them up. I have hers and she just left with mine."

This is what I get for assuming the worst was behind me. A fucking catastrophe. If Mom was around right now, she'd tell me this was a bad sign, bad juju. She might even go so far as to suggest skipping tomorrow's meeting because all signs point to disaster.

Good thing, I don't believe in that stuff the way she does.

Chuck shakes his head, looking exasperated instead of contrite. "Are you sure?"

"I just got a text from a guy named Nick. I don't know anyone named Nick. If I did, do I look like the kind of guy who'd call him 'The Wonderful?' Or does that seem more like something one of those crazy bitches be doing?"

Chuck flinches, then gingerly lays the phone on the counter as if distancing himself from the device will magically solve the problem. "What do you want me to do about it?"

Are you fucking kidding me?

I suck in my lips to keep from spewing obscenities in public. "I want you to switch it back."

The obscenities march through my head anyway. I deserve a medal for not letting them fly.

"But sir, she already left." Chuck scoffs as if I'm the one being difficult here.

"Sweet Jesus boy, could you find two brain cells in there and rub them together? Surely you have a way to contact her."

His eyes harden. "I can't give out a customer's personal information. And there's no need to be rude."

"You mean rude, like having private conversations with coworkers instead of helping customers? Or rude, like refusing to fix the problem *you* caused? If you had simply done your job, we wouldn't be in this mess." Seething, I gather my things, shaking my head. "I'll just text my number and let her know what happened."

Chuck rolls his eyes. "Like texting yourself is gonna help anything. Now look who's being a twat-waffle."

"*She has my phone...*" The words grind past my clenched teeth, and I turn on my heel before I lose control of my mouth.

A blast of humidity slaps me in the face as I step onto the sidewalk. Inhaling deeply, I lean against the building and compose a text, careful not to snoop into more of this woman's life than I already have.

> Hey. There was a mistake at Seaside Mobile. You have my phone and I have yours. When can we meet to switch back?

I hit send and wait, half expecting her to storm around the corner after realizing the mistake herself. She'll probably spew some happy-go-lucky nonsense about things always working out in the end, then go on her merry way. She seems like that sunshiny type who's never met a problem she couldn't ignore. Seconds turn into minutes while I stare at the phone. Now what? Surely, she's figured out the mistake by now. Unless she's just as laidback and dense as JJ and Chuck. I swipe a hand over my face. What if that's just the way everyone is in the Keys?

Fuck me. What does that say about tomorrow's meeting?

Irritated, I send another text.

> Hello? I really need you to respond.

I'm missing calls. Emails. Important messages. There is so much work that needs done and I'm already hours behind. Worse, this stranger has access to my entire life. Vulnerability isn't my thing with the people I know and love, but with some random woman?

Hard fucking pass.

Five minutes go by without a response, so I send another message.

> Look, I don't know if you're getting a kick out of making me wait, or if you think you can get something out of me by holding my property hostage, but come on lady, I really need my phone.

No response. Go figure. I angrily swipe through the screens, imagining her digging through my messages, my photos, and who the fuck knows what else.

A bead of sweat trails down my spine and I let out a long breath, then inhale deeply and let that one out slowly too.

Your anger isn't proportionate to the situation.

I repeat the thought several times while breathing deeply, the way my therapist suggests when my rage ramps up. My fists clench and I consciously release them, then start talking myself down.

There's any number of reasons the woman couldn't respond immediately.

No need to jump to the worst possible scenario.

Everything is going to work out the way it's supposed to...

I scoff at the thought. Isn't that almost word for word what the redhead said before things went to shit? Shows what she knows.

Regardless, I'll go to my hotel and check in. If I still haven't heard from her by this evening, I'll figure out what to do then. In the meantime, I'll answer emails and messages from my laptop. No big deal. With a shake of my head, I push off the side of the building, cross the parking lot, and unlock the rental. Heat boils out of the vehicle, and I swipe a hand through my hair as I lower myself inside and crank the AC.

As much as I hate to do it, I open the GPS on the redhead's phone, then search for my hotel. One of the autosuggestions is the Hutton Hotel which...oddly enough...is labeled as "work."

"Isn't that convenient," I murmur as I start navigation and head out of the parking lot.

CHAPTER FIVE

Angela

A smile curls my lips when I pull into my driveway. I love my house. It's small, but it's mine, set back off the road, surrounded by trees and palms, with a back patio just a few steps from the ocean. I have my own dock, though I don't have a boat. Probably never will. I just love diving into the water, that rush of bubbles and silence whispering past my body, then sitting out there to watch the sun go down while the salt dries on my skin.

As I climb the steps to the porch, two furry faces poke out from under the bushes, then disappear as I glance their way. "Hey, little friends," I coo as I walk past. "It's not quite dinner time, but what if I promise to fill your bowls extra full tonight? Would that maybe convince you I'm not so scary?"

A couple months ago, two kittens showed up out of the blue, stinkin' cute and utterly feral. They wouldn't come near me at first, but I put food out for them every day and we seem to be making progress. The fluffy, brown and white one is brave enough to hop onto the porch while I fill the bowls, but the orange one still won't appear until I'm out of sight. My goal? Get them comfortable enough with me that I can bring them into the house and take care of them properly. The process is taking longer than I want, but it'll pay off big in the end because I already love those silly nuggets with my whole heart.

I step inside, toss my keys into a bowl on a table near the door, then kick off my shoes before pulling my phone out of the box and powering it on. My cousins Micah and Nathan wanted to hang out tonight, and I need to solidify those plans, plus Uncle Wyatt, Aunt Kara, and the rest of the family will want to know Operation Nick went off without a hitch. As the phone powers up, I pad into the kitchen to pour myself a glass of water, then step onto the back porch and curl into the wicker loveseat. A breeze comes off the water and I sigh in pleasure as the palms dance and the waves crash. My mind blips to the meeting I have tomorrow, the one that might save The Hut after my disastrous oversight put it at risk, and a tremor of nerves blasts through my body.

I can't believe I let that happen. I can't believe we might be staring at the end of a The Hutton Hotel and it's my fault. The mistake swims in my gut like poison.

Nope.

Not poison.

Rocket fuel.

After everything went down, I did a lot of research and stumbled across a company called Vision Enterprise. They've got a great reputation, though I don't have a lot of faith they're much better than the company who set this whole thing in motion. The guy they're sending might be perfectly wonderful, but "once bitten, twice shy" is a saying for a reason. My guard will be up—like *all* the way up—and I'll be listening closely to everything he says. I wouldn't even have taken the meeting if it wasn't absolutely necessary.

I will not be the Hutton who set the family business on fire.

The phone comes to life, buzzing like a happy little cricket as multiple messages flash across the screen, one on top of the other. My family is big, weird, and wonderful and we all love each other very much. Maybe a little too much if the plethora of texts coming in has anything to say about it.

I open the message app and tap on the first one without paying attention to who it's from. A picture of a man pops up. He's shirtless, stretched out in bed, staring at whoever took the picture with unadulterated lust blazing in his gaze. His bare torso is a playground for the eyes, with divine pecs, washboard abs, and the perfect amount of chest hair trailing down to disappear under his waistband. One arm is tucked behind his head, revealing a meaty bicep that begs me to bite it.

Like, *begs* me to bite it.

"What the hell?" I murmur, before opening the pic to get a better view.

He's gorgeous.

He's intense.

He's...*the grumpy guy from the phone store!*

My jaw drops.

How did he get my number and why is he sending me half-naked pics? What kind of creepy nonsense is this?

The caption below the image reads, "Remember this?"

The contact photo catches my eye. A woman I don't recognize labeled The Future Mrs. Cooper. Confused, I click out of the conversation as another pic comes into a different thread.

Who the hell is sending me pictures?

A selfie of a strange woman with a strange man

pops up. She's sitting in his lap and has his bottom lip caught between her teeth. He stares into her eyes with a look so predatory, so sexual, so animalistic, I blink in shock.

"Jesus," I whisper before zooming in on his face. "What I wouldn't do to have someone look at me like that." I snuggle into the chair, biting my lip as I hold the phone closer.

I'm no pro in the dating department. I'm talkative and not exactly demure, which apparently is a massive turnoff. Add the fact that I'm not into meaningless relationships and you have the perfect recipe for lots of alone time. Which is fine. I prefer people who are deep, sensitive, someone seeking real connection—and there aren't too many of those out there anymore. I'm no virgin, but I've never been in a situation where a man would look at me like this guy.

Which is fine.

Surging hormones aside, I'm perfectly happy alone. Sure, I may never know the joy of watching my kids on Christmas morning, but that's what my cousins are for. If I do end up devoting my life to The Hut and forsaking a family of my own, I'll live vicariously through them. There will be plenty of little Huttons to go around.

Though maybe I should open myself to the possi-

bility of casual sexual encounters, I think, zooming in on the picture one more time.

Messages buzz in like crazy.

CHARLIE
For shit's sake, Melinda. Really? I mean really????

CONNOR
Did you actually just text the entire family a pic of you with a guy who ISN'T MY BROTHER?

BRENNAN
Are you fucking kidding me? This is a joke, right?

LILY
I don't even know what to say right now

CHARLIE
He told me today he thought she was cheating. You hear that, Melinda? He knows and he doesn't care, right Bear?

THE FUTURE MRS. COOPER
OMG. Bear!!!! I am sooooo sorrrrrrry...... I totally didn't mean to tell you like this...

CHARLIE
Uh-huh. Like we believe that. You're about as transparent as the shirt you're wearing in that pic

THE FUTURE MRS. COOPER
> Bear????? You gonna be okay baby????

Mesmerized, I follow the incoming texts like I'm reading fiction, then realize this is someone's real life drama and close the chat. I study the list of conversations, all from names I don't recognize. One from an unknown number catches my attention and I stare for a long minute before realizing why.

That's *my* number.

"What the hell?"

Baffled, I tap the thread and find three increasingly shitty texts from the stranger whose fiancée just announced she's cheating via group chat. I want to be mad. I mean, why would he assume I'm not responding for the fun of it? Unless that's something he would do...

He did come off as a self-absorbed jerk at the store...

And we do tend to expect people to treat us the way we treat them...

Though this guy seems to be having a bad day, which might explain how incredibly awful he was earlier. The least I can do is cut him some slack. Shaking my head, I type a response.

> Hey! Sorry! I just now powered on the phone. I can't believe this happened! I mean, actually, considering how rude those guys were at the store, I totally believe this happened. Can you meet tonight to exchange?

No one will believe this story. Not Micah, not Nathan, not Nick. Going home with someone else's phone? That just doesn't happen. This Bear guy is probably losing his mind because I made him wait so long.

The phone buzzes with a single word response.

UNKNOWN NUMBER
> Yes.

So, he's not the talkative type. That's perfect. I talk enough for the both of us.

Another message comes in.

UNKNOWN NUMBER
> Where?

I frown. You'd think he'd want to laugh at this crazy coincidence instead of barking one-word texts, but whatever.

After thinking for a second, I suggest my Uncle Eli's bar—The Pact. It's fun, popular, and I can meet Micah and Nathan there after the exchange. Boom. Two birds, one stone. I blow imaginary smoke off a pair of finger guns then stand, stretching, before heading into the kitchen to deposit my water glass in the sink.

Another message comes in.

> UNKNOWN NUMBER
> Be there at 7.

Would you look at that. Four words that time. Four, curt, bossy, not at all polite words.

No wonder Melinda is cheating. Sexy or not, this Bear has the emotional range of a robot. I check the time. There's no way I'm waiting two hours to get my phone back. Not when my entire life is on that thing.

Besides, who does this guy think he is? Demanding I show up on his time without considering what I might want or need?

With a shake of my head and a roll of my eyes, I type back:

> Be there at six instead.

That oughta show him who he's dealing with.

Garrett

One of the perks of devoting myself to my job is that I have a lot of discretionary income. And the perks of discretionary income include booking a two-hour massage to melt away the stress of flying commercial. Wouldn't you know, the redhead finally responds to my texts just as I'm undressing for mine. Her opening salvo is cute. I respond quickly as I remove my shirt, then my pants, and am sitting down to yank off my socks when I ask her where to meet.

I'm standing mostly naked, staring at my phone and urging her to type faster, when the masseuse knocks and starts to enter.

"Wait," I bark, and the door pulls closed.

"Just let me know when you're ready," the masseuse replies in a sickly-sweet voice, while my phone buzzes with a block of text. I skim for the gist; she wants to meet at a bar, blah blah atmosphere, blah blah is she flirting?

There's no way I'm missing my massage, so I tell the redhead I'll meet her at seven, power down the phone, and climb under the sheet.

After the day I've had, you better believe I'm ready to relax.

CHAPTER SIX

Angela

After dropping the mic on my conversation with Bear...*Bear?* Is that his real name? It has to be a nickname. Maybe one he earned by being surly and difficult.

Anyway, after my mic drop, I open my laptop to make plans with Micah and Nathan. With Bear...but for real...*Bear?* I can't even think it without giggling...

Anyway, with *him* swinging by at six, I tell my cousins to be at The Pact by six thirty. Those two are chronically late, which means there's no chance the asshole will still be around by the time they show.

I grab my laptop to read and reread my notes for tomorrow's meeting with Mr. Cooper. Micah would say I'm overprepared, but after the last time, I'd say there's no such thing. I check projections against actuals, cringing as I read through our worst-case scenario.

I won't let that happen.

Step one, assume everything that comes out of Garrett Cooper's mouth is a lie.

Step two, remember he is not my friend, no matter what he says.

Step three, trust nothing, verify everything.

Repeating those thoughts like a mantra, I grab the kitten food and step onto the porch. "Fluff! Orange! It's time for dinner!" I rattle the bag. A little brown and white face pokes out from under the steps, eyeing me warily. "That's right. I'm so totally not scary," I coo as I scoop food into his bowl. "You can just come right on up here with me because a birdie told me you're gonna love some head rubs."

The little guy doesn't seem convinced, so I put the food back in the house, grab my purse, and climb into my car. As soon as I shut the door, the kittens scamper onto the porch and dig in. The sound of the engine startles them and Orange dashes for the steps, thinks better of it, then slinks back to his food. Laughing, I turn on some tunes for the drive, and arrive with ten minutes to spare. Perfect. I can use the time to prep my energy for Bear's arrival. If he's still grumpy, maybe I can turn his day around...

...just in time to find out his fiancée is cheating.

Oof.

I pick a seat with a view of the door, place his phone on the table, then settle in and wait.

And wait.

And wait.

I drum my fingers. Pick up the phone, turn it over in my hands, then put it right back where it was. I had to power it off before I left the house. Apparently, I have trouble respecting other people's privacy, something I learned about myself as the guy received a tsunami of texts. Every time his phone buzzed, my urge to snoop increased.

Was his fiancée apologizing?

Was his family eviscerating her for being awful?

I wanted to know. I needed to know.

But snooping is wrong, so I turned off the phone before the temptation overcame me, which means I can't check the time, but six o'clock has surely come and gone. I order a gin and tonic and stare at the door, drumming my fingers on the table.

Is it possible for steam to actually come out of my ears?

First, this guy's rude. Then he's late. Which just doubles down on the rudeness.

I swirl my finger around the rim of my glass and order myself to stop stressing. When that doesn't work, I take a long drink. Then another. Then one more for good measure. Before I know it, the glass is empty. I flag down my waitress and order a refill. The front door swings open and in steps Micah and Nathan, looking imposing as they scan the place. They're both tall and broad shouldered like Nick, though Micah's the beefiest of the bunch. I've always felt ridiculous standing with them, seeing as my eyes barely make it past their pecs. The imposing factor dissipates when they see me and smile, then head my way as a waitress drops off my second drink.

Micah bends at the waist to give me a hug, before dropping into the chair next to me, his grin warm and disarming. "You do the thing?" He wiggles his fingers. "With the phones?"

"That is one of the funniest stories I've ever heard." Nathan pulls out a chair and lowers himself into it. "I'll be watching my phone like a hawk the next time I need a replacement."

"It'd be hilarious," I retort, glaring at the door. "If I had mine back yet." I take a sullen sip of G&T and slump deeper into my seat.

Micah frowns. "The guy hasn't shown?"

"It's quarter 'till seven." Nathan beckons the waitress over.

"I'd congratulate you two on only being a little late, but I'm too grumpy." I take a long drink and ask for another after the guys order beers. Seems like it's going to be that kind of night. "I really want my phone back."

"Plus, you've been sitting here for forty-five minutes, drinking alone." Nathan leans back, crossing his ankle over his knee. "That's enough to make anyone testy."

Nathan holds up a finger with a wry smile. "Fifty-five. She's ten minutes early to everything."

I laugh despite my growing agitation. "You know me so well."

"What are you gonna do if he never shows?" Nathan asks as the waitress returns with our order.

"Do you think that's even a thing?" I swipe my drink off the table and gulp down a large swallow. "Would someone really just abandon his phone with a stranger and disappear?" I ask, gesturing dramatically, almost knocking over Micah's beer.

"Whoa." He catches it before it spills. "Easy there. How many of these did you have?"

"I dunno." I lean forward to slurp from my glass. "Seems like one too many."

"I'd say more like two too many." Nathan's hearty chuckle deepens my frown.

"If he doesn't show, I'll go back to the store. Maybe get a new number or something." I shake my head and the world gets swimmy. "I just hate it. This guy has access to my whole life. If he doesn't make an appearance..."

The door pushes open and in steps none other than Mr. Sexy Rude and Late, looking just as imposing as my cousins. Even more so because he doesn't smile when he sees me. Oh no. His perma-frown morphs into a full-on scowl and his jaw tightens when he strolls my way.

"D'you have any idea how late you are?" I ask, perhaps a little too loudly as he stops at the table.

"Late?" A frown tugs at unfortunately sexy lips. "I'm ten minutes early."

"No. I was ten minutes early." I drag my gaze to a pair of extraordinarily blue eyes. "You are very, very late."

He checks his watch. "Six-fifty. Ten minutes early."

"We agreed on six." I cross my arms over my chest.

"I said seven." His brows lift.

"That's right. *You* said seven." I smile smugly. "*I* said six."

"And I didn't see that text until I was on my way. I sent a message letting you know that wouldn't work for me." Bear gestures at the powered down phone like I'm the asshole in this situation.

Uh-unh. No way.

"You let me sit here alone for fifty-five minutes with nothing but my good friends, gin and tonic, for company and all you have for me is 'I didn't see the text?' I see you." I point two fingers in front of my eyes then turn them his way. "I see what kind of guy you are. The packaging might be gorgeous, but underneath? It's all shady and slippery. You're only out for yourself and that's it. I didn't think people like you existed in the real world but here you are."

A single eyebrow raises. "Here I am."

Bear's scowly growly face only pisses me off more. My frustration with him joins forces with my frustration over the situation with The Hut and my mouth runs away with the conversation the way it likes to when I'm angry. "That's right. Here you are. In your stupid shirt and stupid pants ordering me around without so much as asking if I was available at seven. Which I wasn't, by the way. I obviously had plans." I gesture at my cousins. "I've signed shitty contracts with people like you and I have a stupid meeting with a guy like you tomorrow and let me tell you, I am not looking forward to it because I'm scared to death I won't be able to ride the rocket to success."

Nathan and Bear's jaws drop while Micah chokes on his beer.

Shit. Did I really just say that out loud?

I hurry on before anyone can speak. "Which I understand has nothing to do with you, but I've had it up to here with people taking advantage of each other." I reach for my drink, but Nathan slides it out of reach while Micah sits back in his chair and grins at the unfolding scene.

Bear sets his jaw, glowering down at me. "I don't know what I'm supposed to say to that."

"She's had a lot to drink." Micah flares his hands. "She's not usually like this."

"Don't apologize for me," I hiss.

"Someone needs to," he retorts.

I turn my attention to the man with my phone. His blue eyes flash and his jaw clenches. It reminds me of a storm coming in off the ocean. It's raw. Charged. Energy shivers through me, followed by a growl of frustration.

"Apparently my companions think I'm being rude. Let's start again. Perhaps an introduction?" I risk a glance at Nathan. He looks shell shocked. "I'm Angela Hutton but my family calls me Angel, a nickname you're absolutely not allowed to use, especially because my college professor told me it sounds like a stripper name." I extend my hand while Micah guffaws, Nathan's brows disappear into his hair, and an emotionally distant robot named Bear blinks in shock.

"Hutton?" Bear's entire demeanor changes. "You're Angela Hutton?"

"That's right. You got a problem with that?"

"I have a problem with everything that's happened since I landed in Florida. Let's just get this over with," Bear says to me, before turning to the guys. "Order her some water and a coffee and make sure she doesn't get behind the wheel like that."

He places my phone on the table and slides it towards me like we're exchanging hostages. I do the same and give him my sweetest smile. "It's a pleasure doing business with you," I say, as he rescues his device and slips it into his pocket.

"It's been something," he mutters before turning on his heel and walking away. The guys stare after him until the door closes on his grumpy ass, then turn to me.

"Sweet Jesus, Angel," Nathan says with a laugh. "You sure told him."

"I did, didn't I." I grin and make grabby hands for my drink.

Micah slides it further out of reach. "That's a conversation he'll remember for the rest of his life. I have no doubt about it."

Nathan shakes his head with a wry laugh. "I'm not sure we can say the same for her."

CHAPTER SEVEN

Garrett

I step out of the bar and run a hand through my hair. *That* is Angela Hutton? Over the years, I built an image of the Hutton family and in one drunken tirade, she obliterated everything I wanted to believe about them.

Not only did she show up an hour early, but she blamed me for being late. Loudly. While sitting there with not one, but two men while Nick the Wonderful is on another continent, holding her hand through the hard parts. Even I smiled when I read his text, and according to my sister, I'm a cold bastard without a heart.

I have no room for cheaters. None. Maybe those

guys were Angela's friends...but something says they're closer than that.

The entire interaction is just more proof that people suck. We're selfish, self-righteous, and willing to screw each other over to get what we want. The older I get, the more it seems like my family is the last bastion of goodness in this world. Everyone else is in a race to the bottom.

I thought the Huttons were better than that, with their entire business model based on the wellbeing of their clients, charity, and giving back to the community.

I thought wrong.

Angela Hutton is loud. And rude. She doesn't have a censor and what kind of woman hangs out with two men when her boyfriend's text is sweet enough to touch someone as cynical as me? She's no better than the Melindas of the world and that truth shatters my last shred of hope for humanity at large.

With a shake of my head, I stride through the parking lot, lower myself into my car, and power on my phone. Who tells a stranger her college professor said she has a stripper name?

My mind conjures up an image of Angela in sky-high fuck-me heels, that fiery hair spilling over her tits as she spirals and writhes around a pole...

They say I'm an angel, imaginary her whispers.

"If only you weren't a devil in real life." I stare at the entrance to the bar, turning the phone over in my hands.

What will she think when she walks into our meeting tomorrow and I'm the guy waiting for her? Will she remember what she said to me tonight? Will she remember calling me shady and slimy? Will she remember telling me how much she's dreading the whole thing?

And here I thought talking to someone interested in giving you a ton of money to save your business was a good thing.

I could have told her who I was. Maybe I should have.

But she was either too drunk or too awful to care.

And if it's the latter, I'll have the upper hand walking into tomorrow's meeting.

Until fifteen minutes ago, I was willing to go the extra mile to ensure The Hutton Hotel lives a long and happy life. Now? After whatever that was? I'm not sure where I stand. I won't do her dirty, but...despite the fond memories I have of the place, if that's the kind of person making decisions, I'll need a lot of convincing before I loan them millions of dollars.

My phone comes on and I tap the map icon to direct me back to the hotel, ignoring the staggering number of waiting texts. Whatever has people that interested in talking to me can wait until I'm in my room. It can't be good news and I'm not dealing with a crisis from my car. Not after what just happened in that bar with its stupid name. The Pact? What kind of asshole calls a bar The Pact?

Resting my phone on my knee, I start the engine and navigate out of the parking lot. As much as I want to put the conversation out of my head, I keep chewing it over.

Slimy?

Shady?

She doesn't know anything about me.

She's the one whose business is in a situation where she needs to accept meetings with shady guys like me. And to think, I fought Branson to make sure he didn't give the job to Jordan Clement. Because *he's* shady. *He's* slimy. I just happen to be good at making deals.

And now? Maybe I won't care so much about making the deal fair to her. That entire interaction was like watching a childhood hero kick a puppy. Years of good faith ruined.

Tension throbs in my jaw, my neck, my shoulders, and I drum my fingers against the steering wheel. Negative thoughts twist and spiral, feeding my frustration until I realize I've just been driving and have no idea where I am.

Fuck! I slap the dash, jaw clenching as I grind my teeth together.

Your anger isn't appropriate to the situation. The words arrive like a friend with unwelcome—though accurate—advice.

I exhale sharply as I pull into a parking lot and drop my head into my hands. Outside my windshield, the ocean stretches for miles, glittering in the evening sun. With a sigh, I climb out of the car and lean against the hood, taking deep breaths of fresh air, closing my eyes as the breeze brushes my temples.

Eager for a distraction, I check my messages, going immediately for the family chat, which apparently blew up while Dirty Angel had my phone. I scroll until I come to an image of Melinda, sitting on the lap of her personal trainer, biting his lower lip. My jaw drops and I laugh out loud. Guess I was right about her cheating on me. Go figure she shared the news in the most dramatic fashion.

I read through the messages, chuckling as my brother, sister, and cousins let her have it. In a world intent on going bad, they never fail to remind me what good looks like. When I reach the end of the conversation, I immediately start a new chat with my family, minus The Future Mrs. Cooper.

> Well that happened.

CHARLIE

Holy shit, Bear. I was worried. You never take that long to reply.

CONNOR

You okay?

BRENNAN

Good riddance is what I say

LILY

I'm so sorry!

> I saw it coming. And it's not like she was anything more than a distraction

CHARLIE

Still sucks. Hate it for you.

CONNOR

I never liked her, but your whole 'distraction' thing is only going to create more of these situations

LILY

Be nice!

CONNOR

I am being nice. It's okay to say bad things about bad people and it's double okay to worry about my brother's health and wellbeing

BRENNAN

How's it going in FLA?

> Oh, it's going...

CHARLIE

Uh-oh. Sounds ominous

> **LILY**
> Everything okay?
>
> I'll just say it's been a crazy few hours. For starters, I'm texting you on a brand-new phone.
>
> **BRENNAN**
> But you just got a new phone.
>
> And now I have an even newer phone. Without the shattered screen. Like I said…rough start.
>
> **CHARLIE**
> Guess that means it can only get better from here.
>
> You sound just like Mom
>
> **CONNOR**
> Like that's a bad thing

I grin, then click out of the conversation, skip over a message from Melinda, and open the thread from Angela because how dare she blame me for being late. I didn't see her text because my phone was turned off, just like she didn't see mine because hers was turned off. Seems to me either no one's at fault or we're both at fault, but she has no leg to stand on, blaming me.

Though, out of context, my one-word responses seem curt, clipped, and downright rude. Sure, I was mostly naked as I sent them, but she doesn't know that.

If I was on the receiving end of that conversation, I

wouldn't have the best impression of me either. Shaking my head, I lock the screen and shove the phone into my pocket.

This is why I don't mess with relationship stuff. Work is easier. Safer.

Although this particular relationship is also work and I'm not exactly killing it. But that's not my fault. Angela blew everything up by being shitfaced and rude. Maybe if she'd let me get a word in edgewise, we could have figured everything out and had a good laugh while I was still at the bar.

Right, just me, her, and the two men she's cheating on Nick the Wonderful with.

Fuck me.

I couldn't make this shit up if I tried.

CHAPTER EIGHT

Angela

I want to be excited for this meeting. I want to feel hopeful and confident and know everything I'm doing means success for the hotel. Only, I felt all those things when I met with the last guy and look where that got me. Staring at the end of an era, knowing I'm the one who knocked the tower down.

Nope.

That's wallowing.

That's swimming in rocket fuel instead of harnessing the energy...

...though maybe the energy would be easier to harness if I wasn't so hungover.

What was I thinking last night? Maybe I could

answer that question if I didn't have giant holes in my memory.

I stare into the mirror, smoothing my red hair into a sleek low ponytail. After a rough start this morning, courtesy of my not-so-good friends gin and tonic, I finally managed to pull myself together, with an assist from coffee, water, and ibuprofen. My makeup is on point. My outfit says I'm capable, while showing off just enough leg to feel beautiful. I twist to check my ass, which is too round for my liking, but whatever. All in all, I'm pleased with what I see. And with the throbbing in my temples turned down to a manageable level, I'm optimistic about today's meeting.

"You can do this," I say to my reflection. "You have the education. You know what you're doing. You've spent your entire life preparing for this and you're good at what you do. Rocket fuel, Angela. Rocket fuel." Mirror me smiles back and my phone buzzes in my hand.

My mind instantly goes to the incredibly hot but utterly awful man named Bear, which annoys the crap out of me. I've had other conversations since getting my phone back. Why can't I stop thinking about *him*?

Probably because I've never had someone be that rude to me for no reason before.

How dare he have the audacity to show up late, then look at me like I was the crazy one for calling him on it. He did try to make an excuse, but it wasn't good enough for me to commit to memory.

Probably because it was a line of bull. (Though maybe because I had too much to drink.)

Either way, he's a pompous asshole.

He's probably used to women falling all over him because he's tall and rugged, while his hair is just long enough to suggest he's sensitive. And those eyes. Like staring into the ocean on a sunny day, deep and endless and warm. Yeah. Well. The ocean is also home to sharks, killer whales, and other murderous creatures, which makes it beautiful on the outside and dangerous on the inside.

Just like that jerk.

With a toss of my head and a mental "So there!" that makes my temples throb, I check my phone and tap on a waiting message.

> NICK THE WONDERFUL
>
> Thinking of you. You've got this. You're smart and strong and good and kind. Square your shoulders. Hold your head high. And remember that we love and trust you.

His words bring a smile and I close my eyes against a tightening throat. When we were kids, he went on and on about wanting to be a superhero when he grew up. Trying to be funny, I dubbed him Nick the

Wonderful when we were sixteen and the name just stuck, mostly because he keeps proving it true. As I'm composing a thank you, another text comes in.

> **NICK THE WONDERFUL** 👍
> But just in case you forgot where you came from...

An image of the two of us as kids fills the screen. Me with my red hair frizzed and crazed after a day at the beach, chocolate ice cream smeared across my face as I give the biggest, gappiest-toothed grin known to man. Him with his arm around my shoulder, equally gap-toothed...scrawny, but towering over me. Our heads are touching, and we look so happy, we obviously had no idea we were smack in the middle of our ugly duckling phase. I save the image and finish my reply.

> Look at you, a pain in the ass from the beginning. Heading out now, but boy do I have a story for you. And I want to hear about wherever you are and whatever you're doing. I'm sure it's classified so you can't tell me much, but I'll take whatever you can give me. Maybe a video chat later?

I wait for a response that doesn't come—typical Nick—so I grab my purse, slip my phone inside, and make the drive to The Hut.

FATE

The office my father shares with my uncle is warm and welcoming. Light streams in through the windows, with pops of color from Aunt Harlow's paintings on the wall. Houseplants cascade off bookshelves and a potted palm warms the corner. When I was a kid, I loved coming in to hang out while the men worked. I'd stretch out on the floor with my coloring books, happy as a clam because the energy in the room made me feel like I belonged. It's why I wanted to grow up and take over the business, to spend every day sitting at one of those desks. When I arrive, the men are waiting, Dad's presence imposing and Uncle Wyatt's less so.

Dad glances up as I enter. "There's my Angel."

I cross the room and hug first him, then Uncle Wyatt. Their blond hair is graying at the temples, and crow's feet crinkle to life when they smile. While some men bear their age like a burden, the Hutton men don it like a crown, growing more distinguished with each year. Their posture is strong and straight, and looking at them, it's clear where my cousins got their broad shoulders.

"You ready for this?" I ask, smoothing my skirt,

worrying that maybe my ass is too round for it after all. My giant smile hides the undercurrent of doubt humming through me.

The last time I had a meeting with an investor, Dad and Wyatt didn't feel the need to sit in. They had as much confidence in my plan as I did. The fact that they're here today speaks volumes.

Not like I blame them.

I just hate that it's necessary.

Uncle Wyatt leans a hip on his desk. "We're only here to listen, Angel. You're still running the show."

"We should have done it like this the first time." Dad leans back in his chair. "We all played a part in what happened, and we'll all be part of the solution."

We've had this conversation time and again and I love Dad for trying to take the weight of my mistake, but it's mine and mine alone. "We're here because of my actions and I appreciate you both for trusting me enough to keep moving forward. I will solve this problem. I promise you that. This guy is not a friend, he's the enemy. I'll assume everything he says or does is designed to make me think he's on our side even though he isn't, and I'll verify the hell out of everything until he proves himself trustworthy." I put a hand to my heart. "Rocket fuel, Dad."

"There's my girl." He dips his head. "Rocket fuel."

Wyatt crosses his arms and gives us a quizzical

look. "You two wanna fill me in? Feeling a little left out of this rocket fuel discussion."

A knock on the door silences our laughter. "Excuse me," says Therese, our receptionist, "but there's a Mr. Garrett Cooper here to see you."

Cooper.

As in The Future Mrs. Cooper.

As in Garrett Cooper, the guy I've been emailing for weeks about this meeting.

How the *hell* did I never make the connection?

Nerves catapult through my system then crash to the floor as none other than an emotionally distant robot named Bear steps into the office.

Our eyes lock. The quirk to his lips tells me he knew.

My jaw drops.

That asshole let me go on and on last night and he knew who I was the whole time.

A hazy memory surfaces of me introducing myself, then calling him shady...slimy...

Oh God. Kill me now.

Why didn't he say anything?

I don't know if I want to facepalm or strangle the guy. If it wasn't so important to look professional, I'd probably do both.

Dad gives me a funny look as I glare at the new arrival. "Please come in, Mr. Cooper," he finally says.

"I'm Lucas Hutton, this is my brother Wyatt, and my daughter Angela. It's a pleasure to finally meet you."

The men shake hands and somehow, I regain control of my body enough to extend one of my own. Garrett's blues zero in on mine. His grip is strong, but brief, though the electricity that shoots through me lasts long after he lets go. I chalk the feeling up to embarrassment mixed with loathing and refresh my smile.

"It's a pleasure to meet you, Mr. Cooper."

"But we've already met." Garrett quirks his head. "I'm surprised you don't remember, considering the circumstances were so unusual."

Oh, hell yes, this guy's the enemy.

I could kill him for the oh-so-innocent look dancing through his evil eyes.

"Of course I remember. I was just..." I glance at Dad and Uncle Wyatt and clear my throat. How in the world am I supposed to recover this?

"Unusual circumstances?" Wyatt gestures for Garrett to have a seat. "That sounds intriguing."

"It's a crazy coincidence," I say with an easy laugh. Look at me, being so light and casual no one would believe I'm imagining a swift kick to Mr. Cooper's balls. "We needed to replace our phones on the same day and the store mixed everything up. I went home with his and he had mine."

"And when I showed up for the exchange, she was completely drunk." Garrett's smile is a challenge and I return it without flinching.

"Only because he was an hour late."

While my dad and uncle exchange glances, Garrett puts two fingers in front of his eyes, then turns them to point at me, mimicking my gesture from last night. If I never understood Nick's need for such a murdery job, I do now. The smile I shoot back at Mr. Cooper is filled with homicidal intent.

I queue up a vitriolic insult, then swallow it back.

Just because he's the enemy doesn't mean I have to sink to his level.

This is a business meeting, after all. At least one of us should remember where we are and what we're doing.

He can lob insults all he wants, but I'm done taking the bait.

CHAPTER NINE

Angela

Standing in the office I've dreamed of inheriting since I was a little girl, I face down my nemesis with a smile. Garrett Cooper can be as rude as he wants, but I will kill him with kindness in return.

On the outside, anyway.

And maybe only for the duration of this meeting.

I'm seething on the inside and have no idea how long I can hold it in, so we'll just take things one step at a time.

I smooth my hair, wrench my gaze from his, and plaster pleasantness across my face. "If all goes well, the way we met will simply be an interesting twist to our origin story, won't it, Mr. Cooper?"

"Interesting indeed." He steeples his fingers under

his chin and deliberately turns his attention to the men. "I've been coming to the Hutton Hotel since I was a kid. If I'm honest, I'm surprised you're in a situation that requires a meeting with a man like me."

Oh no.

He will not dismiss me that easily.

I speak up before Dad can answer. "We are too, as I'm sure you can imagine. Though, once you hear the story, it'll make sense."

I explain that the hotel had grown as much as it could, but I came up with a plan to expand. It was big. Bold. And required going in on a venture with an investment company.

The possibility for success was amazing, though Dad and Uncle Wyatt worried it sounded too good to be true. I, however, was so convinced, I started a new limited liability company to protect my family's financial wellbeing in case the worst happened, then put together the prospective business plan, our share of the startup capital, and presented it to my new business partner. Contracts were drawn and construction on our first satellite location began in Bliss, South Carolina.

Only, no one expected the economy to tank. The investment company went under, and all the players disappeared like a puff of smoke. Worse, the deal *was* too good to be true. I was so confident I had everything under control that when a last-minute change to the contract came in, I made the worst mistake of my life. Instead of passing it to our lawyers for review, I read it, signed it, and sent it back. Buried in the fine print of the contract was a clause that lists the hotel itself as collateral in case of default.

"Expansion of the brand into other markets," Dad says. "The Hutton Hotel isn't just about making money. It's about improving the lives of the people who stay here and giving back to the community that supports us. Angela wants to open more hotels, to better serve more people. Her idea is good. Her plan is solid."

"A noble dream." Garrett meets my gaze with an almost imperceptible smirk. Something tells me he's still laughing at me, but I couldn't guess why.

I glance away and lift my chin. "But without the investment company's money, we're forced to scale back and take things one market at a time."

The truth is, we're barely staying afloat making both halves of the payments with no new business to bring in extra revenue. And given the economy, I'm not sure we'll make it through the off season.

Garrett gives me a long look. "It must have been hard to accept a meeting with me after that experience."

It was even harder not to shove you out the door

with my foot in your ass the second you walked in, but hey, look at me doing difficult things.

Uncle Wyatt folds his arms on the table. "We only considered talking to you because of the positive reputation Vision Enterprise built helping turn Waystar Resorts around after they went through bankruptcy."

I nod, crossing my legs and watching Garrett's expression like a hawk. "And your assertion that you won't do anything to risk the unique charm of the Hutton Hotel sealed the deal."

Which is probably something he said to make him sound like a friend instead of the enemy he is. The surge of disgust following that thought is the best rocket fuel around. Having this jerk contaminating my favorite room has me determined to succeed…simply to spite him.

"As I said, I have wonderful childhood memories here." Garrett's eyes meet mine and they're inscrutable. Probably because he's lying through his teeth to seem like less of a threat. Lucky for me, he proved what he's made of by failing to introduce himself last night. If he had, we'd have walked into the meeting on equal ground. He knew that and chose to use his identity to his advantage.

We share the original proposals I drew up for the first investment company as well as current financials and our projections.

Garrett pours over them, nodding as he reads. "This all looks good."

"We have faith in the project." I watch as he digests the numbers one more time.

"I can see why." He taps the papers. "There's a lot of potential here."

"I agree." I lift my chin because damn it. There's more than potential. He's holding a business plan that is guaranteed to succeed and he knows it.

"I think next steps would be to visit the new site in South Carolina. Get an idea of what's been done and what still needs doing. I came to Florida with a good feeling about this project and today is only confirming that." His smile is wide and genuine for Dad and Uncle Wyatt, but his eyes harden when they settle on mine.

Mr. Garrett Cooper doesn't like me.

Don't you worry about that, sir. The feeling is mutual.

"Do you mind if I take these with me?" he asks, tapping the papers again. When Dad and Uncle Wyatt shake their heads, he continues, "I'll go over the numbers one more time and then call to set a date to visit the new site."

We shake hands, say our goodbyes, and Garrett leaves.

"I think that went well," begins Dad and Wyatt agrees.

But it didn't go well. There's too much left unsaid between Garrett and me and he can't just walk out of here like nothing happened. Not without making it clear I'm not as easy to manipulate as he thinks.

"You know what?" I stand. "I need to say something to Mr. Cooper. I'll be right back."

Without waiting for a response, I hightail it out of the office in time to watch the front door of the hotel swing shut. I race after him as fast as my skirt and heels will allow, sucking in air as I step into a blistering July afternoon.

"Mr. Cooper!" I call, clutching the white porch rail as he stops in front of a car in the lot.

The bastard doesn't even look up, so I hobble down the steps. Whoever made women's fashion so impossible to move in should have a special section waiting for them in hell.

"Hold on a second!" I arrive at his car a breathless mess and lean both hands on the hood.

Garrett's eyebrows twitch upwards. "Is there something I can do for you, *Angel*?" He puts an uncomfortable emphasis on my name.

Oh, God. Please say I didn't tell him about my college professor...

The glint in his eyes can only mean I did.

Okay, then.

If he's willing to play dirty, I have some ammunition of my own.

"I don't know, *Bear...*" I smile so sweetly it makes me throw up in my mouth a little.

His jaw drops. "How did you...did you go through my phone?"

"Not on purpose. I got one of your texts, but I didn't know I had the wrong phone, so I was confused. I read through the conversation until I figured out what happened and..." I wave a hand because I'm babbling and that won't help things. "Look, I don't know if I should apologize for being so rude last night or expect an apology because you could have said something... *anything*...about who you are while we were at The Pact. You knew I'd be shocked when you walked in today. You knew it and used it to your advantage."

"It's not like I could get a word in edgewise."

I pop a hand on my hip. "Yeah, well, it's not like I—"

Garrett lifts a hand, stopping me in the middle of a sentence I had no idea how to finish when I started. I just couldn't let him have the last word. "Why did you chase me out here, Ms. Hutton?"

"Honestly? I kind of wanted to murder you a little, but considering we're going to be working together, I thought it best for us to clear the air. We got off on a very bad foot."

"And how exactly do you intend to do that with someone as slimy and shady as me?" A sly smile curves one side of his mouth. "Those are the words you used to describe me, right?"

Do not take the bait.

Rise above.

Show him how two perfectly reasonable adults are supposed to act in a business situation.

I extend a hand, shaking off my frustration and brightening my smile. "Hello, Mr. Cooper, I'm Angela Hutton and I'm pleased to meet you. If you're still in town tomorrow, is there any chance we could meet at The Pact? Clear the air? Get to know each other under better circumstances?"

Garrett looks as disgusted by the invitation as I feel. He's the last person I want to spend more time with. And as far as clearing the air goes? I don't think I could get much clearer on how big a turd this man is.

"What would Nick the Wonderful say if he knew you're spending so many nights at a bar with other men?" he asks with a sneer.

"My cousin?" I flinch, truly taken back by the question. "Why would he care who I'm at the bar with? And what other men? You mean Micah and Nathan? My *other* cousins?"

There's a moment of stunned silence, and then Garrett scrubs a smile off his face. "I thought Nick was your boyfriend—"

"My *what*?"

"And I thought you were being unfaithful." He sighs, shoving his hands into his pockets. "When I saw you sitting with two other guys."

Is he kidding me? This is really happening right now?

My jaw drops and I shake my head to jumble my thoughts back into logical order. "Not only did you read my texts, then get uppity because I read yours, but you actually thought I'd cheat on someone? With *two* guys?" I sit back on my heel, dumbfounded. "What kind of woman do you think I am?"

Garrett's eyes glimmer as a smirk quirks his lips. "Believe me, Angel, you do not want to know. And yeah. The Pact. Tomorrow. Seven?"

I huff in surprise, unsure if his use of my nickname is a shot at my expense, or if he's trying to be endearing. Combine that with the flutter of energy that courses through me every time his eyes meet mine and I find myself in the rare state of not knowing what to say.

Garrett pulls open the car door and I can't let him leave without saying something.

"Six," I counter. The sooner he realizes I'm not

someone to boss around, the better. "Be there at six. And don't call me Angel."

With a condescending smile and a bob of his head, Garret lowers himself into his car and drives away, leaving me to stare after him, seething and confused.

CHAPTER TEN

Angela

I arrive at The Pact twenty minutes early instead of my usual ten. I must be nervous for my meeting with Garrett.

I hate that he does that to me. He leaves me feeling...I don't know.

I have no words to describe the way he makes me feel.

"Frustrated" comes to mind.

As does "confused."

Along with "asshole," "dickhead," and "Pompous McSmugface," but whatever.

In my experience, people enjoy being with me and I enjoy being with them. I don't think I've ever *not* liked someone before. But with Garrett? The entire world feels electrified, and I can't find my footing. It's like everything's twisted a few degrees off normal and what usually works doesn't. Being with him breaks all my patterns, all my expectations…

He's grumpy. And growly. And he might be an evil shit.

Scratch that. He *is* an evil shit. I have no illusions that he's a friend. Garrett Cooper is the enemy, all right. I could have seen that without Dad's prep.

But if we're going to work together, we need to figure out a way to be in the same room without contemplating felonies. I wasn't at my best when we met, and I'll give him some grace and assume he wasn't either. There have been a ton of misunderstandings and miscommunications. This isn't the way I normally operate.

Surely the same can be said for Mr. Garrett Cooper.

He needs to see me as Angela Hutton, a woman with a strong eye for business and the ability to do more with his money than earn a financial return. We'll improve the lives of everyone connected to the new hotels. I need him to see that's the Hutton family purpose. My destiny.

And *I* need to see *him* as anything but a selfish prick with the most condescending smug face I've ever seen.

As I push through the front doors of The Pact, I bump into Uncle Eli—aka Micah's dad, aka co-owner of The Pact, aka former erotic dancer…at least according to family legend. I've never been sure I believe the stories.

"Sweet Angel!" He wraps me in a warm hug, thumping me on the back before pulling away. "I hate to leave now that you're here, but I have a big night planned with my beautiful wife."

"You guys celebrating a special occasion?"

"Every day with your Aunt Hope is a special occasion." Love radiates off him like a beacon of light. What would it be like to have someone love me that much?

"What are you wasting time talking to me for? Go! Go!" I shoo him towards the door. "I'm here for a business meeting anyway. I won't be much fun to talk to."

A smile crinkles Eli's eyes. "Of all the things I hoped this place would be, I never imagined my fancy pants niece holding business meetings at my bar. Very cool." He presses a kiss to my forehead, then waves goodbye before stepping through the door.

After a moment's hesitation, I choose a seat at the bar instead of a table. It's a psychological tactic I learned in business school. Sitting face-to-face can be perceived as combative while sitting side-by-side feels more like partnership. Tonight, Garrett and I need to focus on getting along. Just two people having drinks while figuring out how to work with someone they hate. I even chose my outfit with that in mind, the perfect blend of business and casual. A little fun, a little flirty, but nothing over the top. My hair is down, and I let the natural wave take over. All of which I hope says, "Hello there! I'm friendly and not into doing two guys at a time, so why don't we call a truce and figure out how to save The Hut."

I claim a stool and order a gin and tonic, promising not to drink more than a quarter of the glass before Garrett arrives. No need for a replay of the other night, especially because there's no guarantee he won't be late again. I get the feeling he enjoys pissing me off.

Movement catches my attention as someone slides onto the stool next to mine. "This seat taken?" rasps a masculine voice.

I turn, expecting to find Garrett, but my smile crashes to the ground when I find a man I don't recognize leering my way. His dyed black hair swoops off his forehead and a black V-neck clings to a chubbier-than-he-thinks torso. I don't know what's worse, his cologne or his slippery grin as he extends a hand.

"Name's Tank and that drink's on me." He clicks his tongue as he finger guns my gin and tonic. "So's the next one. As if that needs said."

I blink in shock. Tank? Finger guns? Is this guy a real person or am I hallucinating?

"I see I've stricken you senseless with my charm." He takes the hand I didn't offer and plants a sloppy kiss on the back.

"You've stricken me senseless with something." I pull my hand from his grasp and wipe it on my pants. "And that seat's taken. I'm meeting someone."

"It's your lucky night, baby girl. Fate intervened and sent me instead." His grin says he thinks he's marvelous while he manages to invade my space even further.

"No, see, I'm meeting—"

An arm slips around my shoulder. "Me," growls a familiar voice. "She's meeting me."

I turn to find Garrett Cooper looking murderous as he stares Tank down. Garrett's got a good three inches on the guy and after seeing that picture of his bare chest, he has the body to back up the threat. One look at Tank's face says he knows he's beat.

"Sorry, man." He holds up his hands and removes himself from my personal space. "But you can't fault me for trying."

"I do fault you for trying. She's clearly out of your league." Garrett lifts one unimpressed eyebrow. "And I'm not the one you need to apologize to."

Tank's shoulders droop as he mumbles an apology to me and slinks away.

Garrett watches as he leaves, still holding me

close. His cologne is subtle yet delicious, and I inhale deeply to wash away the stench of cheap pickup lines. As soon as the coast is clear, he releases me and claims the vacant stool. He's wearing a white button down with the sleeves rolled up, a pair of black slacks, and an air of indifference that makes my blood boil.

"I was handling that."

"Is that what you call it?" Garrett orders a whiskey and casts an amused smile my way.

"That's exactly what I call it. I made it very clear I wasn't interested."

If there was a picture next to the word "underwhelmed" in the dictionary, it would be the look on Garrett's face as he folds his arms on the bar. "Guys like that don't care if you're interested or not, Angel. It's a numbers game. He knows if he talks too long or gets you to drink too much, there's a chance you'll give in out of sheer exhaustion."

"That's a despicable way of doing things." I glance across the bar and sure enough, Tank has another woman cornered. "And don't call me Angel," I say as the bartender arrives with Garrett's whiskey.

He takes a drink, his eyes meeting mine over the rim of his glass. "I hope you didn't have to wade through that shit too long before I got here."

The intensity in his gaze has my entire body on

alert but I refuse to let him see that. What is this? Some kind of intimidation tactic?

With my sweetest smile, I sip at my gin and tonic. "I would've been wading a lot longer if you showed up late again..."

"As I said the other night, I didn't think I was late." I start to protest, but Garrett holds up a hand. "Let me explain before you jump down my throat."

I huff but lift an eyebrow and gesture for him to continue.

"I was...indisposed...when you texted, but I'd been waiting for hours and didn't want to miss the chance to make plans with you. I suggested we meet at seven, considered it a done deal, and turned off the phone. I didn't see your reply."

"Suggested?" I laugh, crossing my legs and twisting to face him. "You mean ordered."

Garrett's brows draw together. "As I said. I was—"

"Indisposed." I tap a finger to my chin. "How very vague of you."

"So you see," Garrett says as he turns his full attention to me, "from my point of view I arrived on time, but I understand now why you thought I was late. I tried to explain, but I don't think you were listening."

A hazy memory of me screeching about being left alone with my good friends, gin and tonic, surfaces, and I inwardly grimace. I could concede his point, but where would the fun be in that?

"I didn't just *think* you were late." A smile tugs at my lips. "You *were* late. You can't demand people show up on your time and consider it done without waiting for confirmation."

"I'm trying to apologize here." Garrett tosses back the rest of his whiskey.

"You're right. Silly me for making it hard."

A strange look crosses his face. There's this intense moment of eye contact while his gaze sears mine and my brain helpfully serves an image of something else I'd like to make hard.

Shit. Where did that come from?

And why do I get the feeling he's thinking the same thing?

Uncomfortable, I look down, then cover my embarrassment by taking a drink.

So much for finding my footing.

CHAPTER ELEVEN

Garrett

I can't explain what came over me when I stepped into the bar and saw Angela with that creep invading her space. Her body language said she wanted nothing to do with the guy while his told me he didn't give two shits what she wanted. I acted without thinking, sliding an arm around her shoulder rather than punching the guy in the face.

I haven't wanted to hit someone like that in years. Not since I found Elizabeth with…

I stop that thought with a shake of my head.

What I can't figure out is why I wanted to hit a man for touching a woman I can't stand. I'm chalking it up to my protective streak until I find a better answer.

"Since we're handing out apologies…" Angela

smiles wryly, bringing me out of my thoughts. "Assuming that's what just happened. You apologizing for being late the other day." Her brow arches as a half-smile lifts full lips.

She's a spitfire, that's for sure.

"You mean, you don't know?" I ask, then signal the bartender for another drink.

"It's just that generally, apologies come with the words 'I'm sorry' somewhere in there." Angela rests her chin in her palm. "That's what really seals the deal. Otherwise, it's just a lot of words that don't really amount to anything."

She's got balls. I'll give her that. I may not like her, but I am starting to respect her.

The bartender returns with my drink, and I take a sip. "And I didn't say that?"

Angela pretends to think. "I seem to remember an explanation. A vague one at that. There was something about you being indisposed, and then somehow you blaming me for not knowing, but no...I'm sure I never heard anything that sounded like 'I'm sorry.'"

The sparkle in her eyes says she likes getting under my skin just as much as I like getting under hers. She's expecting me to push back. To dig in and put up a fight. But I know how to throw her off her game.

Shifting to face her, I meet her eyes, purposefully softening my expression into a look of absolute contrition. "Angela. Please accept my sincerest apologies for being late. I hope you'll understand the slight wasn't intentional as I didn't see your counter-order of meeting at six instead of seven."

"Counter-*order*?" Her eyebrows hit her hairline as a laugh escapes sultry lips.

"'Be there at six instead.' That doesn't sound like an order to you?"

"It sounds as much like an order as 'Be there at seven.'" She leans both elbows on the bar and quirks her head. "I wanted to make sure you knew who you were dealing with."

"And who am I dealing with?"

"Someone who doesn't like being ordered around." Her gaze is fire and ice, an invitation...and a challenge.

"That's too bad, Angel." My voice is low, my smile wry. "I like giving orders."

Color rises in her cheeks and her eyes dilate as they lock on mine. She wants to say something. I see it in the way her lips part, hear it in her sharp intake of breath. Instead, she blinks, swallows hard, and gives her attention to her drink.

I sip my whiskey and lick my lips.

Where the fuck did that come from? I walked into this bar to meet a woman I can't stand, and now I'm flirting? With a business associate? The Florida sun must be melting my brain.

"Anyway..." Angela switches back to her customer service smile. "I do owe you an apology. As I said before, I accidentally read some of your texts. I know about your fiancée, and I feel like I need to put that out there." She casts a sympathetic glance my way. "So, in the spirit of apologizing properly, I'm sorry about what happened."

"Fiancée?" I frown, confused. "You mean Melinda?" The name enters the conversation on a laugh because the idea of her being anything close to permanent is hilarious.

Angela nods. "The first text I got was that picture of her with another man." She grimaces. "Well no, the first text..." She stares dreamily into her drink, then shakes her head. "That's not important. What I'm trying to say is I've been feeling so bad for you, finding out about her cheating like that. And it doesn't seem fair that I know, and you don't know I know. So now you know I know, and I can stop feeling bad for you know, knowing."

"Melinda wasn't my fiancée." Still chuckling, I swipe my drink off the bar and shake my head. "Not by a long shot."

"But her contact name...The Future Mrs. Cooper..."

"My sister did that as a joke. Melinda is a lot of

things, but wife material isn't one of them. She was—" I make a dismissive gesture "—a distraction."

"A distraction?" Angela wrinkles her nose. "That sounds awfully..."

"Detached?"

She gives me a look like I'm full of shit. "That's a nice way of putting it."

"My sister agrees with you. She changed Melinda's contact name to The Future Mrs. Cooper to make a point about the women I associate with."

Angela bobs her head, clearly siding with Charlie. "Are you guys close? You and your sister? I get the feeling you must be."

"Why's that?"

"I can't imagine anyone else having the balls to come near your phone without fear of losing a hand."

"Funny," I deadpan, lifting my drink with a sarcastic shake of my head, then bring the glass to my lips. "She and my brother are the only people I trust in the world. Well, and my parents. And Brennen, and Lily. They're family friends, but we grew up together, so I consider them honorary cousins."

"I'm close with my family too. No brothers or sisters, but Nick?" Angela quirks her head in question.

"The wonderful?" I half-smile, remembering how angry I was on his behalf when I found her sitting with her cousins the other night. The conclusion that she was cheating seemed so obvious at the time.

Funny how that works when you don't have all the information.

"That's the one. We were born one day apart, and I don't know...I think he might be my person. He's overseas right now. He's a Marine, and works in intelligence, so I never really know where he is or what he's doing. Which means I'm simultaneously proud of him and scared to death all the time."

"And your other cousins?"

"Which ones? There are so many." She laughs, her face brightening at the mention of her family. She's prettier than I gave her credit for, especially when she smiles. "But for the sake of argument," she continues, "I'll assume you mean the guys you met the other night. Micah—his parents own this bar—he's just this ball of energy. A firefighter. He's a lot, his humor is its own brand, like it's this whole thing, but he's amazing. Nathan works for my Aunt Maisie's charity and..." Angela's features tighten as she finishes her gin and tonic with a shake of her head.

"Not a fan of your aunt's charity?"

"No, it's not that. Nathan's dating this woman and she's..."

"A distraction?" I lift a brow.

"Worse. I'm afraid she's angling to be permanent."

"The horror!" I clutch imaginary pearls.

"Nothing wrong with marriage if you're with the right person. But...Nathan's a great guy who'd do anything for anyone and this woman..." Angela clicks her tongue. "She's got these two little girls and, you know, nothing wrong with that either. Just everything about her feels off." She shrugs. "I don't know what it is, but I get the feeling she's taking advantage of him."

I nod, returning my focus to my whiskey. "And that is why I prefer my relationships in the form of distractions. No commitment. No feelings. If someone feels taken advantage of then everyone is cool to walk away."

"But are you though?" Angela wrinkles her nose. "Cool to walk away?"

"Do I look bothered by the Melinda thing?"

"Not particularly, but didn't it hurt to see her with that other guy? Even a little? Maybe deep down in this region?" She waves a hand over my chest.

Laughing, I pivot to make eye contact. "Not even a little."

"I don't believe you." She lifts her chin and it's another challenge. *Prove me wrong*, says the twinkle in her eye.

Ask and you shall receive, says the half-smile quirking my lips.

"Fine. Let me demonstrate." I put my glass down on the bar, then lean close. "Do you trust me?"

"What?" Angela's voice is low. Guarded. She leans closer.

"Do you trust me?"

"No offense," she says with a laugh, "but I really don't know you well enough to trust you."

"Good answer. Would you say we have a connection?"

"Garrett..." Angela draws back. "Where are you going with this?"

"Just answer the question."

Her eyes search mine for several seconds, then she brings out her customer service smile. "I'd say we have the beginnings of a wonderful business relationsh—"

"Is there a connection, Angel? Chemistry?"

"I don't..." She shakes her head. "No. We only just met. I'm not even sure we like each other. And don't call me—"

Gripping the back of her neck, I lean down and press my lips to hers, intending to demonstrate how perfectly normal it is for me to be unbothered by my relationship with Melinda coming to an end.

But that isn't what happens.

Angela tastes of lime and feels like lightning, her gasp sending a jolt of lust to my cock.

I thought I'd stop there. Make my point and pull away.

But I don't.

I kiss along her jaw, using my hand to tilt her head and damn if she doesn't give in, closing her eyes and sighing in pleasure.

I didn't expect this.

The surge of lust swelling my dick.

My hand fisting her hair.

"Does it feel good, Sweet Angel?" I whisper, my voice rough, commanding. "Do you like it when I take what I want?"

Her hair smells of coconut and I adjust my grip on those red locks, savoring the taste of her skin as my lips find hers again. I didn't think I'd growl into her ear. I didn't think I'd want to strip her naked, bend her over the bar, and bury myself in her silky warmth. I thought I'd kiss her, prove my point, and sit the fuck back down.

Angela's breath hitches and when I pull away, her lips are parted, her eyes wild, burning with a heat I wasn't prepared to meet. I stare into her blues, desire boiling inside me.

I blink.

Clear my throat.

Return to my seat and finish my whiskey.

"Now," I grit out, as coolly as I can muster. "After that kiss, if you saw me in a picture with another woman, would it hurt?"

Angela licks her lips.

Releases a shuddering breath.

Forces a smile.

"Not even a little." Her voice is strained. Her eyes wide. Her lips parted and swollen as she swallows hard and looks away.

She's lying. Or she's considering filing a sexual assault charge.

Either way, I crossed a line...

...I *obliterated* a line...

And there's no going back.

CHAPTER TWELVE

Angela

Holy fucking shitballs. What the fuckity fuck just happened? Garrett kissed me. Public enemy number one had his lips on mine...*and I liked it.*

He only did it to make a point. Not because he wanted to, but because he plays dirty.

And maybe I could have laughed it off and moved on if that was all that happened.

But that isn't all.

He didn't just kiss me.

Garrett Cooper looked at me like he owns me. Like he claims me. Like I belong to him and he fucking loves it. His kiss was heat and passion. It was raw and charged with energy.

I can still hear his voice rasping in my ear.

Hot.

Demanding.

I shiver just thinking about it.

I've never been kissed like that. Not once in all my life. I've never felt anything like the aftershocks of desire still coursing through me, my lower belly throbbing, begging for more.

As he returns to his seat and takes a drink, his shitty smirk reiterates he only kissed me to prove his point: sex and connection don't go hand in hand. But that isn't the only point he made. I am now officially aware Garrett Cooper doesn't play at my speed. He kisses acquaintances like he's ready to fuck and I don't want a relationship without meaning...

Hold up now.

I don't want a *relationship*...?

What the hell is that word doing in my head?

I hate the man. And what just happened is a bigger violation than anything that Tank guy said or did.

So why, in the name of everything holy, am I thinking of ways to make Garrett kiss me again?

Shouldn't I be indignant? Disgusted? Maybe a little traumatized?

"So yeah. I think I see what you mean." I run a hand through my hair and lick my lips, tasting a hint of whiskey. "Point made. You're definitely not hurt after the Melinda thing."

Garrett nods, his eyes blazing into mine and I have to do something if I'm going to regain my footing. I feel utterly out of control, like I'm tumbling down a hole without end, head over heels, over head, over heels.

I want to say I hate it…

No. I *do* hate it. I loathe it. I hate *him*.

I lift my chin. "For the record, don't ever do that to me again."

"Noted." His voice is low. Tight. Almost a growl. He takes a long drink, then his eyes sparkle with dark humor. It's like he knows I'm not gonna like what he's about to say…and loves it. "Do you think we could do the other thing, though?"

My heart stutters. "Do I think we could do what other thing?"

"Work together. After everything we just shared." His eyes cut my way, dancing with self-satisfaction.

"I know without a doubt we could work together because we haven't shared anything." Except a kiss that'll fuel my fantasies for the next six months, but whatever.

"Good. Because I looked over the paperwork again. It's good. I have as much faith in the project as I do in the Hutton Hotel itself. And that's saying a lot." He raises his glass, a rare smile gracing his face. "To bright futures."

Grinning, I lift my glass to his. "And strong partnerships."

And to the best kiss of my life, I think as I finish my gin and tonic in one long swallow.

It's nearly eight o'clock by the time I get home and the flash of fur dashing off the front porch reminds me I forgot to put food out for Fluff and Orange before I left.

"Oh you guys! I'm so sorry." I let myself into the house, drop my purse near the door, and grab the food before hurrying back outside. Fluff waits for me on the top step, keeping a watchful eye as I bend to scoop food into the first bowl.

"You know I've never been this late before. I just, well, I had a really confusing evening with a man I don't even like." I fill the second bowl, then step into the house, closing the screen door. The moment I'm inside, Fluff dashes over and chows down.

"And he doesn't like me as much as I don't like him," I say as Orange slinks up the stairs.

That kiss said he likes me...

I laugh out loud at the thought. What is this?

Elementary school? He doesn't have to like me to want to sleep with me and the way he touched me? He wants me. There's no way around that. A man doesn't touch a woman like that unless he wants her.

But that could have been all for show. Garret Cooper is impossible to read. Besides, don't men think with their dicks as a rule? Case in point, Tank the Friendly Date Rape Guy?

I watch as the kittens scarf down dinner. The fact that Fluff was on the porch while I was outside is a major win.

"We're one step closer to the three of us being a big happy family," I say as I stand and head into the kitchen to pour myself a glass of water. Nick couldn't get free for a video chat yesterday, but he promised he'd be good to talk today.

I step onto the back porch and curl into the love seat, sending him a text to see if he's available. The sunset slips the world into twilight, the rhythmic company of the ocean sparkling darkly. It's my favorite time of day. A time without responsibility or deadlines. A time for resting. For relaxing. For simply being a creature on this earth, enjoying the beauty stretched before me. After a few minutes, my phone lights up with a video call. I hit accept and beam when Nick's giant smile fills the screen.

I grin in return. "There's my favorite face in the whole wide world."

"Man." His video jostles as he settles back in his chair. "It's gonna hurt when you fall in love and that's not true anymore."

"I don't think we need to worry about that any time soon. Love isn't in the cards for me. Not when I have a business that requires my full attention." Garrett's face flashes through my mind, his eyes searing mine as he leaned in for that kiss. I hear the rasp of his voice against my ear and my nipples pebble, my body tingling with the memory. "Besides," I say to Nick, pushing away the thoughts with an internal roll of my eyes. "No one could ever take your spot."

"Correct answer." He nods decisively. "Now, I believe you had a crazy story to share with me?"

"I do. But I want to hear about you first. How is it out there?"

What I'm really asking is "Are you gonna be okay? How safe are you?" but questions like that make Nick as uncomfortable as goodbyes.

He gives me his best non-answer, grinning widely as he navigates telling me about his days while avoiding anything that might clue me in on what he's actually doing. This is a man who loves what he does. His protective streak runs so wide, it encompasses the entire world. He's a ray of light in comparison to the murky darkness surrounding Garrett Cooper.

"What?" Nick asks, interrupting himself mid-sentence. "Did I say something weird? You're smiling kinda funny."

"I was just thinking about how hero-ing suits you. You look happy and that makes me happy."

"Life is good, Angel. I have a job that gives me purpose. My family loves me, and I wake up content with my place on this beautiful rock hurling through space. Name one reason not to smile."

You're in danger every day.

You're thousands of miles from the people who love you.

I might be in the process of ruining the business and the one person who always makes me feel better isn't here.

The enemy kissed me today and I can't stop thinking about ways to make him do it again.

"I guess there isn't one," I say, hoping he can't see the lie in my smile.

CHAPTER THIRTEEN

Garrett

Charlie meets me at the airport, lifting up on tiptoes to wrap me in a giant hug when I step into a gray New England day. After squinting against the sun in the Keys, I welcome the dreary weather. The energy is different here. Subtler. Less intense.

Or maybe that's because Angela Hutton is thousands of miles away.

She's...shit...what is she?

She's facing down this career-ending problem and doing it with a smile on her face and hope in her heart. She's smart, though overly optimistic. She's funny. She calls me on my shit and manages to annoy the crap out of me while doing it.

I can't stop thinking about her and I hate it.

"How did you spend four days in the Keys and not get tan?" Charlie shakes her head, her dark curls bouncing around her shoulders. "Please tell me you did something that wasn't work related."

"You mean on the trip I took for work?" I fight back a smile because I don't want to encourage her. This topic is getting old.

"Yes, Bear. Fun can happen, even on the trips you take for work." She pops the trunk on her car. "You're allowed to enjoy yourself from time to time. You should try it. In fact, this is me officially giving you permission to let loose. Start small, if that would help. Maybe have a cup of coffee simply because you want it and not because you meet someone at a café to negotiate a deal."

I deposit my suitcase in the trunk and close the lid as the wind picks up and the clouds darken. "I have fun."

"Name one thing you did that made you smile while you were in a tropical paradise, not getting tan." The twinkle in Charlie's eyes says she thinks she's got me. Little does she know that messing with her is my number one way to have fun.

"I met a woman at a bar," I say as I yank open the passenger door. "Twice."

My sister's wide eyes meet mine as we lower ourselves into the car. "You did not."

"I did. She's smart and funny and is a surprisingly good kisser."

"You sure are fast at finding distractions." Charlie shakes her head as she fastens her seatbelt.

"She's more than a distraction. I intend to see a lot more of her. And soon."

In my mind, Angela's gaze locks on mine, burning with lust after our kiss. It's been just a few days and I haven't stopped thinking about her. Jasmine perfume mingling with coconut shampoo, the hint of lime on her lips. Soft skin and sweet vulnerability in eyes as blue as the Florida sky.

I wasn't supposed to like that kiss so much. And neither was she. It annoys me that I'm still thinking about it.

Charlie gives me the side-eye. "You're talking about someone you met for business, aren't you?"

"You say that like it's a bad thing."

"It is a bad thing! Here I thought you were having a little fun with the next Future Mrs. Cooper, and you're talking about business meetings with a potential partner. That was a dirty trick, making me think you kissed her." She shakes her head as she pulls into traffic. "You're officially hopeless."

Outside the window, travelers blur by as the car picks up speed. "How about you? Anything exciting happen while I was gone?"

"It basically rained the whole time, so that was fun. But it's Friday, so you know, it's Cheers 'n Beers time. You're coming, right?"

Every Friday, there's a standing invitation from my siblings and cousins to meet for drinks at the bar. I don't make it as often as they'd like, as they are quick to tell me every time I pull a no-show. Tonight though...?

"Of course I'm coming. Why wouldn't I?"

"I was worried you'd be all funned out after your adventures." Charlie's smile is sharp, though her eyes are soft.

I've had as much as I can take of the jokes about me being a workaholic. I enjoyed my nights with Angela. Well, the second one anyway.

Kind of.

Maybe.

Fuck, I don't know.

Sure, everything about her is work related, which means there's no chance of her becoming another distraction, but shit...

...that kiss...

I was not prepared to lose control like that. Our lips touched and I wanted more. So I took it. And if we hadn't been in a public space, I would have taken a lot more than that...

I swipe a hand through my hair before the thought can go anywhere. "A night at the bar sounds great."

My sister drops her jaw and widens her eyes, placing her hand to her cheek in mock surprise. "We will be *so* honored by your presence, but are you sure you won't overdo it? I'd hate to swell that organ you keep in your chest into something resembling a normal human heart…complete with feelings and everything."

Her joke echoes the one Angela made when we were talking about Melinda. The comparison is a spark, setting my annoyance ablaze.

"That's enough, Charlie." The edge to my voice surprises even me and I turn my attention back to the window.

"Geeze. Sorry. I didn't mean to push a button."

"I know." I swallow hard. "You just gotta know when to stop."

"I'd say you gotta learn how to take a joke—"

I turn, anger flashing across my face, and Charlie holds up a hand.

"Okay, okay. Message received. I'll drop it. Guess it's true what they say about poking the bear."

I laugh despite myself. "You're lucky you're my little sister."

"I think it's more like, *you're* lucky I'm your little sister, but whatever."

"For fuck's sake," I say with a laugh. "Just drive."

Charlie drops me at home, a two-story house on the outskirts of Wildrose Landing, the small coastal town where we grew up. When I got the job at Vision Enterprise, I immediately rented an apartment in the city. Said goodbye to my family and put all my chips in the work basket. After Elizabeth…

…after I found her with…

…and she…

…she…

I couldn't stand to be in the city anymore. I kept my apartment and I'll spend a week or two there if things are busy, but my primary residence is right here in good old WRL. I like being this close to family and the simple energy of Wildrose suits me. I don't like people and they don't like me. Out here, I can kick up my feet and everyone leaves me be. Branson isn't a fan, but I'm too good at what I do for him to make it a thing.

I unlock my front door and hang my keys on the hook near the door, then wander through the quiet house to deposit my suitcase in my bedroom before checking email and giving the projections from the Huttons another read. They're solid. If this was all Angela's doing, she has a good eye for business—when she's not making catastrophic rookie mistakes.

After I unpack, I grab a shower, with Angela prancing into my mind as warm water slices down my chest. Tonight, she's the perfect blend of Dirty Angel and Pencil Skirt Angel, wearing red fuck-me heels with a tight skirt and blouse, her lips painted a fiery red and her hair tousled around her shoulders.

Her eyes are wide and innocent, like they were the night I kissed her and fuck if that blend of sweet and sexy doesn't send a jolt of need to my swelling cock. I lean my arm on the cool tile and take myself in hand, imagining her graceful fingers undoing the buttons on her blouse, her full tits spilling out of a black lace bra.

What the hell am I doing? It's bad enough I can't stop thinking about the woman. Now…this?

A better man would be appalled enough to stop what he's doing.

But me? I remember the taste of her lips. The fire in her eyes. The heat of her skin as I whispered in her ear. *Does it feel good, Sweet Angel? Do you like it when I take what I want?*

Water beats against my shoulders, rolling off my chest, down my back.

Maybe all I need is to get her out of my system. Maybe then I can stop thinking about her, stop being so frustrated all the time…

My hand slips and slides along my dick and I pretend it's her mouth, my hand fisted in her hair as I press all the way to the back of her throat. Except that isn't enough. I don't just want her mouth. I want all of her, stretched out in front of me, moaning my name. I imagine her naked body, writhing beneath me, her eyes rolling shut as I bury myself to the hilt.

I'd slam into her, my balls slapping her ass. She'd beg. She'd moan. She'd cry my name as I work her clit, claiming that body as mine. She's heat and warmth and she'd look up at me with those blues...

This is bad, whispers a quiet voice in the back of my mind. *This is wrong. I shouldn't be thinking of her like this. We're going to be working together.*

Me and my Dirty Angel.

My balls clench and I grunt in release, coming so hard my knees go weak.

CHAPTER FOURTEEN

Garrett

I pull into the parking lot of Cheers 'n Beers, the bar Brennan's older brother opened around the time I was born, and park next to Charlie's car. The rain promised by the gray skies finally starts to fall and I race for the entrance, shaking water out of my hair as I step through the front door. My sister waves from a table in the back and I make my way over.

"Early as usual." She smirks as I take a seat.

"Says the woman who got here before me."

"Only because I knew you'd pick a spot at the bar and things are so much better at a table." She laughs, her attention flicking to Connor as he comes through the door. He smiles when he finds us, lifting a hand and crossing the room. Where Charlie got our dad's dark features, Connor and I took after our mother. My hair changed from blond to brown as I aged, but his didn't. My memories of my mother are blurred, but seeing him always makes me feel closer to her.

"Hey there, big brother." Connor drops into the seat across from Charlie. "How was the trip?"

"Don't mention the word fun," our sister says with a laugh. "He doesn't like that *at all*."

I shoot her a warning look. "You know, I've been thinking about it, and you might be right. Maybe I do have something against enjoying myself."

She narrows her eyes, sensing a trap. "What makes you say that?"

"I'm here with you, aren't I?"

Charlie laughs lightly and slaps me on the arm as Brennen arrives with his wife Maya, followed by Lily. We order drinks and shoot the shit, filling each other in on our lives and discussing world events. While only two of the people at the table are related to me by blood, these people are family. We grew up together. Stood up for each other through hard times and celebrated wins together. I should really come out with them more often.

I smile, thinking of Angela and the way her face brightened when she talked about her cousins. I get that. I really do. Like it or not, she and I might have more in common than I thought.

"What's got you grinning so big?" Connor asks and I snap my attention his way.

"Just thinking about someone I met in the Keys."

"Don't get your hopes up." Charlie sits back, shaking her head as she sips her drink. "He's talking about a work someone. One of the Huttons."

"Still." Lily leans on the table and points my way. "If she has him smiling like that..."

Charlie frowns, gives me the onceover, then cocks her head. "She does have a point. Maybe there's more to Angela Hutton than meets the eye?"

I shake my head and stare into my whiskey. What am I supposed to say to that? I kissed her to make a point and now I can't get her out of my head. I jacked off in the shower, imagining her on her knees, begging for my cock because that was supposed to make me stop thinking about her, but she's still in my head, driving me even more crazy than before. I'm going to work closely with her and don't know how to pull that off since my dick thickens every time I hear her name.

Yeah. That ought to shut everyone up.

I take a drink to buy myself time when I hear a voice that makes my balls climb back into my body.

"Oh, shit. *Bear*? I didn't think I'd see you here."

I turn to find Melinda, tucked under her personal trainer's arm, her mouth drawn into a too-big-to-be-real frown. Her tits are pushed up to her chin and her dress is so short and tight, there's nothing left to the imagination. Did she always look this trashy?

"Really?" I ask. "You didn't think I'd be where I always spend my Friday nights when I'm in town?"

"You barely come to these things." She flicks her hand at the table with disdain. "Besides, I...you know... I thought you'd still be in Florida."

"Of course. It's not like I told you when I'd be back in town." I shrug. "Oh, wait. I did."

This whole thing is a typical Melinda move, designed for maximum drama since her ego can't stand not being in the spotlight. She's here in the hopes that I'd want to lick my wounds with family tonight, so she showed up with her new boy toy to twist the knife a little deeper and suck a little more attention out of me.

"I sent you a text," she purrs, snuggling closer to Gustavo—the personal trainer she swore was gay.

Unfazed, I let out a long breath. "I think we all saw that one."

Melinda rolls her eyes. "I mean I sent one just to you. You never responded."

"Didn't have anything to say. We knew what we were to each other. You moved on." I turn my attention to Gustavo. "Enjoy it. It won't last long."

Melinda's jaw drops. "Don't listen to him, baby. He's just bitter." She puts a hand on his chest, then leads him to a table at the other side of the bar.

"Wow." Brennan throws an arm over the back of his chair. "That was cold."

"That's just how she is." I finish my whiskey and signal for the waitress. One isn't going to do it tonight, not with Angela and Melinda taking up so much mental space.

"No, I mean you. That was..." Brennan shakes his head. "I guess I thought somewhere, you must have cared about her at least a little."

"I guess you thought wrong." I sit back, frowning. Our waitress returns with my order, and I take a long drink. Between my sister harping on my devotion to work and yet another person I care about calling me cold, I'm starting to feel misunderstood.

Charlie sighs deeply, the twinkle in her eyes signaling she's in love with whatever she's thinking. "I wonder how long it'll take."

"How long what'll take?" I growl, bracing myself for yet another dig at my expense.

"For Melinda to realize you make way more money than that guy and come crawling back to apologize."

"Wow." I huff a laugh, surprised to hear something like that come out of my sister's mouth. "It even comes down to money for you."

"Oh no, no, no. I want you to find someone who sees what a great guy you are underneath that prickly exterior and loves you for all the things that make you awesome, but that woman?" Charlie points a finger Melinda's way. "She only cares about what's in it for her."

"Amen to that." I lift my glass. "Now, let's forget about my love life—"

"How can we forget something that doesn't exist?" Connor quips and the rest of my friends laugh.

"Remind me why I still hang out with you guys?"

"Because we keep you humble," Brennan says.

Connor grins. "And remind you where you come from."

Charlie lifts her drink. "And you love us immensely because we are fucking awesome."

I laugh and the conversation moves on. Across the bar, Melinda makes a show of enjoying her new boyfriend's company, giggling loudly at his jokes, and sitting so close to him she's almost in his lap. Oddly enough, the one time I happen to glance her way, her eyes are locked on me. I snort and look away.

How did I ever find anything about her appealing?

She's cheap. Tacky. How did I not see that before?

And Charlie's right, she's only interested in herself.

Maybe it's the comparison to Angela I find so jarring.

Where Melinda is fake and superficial, Angela is who she is without worrying how she's perceived. Instead of working angles to manipulate things to her advantage, she works hard to do the right thing. Instead of every move being about what she can get out of someone, it's about what she can give back.

Melinda is a distraction. Angela is...she feels real. Solid. Like someone I can trust.

Maybe, I'll text her when I get home tonight.

Shit. Nope. That has to be the whiskey talking.

I don't even like her. Why would I text her? And why am I eating up more mental energy by comparing her to Melinda?

The version of Angela Hutton I met at The Pact was on her best behavior. She wants to win me over because of the business deal, nothing more, nothing less.

The only thing I can trust people to do is look out for themselves. Only a fool would expect anything different.

CHAPTER FIFTEEN

Angela

Dad's frown etches deep lines into his forehead as he stares at his computer. He sits back, threading his fingers through his hair. "I don't want to worry you, but actuals aren't holding up to projections. Revenue is significantly down from previous years. If something doesn't change soon, we're going to be in a tough spot."

The words knock the air out of me on a day I already feel off my game thanks to stupid Garrett Cooper and the even stupider kiss I can't stop thinking about. A weight settles into my stomach as I watch dust motes dance through the sunlight.

If something doesn't change, we're going to be in a tough spot.

A tough spot we wouldn't be in if it wasn't for me.

One mistake. One simple oversight that I knew better than to let happen...

I swallow hard, my gaze flicking to Dad's. "I'm so sorry."

"This problem doesn't rest on your shoulders alone." He offers a gentle smile. "Now is not the time to focus on what went wrong. It's time to focus on the solution. With the economy down, people aren't traveling, and this is our slowest summer in decades. The off season is only going to make things harder. None of that is your fault, but if we don't find a way to increase revenue soon..."

"We will." I lift my chin, shoving down a hitch of panic. Dad's right. Now is not the time for nerves. It's time for action. For solutions. Emotion has no place in these decisions.

"We have to." Dad's eyes harden into the look that used to unnerve younger me. I've since learned his outward expression doesn't always sync up with what's in his heart, but his intensity can be hard to handle when it's aimed your way. When he meets my eyes, his entire face softens. "Don't be so hard on yourself, Angel. Whatever happens, we'll be okay."

Outside the window, the ocean rolls onto the shore, oblivious to the dramas playing out in my heart. I cross the room and put my hand to the glass. "I don't want to be the one who killed the family legacy."

"You won't be."

I meet his eyes, huffing a laugh. "I delivered a killing blow as my first big move."

"The Hut withstood the test my father put it through. It'll withstand this as well."

My grandfather brought our family to its knees. Being likened to him, even a little, feels like a slap in the face.

"I don't want you to think less of me." The words are small, barely loud enough to be heard, but Dad is out of his chair in a heartbeat.

Gripping my arms, he gently turns me to face him. "I think the world of you. Nothing will change that. You're my daughter and I'm so very proud of you."

Would he feel the same if he knew Garrett Cooper kissed me to prove a point and I can't stop thinking about ways to make him do it again? That even knowing he's the enemy, I can't get him out of my head?

Would he be proud of his daughter, then?

"I just hope that stays true." I fold my arms over my chest and return my focus to the window, watching a couple stroll hand in hand across the beach. I noticed them when they checked in. They could barely look at each other, let alone touch. After a week at our resort with access to Reiki, massages, healthy food, fresh air, and meditation, they look glad to be together, laughing at something one of them said. They're lighter. Happier.

This is the legacy I want to protect.

There has to be a way to ensure The Hut is strong enough to reach more people. To ensure my dad stays proud of me.

I scour my brain and find an easy answer almost immediately:

Don't allow things with Garrett to escalate.

He's a business contact and needs to remain that way.

Dad leans against the wall, sliding his hands into his pockets. "Have you heard anything from Mr. Cooper?"

His name brings the memory of his lips on mine, his voice whispering in my ear.

Does it feel good, Angel? Do you like it when I take what I want?

My body throbs with want and I hate myself for it. Not only is Garrett Cooper a selfish ass, but our relationship is business. He has the power to solve the problem I created. How dare I jeopardize the deal, the future of my family, just because he kissed me like I've never been kissed?

Clearing my throat, I refocus on Dad. "Not yet, but he only just left. I'll give him the weekend and then reach out if we haven't connected."

"I agree with you on that timing." He turns his gaze out the window. "If we could finish construction on the satellite facility in South Carolina, things wouldn't look so grim. Multiple streams of income." He bobs his head. "That's the only way forward."

Later that night, after the kittens have been fed, I curl into bed with my phone, intending to finish my audiobook. Instead, I open my texts, my finger hovering over Garrett's name before tapping on the conversation. Scrolling to the top, I read through the curt back and forth while our phones were mixed up. His one-word answers send my imagination into overdrive.

He sent those clipped responses because he was indisposed.

What could he have been doing?

That word conjures images of something private, something that might not require clothing. I like the idea of Garrett Cooper without clothing, especially after seeing that pic of him without a shirt.

I told Dad I would wait until Monday to reach out, but I want to text him tonight.

And I don't want to talk about work.

"What do you want to talk about then?" I murmur as I stare at the blinking cursor.

I want to talk about that kiss, I type into the message box. *It left me breathless. The way you grabbed my hair, tilted my head to the angle you liked best. Your hot breath brushing against my skin as you whispered in my ear. Your body made a promise that night and I can't stop thinking about you. And fuck you for that because how dare you? How dare you get in my head? How dare you make this physical when this? Us? We're enemies. We may look like we're fighting on the same side, but we both know we're not. Something tells me you'll ruin me Garrett, and as much as it makes me hate myself, I want you to. You said you like giving orders. So I ask you, what would you order me to do if you knew how much I wanted you to fuck me?*

I stare at the text for a long second, my thumb suspended over the send button. Jesus. What am I thinking? I barely like the guy...

Though I didn't totally hate my time with him at the bar...

And he did manage to scare off that creepy douchebag...

And that kiss was...

Nope. Garrett Cooper is not for me. He's...he's

rocket fuel, and not in the good way. He'll come into my life. Combust. And take all of us down with him.

I move to delete the text—because really Angela? That seems like your next best move?—when my phone bumps with a new message.

GARRETT

> What are you doing?

My heart pounds as I read his words. Breath held, I triple check I didn't hit send on that stupid, *stupid* text, and I didn't. I can see that I didn't. That horrifying message is right there, waiting for me to delete it.

I feel like I've been caught red-handed. Like Garrett knows all the dirty things I want him to do to me. Like somehow, by wanting him to ruin me, I've ruined my chance at saving The Hut, instead.

Obviously, that's ridiculous. There's no way he could know what I typed, but I'm struggling to convince myself of that.

Careful to avoid the send button at all costs, I delete my message and type another.

> Just a quiet night at home.

> Is there something you wanted to say to me?

What the hell? I deleted the damn text. It's quite clearly not there. There's no way he knows. I sit up straight and stare at the screen, then craft a perfectly nonchalant response.

> Umm...not that I can think of

I grimace. Not exactly wordsmithery, but hey, I'm half convinced this guy can read a message I didn't send, so...you know...

> I saw you were typing something.
> Waited but got impatient

Sweet Jesus, he basically watched me beg him to fuck me. I mean, not really... He never saw the words, but as I was typing them in, he was right there. Watching the bubbles dance. Nerves spin in my stomach and my body goes on alert. I bite my lip as I respond.

> That's strange. I mean, I clicked into the conversation, maybe that's why it looked like I was typing?

> maybe

I chew on my lip as I wonder what to do. The smart play would be to wait for him to bring up work.

If he doesn't, I'll say goodnight, wait until Monday, and ask him about the contract as planned.

> What does a quiet night at home entail?

My brows lift in surprise. We're chatting now?

> I'm in bed, getting ready to listen to an audiobook

> Who would have thought we'd be in bed together so soon?

My eyes go wide. What is happening? Is he flirting with me? I sit up cross-legged and cradle my phone as my stomach flutters in excitement.

> Certainly not me. Is there something you wanted, Mr. Cooper?

> I want to know what you're really doing

> What's that supposed to mean? I just told you…

> You were typing something to me.

I swear to God, it's like he knows. Think, Angela.

Think! There's a perfectly reasonable explanation somewhere.

> I was going to ask when you'd like to see the new location

There's no way he won't buy that.

> You were going to bring up work at 11:45 on a Friday, while in bed, listening to an audiobook? I don't buy it Angel

I've told him so many times to stop calling me Angel, and I'm halfway through typing those words into the message box when I realize I like the familiarity coming from him even though I shouldn't.

I shouldn't, shouldn't, shouldn't.

Instead of calling him on it, I switch the focus to him.

> What were YOU doing? Also in bed at 11:45 on a Friday, looking at our conversation

> I was thinking about you.

My heart stops.
My jaw drops.
I read, re-read, and read his text again.

Oh, shit. Is this really happening? I chew my lip, trying to come up with an appropriate response

"Don't overthink it," I murmur, before asking the only question on my mind.

> What were you thinking about?

> I was thinking about how much I liked kissing you

I flop back onto my pillow and grin, letting that sink in. Well, there's that. At least I'm not the only one who can't get that night out of my brain.

My hands tremble as I type.

> Well I was texting you to let you know I was thinking about filing assault charges.

That should shut this conversation down.

> I don't believe you.

Or not.

> Fine. I was thinking about texting you because I can't get you out of my head either.

> What made you stop?

> I decided it wasn't appropriate and what I had to say was completely unprofessional

Ahh. I see.

> I didn't want to complicate things

And telling me you liked kissing me would complicate things?

> Are you implying it wouldn't?

Only if we let it

> And how do we make sure that doesn't happen?

We simply don't let it happen.

I snort at my screen because, yeah right. That's exactly the way it works.

> It's that easy?

It's that easy.

> Okay. Fine. I liked it when you kissed me.

And...?

> And I wouldn't mind doing it some more.

> That's what you wanted to tell me. You liked kissing me and you want to do it again? Come on, Angel. I'm not buying it.

I blow a puff of air past my lips. Am I really doing this? My fingers fly across the keyboard, acting on their own volition.

> Fine. I said your kiss left me breathless. That I loved the way it felt when you grabbed my hair and growled in my ear. That night you said you like giving orders. And I wanted to ask what you'd order me to do if you knew how much I wanted you.

I stare at the message for a long time, thumb hovering over the send button before I finally touch the screen. The text sends and I hold my breath, waiting for a response.

Seconds later, the phone lights up with a call.

CHAPTER SIXTEEN

Angela

"Hey," I breathe as I answer the phone. I'm shaky from excitement, from anticipation. I don't know what to expect, but I'm damn sure this call has nothing to do with business.

"Do you mean it, Angel?" Garrett's voice is husky. Needy. "Did you mean what you said?"

"I can't stop wondering what would happen...if we...if you..." I swallow hard. "What would you order me to do?" I whisper. "The thought just goes round and round and I don't know how I'll handle myself professionally the next time I see you because that's all I can think about."

Garrett clears his throat and I'd do anything to see his face. I have no idea what he's thinking, and the seconds of silence drive me crazy. Though, seeing his expression wouldn't help that much. He's probably glaring, doing that growly and intense thing he's so good at.

The thought makes me giggle and I clamp a hand over my mouth.

"If you're serious," he says, "I'll give you my first order right now and we can get whatever this is out of our system."

"Just like that, huh? One order and this whole thing will be out of our system?"

A little voice reminds me that the kiss he used to prove his point set whatever this is between us on fire. If one kiss can do that, what would a little phone sex do? Assuming that's what he's talking about.

But what else could he be talking about?

"Like I said before, this will only become what we let it. Maybe releasing some of the tension is exactly what we need. But only with your permission. This only works if you want it too. Consent matters. Even on the phone."

Nerves flutter in my belly. Not only am I now positive he's talking about phone sex, but I've never done it before. I've never even considered it before, especially with someone I barely know and don't even like.

"I'm not a talker in...in umm...this kind of, well, you know, sexual situations." I drag a hand down my face. Sexual situations? Really? "Quiet as a mouse. That's me. It's the only time you can get me to shut up."

"It doesn't matter, as long as you're good at listening." Garrett's deep voice sends a shiver of desire through me.

"Tell me what you want me to do." The words are so quiet, it's like someone else is speaking.

"Put me on speakerphone. You're gonna need your hands."

My nerves pitch into overdrive and I suddenly feel ridiculous. All the reasons this is a bad idea come rioting back through my head. He's a business contact and he's playing for the other team. He deals with distractions, and I want real connection. Nothing good can come of this.

"Garrett..."

"Do what I say, Angel." He speaks firmly yet gently and something about the combination breaks my resistance. People have casual sexual encounters all the time. Why can't I?

I tap the speakerphone button then place the device on my knee.

"It's done."

"Good girl."

My breath hitches and a smile tugs at my lips. I drop my gaze, overwhelmed by the heat those two little words ignite in me. Why do I like it so much and how can I make him say it again?

"What are you wearing?" Garrett asks. There's a rustle of fabric on his end of the line...the hiss of sheets? Is he settling into bed? Taking off his clothes?

"A pink tank top and silk shorts."

"Imagine I'm standing at the edge of your bed, watching you take them off."

I envision Garrett, tall, imposing, wearing the black slacks and white button down he seems to love so much. His shirt is undone, revealing the powerful chest I saw in the picture, with his tie draped around his neck. His hands are shoved into his pockets as he watches me pull my tank top over my head, then shimmy my shorts over my hips and toss them on the floor. In my mind, he smiles darkly, his eyes locked on mine.

"Okay," I breathe. "Clothes are off."

"Imagine I'm kissing you. I start at your mouth, then work my way down your throat and take a nipple between my teeth." He pauses while I trail my fingers down my chest. "Would you rather I bite? Or lick? Pain or pleasure, Angel?"

"Both," I manage. "I like both."

"Good. Pinch your nipples, Beautiful. Let me hear you moan."

I do as I'm told, moaning in pleasure that's only amplified by Garrett's growl of approval.

"I'm taking off my clothes now. I'm so fucking hard for you."

I close my eyes and see him lying back in bed, his hand stroking his dick as his eyes burn with pleasure.

"Are you using your hands on yourself?" he asks.

His voice is tight. Low. My body throbs with desire. "Yes."

"Good girl."

The words have me clenching in satisfaction and I smile as my eyes slide shut. "I like it when you say that."

"Then give me another reason to say it."

"What do you want me to do?"

"Rub your clit and imagine it's my tongue."

I slip my hand between my legs, rubbing the tight bundle of nerves hidden there.

"Are you touching yourself, too?" My voice hitches with need. For him, but also for validation, for confirmation. My brain is certain I'm making a mistake, but my body is beyond caring.

"I'm stroking my cock, Angel. It's so hard for you."

I close my eyes, imagining myself trapped beneath him, his dick slipping into me so slowly I can't stand it. "I'm close, Garrett," I groan. "Oh God. I'm so close."

"Keep going. I want to know what you sound like when you come."

I moan, cursing, as his breathing sounds rough and ragged in my ear.

"There. Yes!"

As I tumble over the edge, my body clenching and bucking, Garrett's words fall away, leaving only his breath. I focus on the sounds he makes as he chases his release, until his breathing stalls and he grunts, then falls quiet.

I stare at the ceiling, melting into my pillow as I catch my breath.

Holy fucking shit.

My first casual sexual encounter.

But wait...

How was that a "casual encounter" when it was the single hottest thing in my life? Nothing about what just happened feels casual.

There's silence on his end, and then, "Still with me?"

"I think so," I say with a laugh, tapping the speakerphone button and putting the phone to my ear. "So... that's a thing we did."

"Do you regret it?"

I slip under the sheet, pulling it up to cover my breasts. "No. Do you?"

"Not even a little." There's a smile to Garrett's voice and it brings one of my own.

"You really don't think this'll change things between us?" I ask, because how can it not? How will I look at him the same now that I know what he sounds like when he comes? Now that I'll crave those two little words in that rasping voice...*good girl*.

"It'll only change what we allow it to change." He sounds so certain, but I'm still not convinced.

"We're still business partners?"

"Business partners who have phone sex." Garrett laughs teasingly and I roll my eyes. I like this lighter version of him. It feels personal, like I'm getting a glimpse of him with his guard down.

"Very funny."

"I thought so."

"I just don't want this to interfere..."

"Honestly, Angel? It would've been worse if we didn't get that out of the way. I couldn't stop thinking about you."

"And now you can?"

"At the very least I'll be able to focus when we meet in South Carolina to check out the new site. Otherwise, I would only have been able to focus on how much I wanted to fuck you."

"Yeah." A nervous giggle. "Same. Good thing that's out of our system."

"Exactly."

Only, it doesn't feel like this is out of my system. If anything, I want him more now that I know what he sounds like when he comes.

It's safe to say Garrett Cooper is firmly lodged in my system.

We plan to meet at the South Carolina site in two days and end the call. I stare at the phone for several long minutes, unable to process what I just did. Instead, I focus on the fact that I have a trip to plan. I need to book a flight. A hotel. Oh shit! I can't just leave the kittens! I text Nathan and Micah, asking if they'd mind feeding them while I'm gone. It's too late for them to respond, but I'm sure they'll give me hell about it first thing in the morning.

Once that's over, there's nothing to distract me from what I just did with Garrett.

I can't believe something like that happened and I don't have anyone to talk about it with. There's no way I'm telling Nick I had phone sex with a guy I've known only a handful of days. That's not something you bring up to a male cousin, no matter how close you are.

Right?

I try to imagine the look on his face as I share the story and burst out laughing.

Yeah. No. That's not something I'll be telling Nick the Wonderful.

What does it mean that Garrett's phone call was the single hottest thing that ever happened in my life?

Does it mean I'm sheltered? (Probably.)

Inexperienced? (Definitely.)

Or does it mean there's something special about the guy?

"You mean something special like he lives in another state?" I ask myself. "Or something special like we're gonna work together and the only reason he called was to get me out of his system?"

Of all the stupid, boneheaded things I've ever done…

Shaking my head, I place my phone on the nightstand and pad into the bathroom to clean up. Garrett might have gotten me out of his system, but what we did tonight injected a heavy dose of "Yes please, Mr. Cooper" into mine.

Hearing his moans. His grunts. His deep voice ordering me to touch myself. To make myself come…

I already want to call him back and beg for more.

"Out of my system, my ass," I say to my reflection as I reach for my toothbrush.

And we'll be seeing each other again in just a handful of days. How will I make it through without jumping his bones?

CHAPTER SEVENTEEN

Garrett

Tonight did not work out the way I thought it would.

After thinking about Angela the entire time I was at Cheers 'n Beers, I told myself one text conversation would jog my memory on how much she irritates me. But she said what she said, and I did what I did and now here we are.

Whatever the fuck that means.

She's in the Keys and I'm in Wildrose. In two days, we'll be in South Carolina and then what? We pretend we don't know how we sound when we come?

"Yes, asshole," I murmur. "That's exactly what we do."

That's what I told her would happen.

And that's what I *want* to happen.

Listing every reason Angela is a bad idea, I put myself to bed, only to stare at the ceiling for at least an hour, replaying every word she said…

…every sound she made…

The phone rings and I lurch awake, slapping it off the bedside table in my haste to answer. Annoyance has me flopping back on the pillow when I see Branson's name on the ID.

Pinching the bridge of my nose, I answer. "It's early."

"Where are you?"

"In bed."

"Which bed? The one in the city? Where you belong? Or the one in that little town you run to when you need to lick your wounds."

If he wasn't my boss, I'd tell him exactly what *he* could lick for saying something like that. Instead, I push up onto an elbow, rest my head in my hand, and bite my tongue. "I'm in Wildrose."

"Jesus, Cooper. When are you gonna pull it together? Get your head on right? A man with your talents needs to be where the action is."

"A man with my talents brings the action to him." I run a hand over my face. "Is there something you need?"

"Yeah." Branson clears his throat. "I need an update on the Hutton Hotel. Things good there?"

Angela's smile. The flash of wit in her eyes. The way she moaned my name.

"When was the last time I didn't close a deal?" I sit up, wiping the sleep out of my eye.

"Never."

"I'm glad you remember because, when you're calling, I'm not making money. Don't babysit me. Don't check up on me. I've got this."

Branson sighs. "If anybody else talked to me like that, they'd be gone."

"Good thing I'm not everyone else."

"That you're not. But why don't you give me an update anyway."

"Things are moving forward." I swipe a hand through my hair. "Financials look good. I like their plans and their projections. And, you know, the family seems decent."

"Why would I care if they're decent or not? What I

want to know is if this investment is going to earn out for Vision Enterprise."

Of course that's what he wants to know. How could I forget that all anyone cares about is what's in it for them?

Not Angela. She wants to expand her business to give back to the community...

I scoff at the thought. That's what she said to sell me the idea. But underneath?

"They're gonna make us a shitload of money," I say. "I'm meeting Angela Hutton in a few days to look at the new site."

"The daughter." Branson sounds like he's smiling. "Now that's the kind of shit I keep you around for. You're a good-looking man. She's young and naïve. Maybe a little flirting. A little wining and dining. Make her fall in love with you and skew the contract in our favor. I like the way you think."

And I hate the way he thinks. Toying with someone's emotions to get what you want? That's not my way. Though, I definitely got what I wanted last night. And there was a lot of flirting, though I skipped the wining and dining and went straight for the gold.

Fuck.

I feel dirty.

My therapist would have a field day with the story.

Tearing it to shreds, looking for hints of mommy issues or counting the echoes of Elizab—

"Keep me in the loop, Cooper," Branson barks. "I like this deal. Do what you need to do to make me love it."

He ends the call and I drop the phone on my bed, swinging my legs off the mattress and resting my elbows on my knees. I scrub my face and stand, making my way to the bathroom with a head full of questions. Maybe I won't tell my therapist about this whole situation. She already wants me to find a new job, preaching I've made so much money that I don't need to work. She can fuck off very much about that. I don't care how many millions I have in my account; I still like seeing that number grow.

Besides, she's my therapist, not my keeper. And I don't even know if I need her anymore.

I'm fine. I've been fine.

No more angry outbursts. I'm spending time with my family, just like she suggested.

And hey, I even made a new friend. Kind of. Can you be friends with someone you don't like, but ordered to take off her clothes anyway? I splash water on my face then stare at my reflection, droplets running off my nose, my chin.

"Pull yourself together, man." I grip the porcelain

sink and meet my eyes. Dad likes to remind me they're the same shade as my mother's. What would she say if she met me now? Would she like who I've become?

As much as I want that to be true, something tells me she'd be as disappointed as the rest of my family.

CHAPTER EIGHTEEN

Angela

The trip to Bliss, South Carolina is an easy one. A quick flight, a short drive, and tada!

Here I am!

The town is adorable. It's small, right on the coast, and the perfect blend of quaint and serene. Tourists have yet to discover it, so The Hut will be the first and only hotel here, which serves our mission statement ridiculously well. People don't come to the Hutton Hotel for tourist trap stuff. They come to rest. To recharge. To focus on their emotional, physical, and spiritual health and be pampered while they heal from the stress of our purposeless contemporary lives.

The great thing about Bliss is that if our guests do choose to venture off the resort, they'll find plenty to keep them occupied. From casual coffee shops and bars, to a luxurious restaurant called Harrison's right on the water, to a skydiving facility a few miles outside town for any adrenaline junkies who might book a stay with us, Bliss has something for everyone. As I pull my rental car to a stop in front of a sprawling stretch of beach, I'm struck yet again by how perfect the area is. It's a one-in-a-million blend of *away from it all* and *modern conveniences.*

The location for our new hotel is set back from the main road, following a long drive through lush black oaks. When the road ends, the trees open up, offering a stunning view of the ocean. Waves serenely lap the beach. Palms bend in the breeze. Sunlight sparkles over the water.

It feels like a little slice of paradise and this...

I inhale deeply, closing my eyes and taking it all in.

...this spot is the beginning of our future.

I know it.

I feel it.

Deep down in my gut.

This is right.

This is what the business needs to take that next step forward.

"This is where it all begins," I whisper, holding my hair out of my face as it catches in the wind.

A car rolls to a stop beside me and I glance over as

Garrett kills the engine and climbs out. He looks fine as fuck in a dark blue button-down. The shirtsleeves hug his arms and chest, highlighting everything I imagined while touching myself for him a few days ago.

I'm nervous. How are we supposed to handle ourselves? Do we ignore what we did? Put it behind us never to be talked about again? Or will things be different now? They feel different for me, but maybe this is just another day in the life for a man like him.

Garrett approaches and I lift a hand with a smile. "Hey."

He dips his head in my direction and folds his arms over his chest, taking in our surroundings. Sunlight glints in his hair, illuminating streaks of gold I hadn't noticed before. "This is good," he says, nodding. "I like it."

Okay then. We're gonna ignore what we did. I can get behind that.

"I'm glad you think so." I stand beside him, mimicking his posture as I survey the area. "This expansion could end up better than our original location. We broke ground with a plan here and know what we want the finished product to look like. The one at home is chaotic because it started out as just that...a home. The rest is history. A very successful history that's only getting better with time."

That feeling of legacy sweeps over me again, the

one that makes me heady and dreamy. The one that makes me certain I'm doing the right thing—not just for me, not just for the family, but for everyone who meets us. This is what I was made for.

Garrett looks at me like I've lost my mind. "You mean successful save for the hiccup of not having enough money to complete the project without my assistance."

"A hiccup's a hiccup, right? A short annoyance that's over as soon as it starts." I smile because damn it, why not? Being here makes me feel like I'm swimming in possibility, like the future I've dreamed of has finally arrived. "I have a sneaking suspicion you're going to give me the money. You wouldn't be here otherwise. My little setback is over, and things can only get better from now on."

Garrett turns his focus to the horizon, his jaw tight, his expression unreadable. "Do you always do that?"

"Do what?"

He arches a brow, a hint of a smile lifting his lips. "Ignore reality to focus on the positive."

"How am I ignoring reality? You saw the projections. This?" I gesture around the area. "This is nothing but good."

"Once I give you the money."

I nod. "Once you give me the money."

"You and I have very different views on reality.

You look around and see 'nothing but good.' I see a project that failed before it got off the ground."

"But that's the thing." My voice rises in excitement. "It didn't fail. It stalled. Things happen and we can label them as 'bad,' or we can label them as 'opportunity.' My parents always taught me that everything in life comes down to mindset."

Garrett slides his hands into his pockets, regarding me with curiosity. "And this financially devastating pickle you find yourself in. You see it as an opportunity?"

"One hundred percent," I say with determination. "The original investors? They were wrong for us. For me. But you? This? This feels right, you know? We stalled for a reason. To bring you and me together."

Shit.

That could one hundred percent be taken the wrong way.

"And the family of course," I add quickly. "All of us. Not just…you know…you and me."

Garrett stares for a long minute before bobbing his head and looking away.

Relief softens my posture. He could have called me on that verbal blunder but didn't.

Working together might actually be as easy as he promised. We'll just…talk about business and ignore all the other stuff.

Look at me go, having a casual sexual encounter and not letting it turn into A Thing.

"For the record—" Garret folds his arms over his chest "—the chaos of the original hotel is part of its charm. I suggest you replicate it here. The only changes I'd make would be to put your highest margin features in the center of the chaos. Like they do in casinos. If guests are walking past the onsite bar and restaurant, or the luxury massage suite fourteen times a day on their way to and from everything else..." He levels me with a knowing look as he pulls his phone out of his pocket. "You'll double your profits from those segments within six months."

"Smart."

"That's what I do." Frowning, Garrett stares at his screen. "Sorry. One sec. Business." His thumbs tap, tap, tap away as his jaw pulses. He looks so serious, so intense, I try to imagine him joking, or being silly, or doing something ridiculous just for the fun of it and I can't. It's like a peanut butter and orange slice sandwich. Some things just don't go together.

Garrett finishes his text and slides his phone back in his pocket. "Now come on. Show me what's been done and talk me through what's left."

"You can see what's been done." I wave a hand around the site. "This is everything."

"This hole? That's it?" Garrett lifts a brow and huffs a laugh.

"Clearly, we didn't get very far. We basically paid a fortune to drive a construction crew out and dig the foundation, then the economy went south, the investment company disappeared, and we had to pull the plug."

"I'm sorry, but I have to ask." Garrett pinches the bridge of his nose. Everything about him oozes judgment and frustration. "If this is all you've done, why are we even here? There's nothing for me to see. We could have covered all this before I left the Keys."

But we couldn't cover it all. Some things you have to experience to understand. I could show him all the pictures in the world, but they couldn't convey how it feels to stand here, in this perfect spot, and *know*.

"There's plenty for you to see," I say. "This town. This site. You can't tell me you don't feel that."

"Feel what?" Garrett shades his eyes with a hand as he surveys the area.

How can he not instantly know what I'm talking about? I'm surprised I have to explain it, although I shouldn't be. Everything about the man screams "practical and not into listening to subtle inspiration."

"That...I don't know if there's even a word for it. This sense of...right. Of good. Of, you know, magic."

The arch to Garrett's eyebrow says I just lost about a thousand cool points. "Magic?"

"Yes, Mr. Serious. Magic. Humor me for a second and hear me out." I step onto the broken ground, talking as I point out the general locations for the main building and the private bungalows. "We thought we'd add a dedicated meditation hall here. And the open-air massage stations have been a hit back home. They'd go there." I wave a hand to my left, not looking where I'm going, and stumble over a rock.

With a gasp, I brace to go down, but Garrett catches me, his steadying hands on my back and arm, his touch sending a shuddering jolt of "Oh shit, he is *so* not out of my system!" through my veins.

But why?

Why is he still in there?

He's been completely professional since he arrived. He's done nothing to indicate he wants anything to do with me outside of business and I have to wonder why I don't feel the same. Garrett and I have nothing in common. We live in different states. He's all about casual distractions and I'm looking for a serious connection—and I'm not even looking. Not while the hotel requires my attention.

For all that to add up to me still wanting him makes me feel small. Powerful women don't lust after bad matches.

"Careful now," Garrett murmurs, his eyes dark and hooded as they lock on mine. "You okay? You didn't twist an ankle, did you?"

His attention darts to my mouth and back again. His hands linger longer than a professional relationship should allow. Maybe I'm not the only one struggling to ignore whatever this is.

"I'm good." Carefully, I step out of his arms and shake my head, laughing. "Sorry about that. Clumsy me."

But I'm not sorry. Not at all. I want to orchestrate a hundred new reasons to fall and have him catch me. I'll be a klutz if it makes him touch me. I'll swoon like an eighteenth-century debutante if that gets me into his arms.

I let out a long sigh, inwardly rolling my eyes. Instead of a mental debate on the merits of swooning, I'm better off keeping things professional and congratulating myself on not turning this into A Thing.

"I think that's all the magic I need to see." Garrett bobs his head, his face maddeningly inscrutable. "You feel like you can make your way back to the cars safely, or do I need to carry you?"

I laugh. "I think I can make it."

"Suit yourself," he replies with a scowl.

Still, he places a hand on the small of my back to steady me and it's a miracle I don't fall flat on my face because that one point of contact is all I can focus on. His touch sends a surge of "Thank you for calling me a good girl." through me and I bite my lip, fighting a smile and dropping my gaze to my feet so he can't see me blush.

CHAPTER NINETEEN

Garrett

This is bad.

Choosing to meet Angela today—the anniversary of the *first* worst day of my life—was risky in the first place. I knew that and fooled myself into thinking it wouldn't matter. But the minute I pulled up to the construction site and saw her standing there, I realized I was in trouble. Her fiery hair caught in the wind. A pair of dress slacks hugged her ass, and a white blouse highlighted her perfect tits. The wind whipped the thin fabric against her chest, perking her nipples under the hint of a white lace bra.

Fucking white lace.

I'd guess she dressed like that to taunt me, but

Angela doesn't play mind games. That's more of a Melinda move.

Just like going to a bar with two guys while her boyfriend is overseas is more of a Melinda move. One of Mom's favorite principles is that we become an amalgamation of the people around us. If we surround ourselves with goodness, we'll come to expect it. And, apparently, if you surround yourself with people like Melinda, you'll come to expect the worst out of everyone.

Compared to The Ex-Future Mrs. Cooper, Angela's optimism, her view of the world, it's a breath of fresh air. In a way, she reminds me of home—of Charlie and Connor, of Dad and Mom.

I like who I am when I'm with her.

And that scares me to death. I don't do relationships for a reason. I can't stand being vulnerable. Letting someone in guarantees I'll end up hurt when I inevitably lose them.

But worse than that, what if the deal falls through because I'm being stupid? I mixed business with pleasure once and it nearly ruined me. What kind of fool would try it again?

What a disaster. I tangled things up with that phone call. All I can think about is seeing her naked. I know what she sounds like when she comes, and now I want to know what she looks like. I want my hands on her. I need to touch her. To taste her. To pin her to a bed and worship her body the way she deserves.

And now, after just twenty minutes staring at a hole in the ground so we can appreciate "the magic," we're supposed to check in at the hotel one town over and that's that? We'll sign some contracts, I'll fly back to Wildrose and she'll head home, and we're just business from this point forward?

That should work for me.

It should.

It really fucking should.

But it won't.

I lean on the hood of my rental, almost hating myself for what I'm about to do. "You wanna grab something to eat? There's this restaurant a few miles from here. Harrison's. I hear it's pretty good."

My therapist would say I'm distracting myself from bad memories on this shitshow of a day, but she'd be wrong. I'm choosing to spend time with someone despite the memories. Not because of them.

Angela studies me for a long time, eyes searching —*questioning*—as she chews her bottom lip. "This getting of something to eat," she says with a quirk of her head, "are we talking business or pleasure, here?"

"Business, obviously. You're officially the only person I know in this state, and I hate eating alone. We can go over the contracts. Maybe forward them to your lawyers if everything looks solid to you."

"Right. I see." She looks away, a flash of disappointment in her eyes. "Then sure. Yeah. Dinner sounds great. I heard about Harrison's when we first scoped this location. Been wanting to check out the menu ever since."

"Wonderful. I'll lead." With a grunt of frustration, I push off the car and yank open the driver's door.

It shouldn't be like this. If it wasn't for the fact that I can't get enough of Ms. Angela Hutton, we'd drive back to the hotel, sign some papers, and move the fuck on. This is different.

Because of her.

I haven't felt so off my game since everything blew up with Elizabeth.

"Great." Angela gives me a funny look as she passes me on the way to her car. "I'll meet you there."

I use the drive to Harrison's to get myself under control.

This thing between us? We'll make it work somehow or another. I'll look at her like I would any other person I'm doing business with, and she'll do the same. It doesn't matter how beautiful she is. Or how funny she is. Or how much her stupid positive outlook makes me want to forget that hope is a dangerous, fickle beast. It doesn't matter how much she aggravates me or how much it drives me crazy to be near her. I will look at her as Angela Hutton—future owner of The Hutton Hotel. Not Dirty Angel. Not Pencil Skirt Angel. Not Hot Phone Sex Angel.

She's a colleague.

And that's the end of that.

We arrive at Harrison's without issue and find two parking spots beside each other. Angela shuts her car door and stretches, the evening sun glinting in her hair as she closes her eyes and reaches for the sky.

Fuck, she's hot. I can still hear her moans in my ear, those sweet gasps—

She catches me staring, lifting an eyebrow while a secretive smile plays across her mouth. So much for treating her like any other colleague.

"You ready?" she asks, looking as uncertain as I feel. She doesn't think we can be professional either, which makes me all the more determined to pull it off.

"Let's do this." I fight the urge to put my hand on her back instead of walking calmly beside her. When we arrive at the front door, I pull it open, gesturing for her to enter. The atmosphere is sophisticated, and the hostess greets us with a polished smile.

"Two this evening?"

I nod. "We'd like a table with a view of the ocean, if that's possible."

"Right this way, sir."

I gesture for Angela to walk in front of me. As she

strides ahead, my gaze lands on her luscious hips, swaying with each of her steps. I imagine my hands gripping her ass as she rides me, her lips parted, her tits bouncing. She glances over her shoulder and catches me looking, a twinkle settling into her eyes.

She likes that I like looking at her.

Good. Because I couldn't stop if I tried.

CHAPTER TWENTY

Garrett

Over the course of a delicious meal, Angela and I talk about Bliss and all the reasons it's perfect for her hotel. We talk about the weather. We talk about the economy and the toll it's taken on her business, on mine, on the world at large. She reads through the contracts and my proposal, her eyes narrowing shrewdly as she questions me on details. After she's satisfied with my answers, she forwards them to her lawyers for review.

And that should be enough.

But it's not.

While the banter is fun and the conversation clicks along, it's not doing it for me. For as much as I resist, I want to know her, and I want to be known by her.

And I don't just mean sexually. I find myself asking about her likes and dislikes, her childhood, her time at school.

I want connection.

I'm such an idiot for feeling that way.

People are good at one thing and one thing only, letting each other down. Judging each other for our worst traits and failing to see the good, the humanity, the struggle. We take what we want from each other and move on.

Letting Angela know me will not end well.

It never does.

"This has been really nice." She rests her elbows on the table and her chin in her hands. "For someone who claims to be all business, you're easy to talk to."

"That's because business is easy to talk about."

Her eyes darken and she buys time by taking a drink. "And here I thought you might actually be enjoying my company."

I watch, transfixed, as her tongue darts out to moisten her lips. "I am. I'm enjoying it a lot. But that doesn't change the fact that this evening was just business."

I don't know if I'm repeating myself to remind her, to remind me, or to remind us both, but the statement puts a damper on the atmosphere.

"Look. Garrett." Angela sits back, sighing in frustration. "It's clear there's something going on here. And I'm not saying we need to do anything about it, but...I don't know...do you really think ignoring *this*—" she gestures between us "—is the best way forward?"

"I do. It is." I finish my whiskey and set the glass on the table. I want another, but still have the drive to the hotel ahead of me. More importantly, *Angela* still has the drive to the hotel ahead of her. If I order another drink, she might too, and previous experience says Angel's a lightweight.

I push my glass away. No more whiskey tonight.

"Shouldn't we at least talk about what we did? On the phone?" She leans closer, lowering her voice. The flickering candle casts a dance of light and shadow across her face. She's really quite beautiful.

"What's talking going to do for us?" I spin my glass on the table, watching as the ice catches the light. "I like my women in the form of distractions, and that's not what you're looking for."

Resist, Garrett. Resist. Don't let her see that she's becoming a different kind of distraction. One you can't get out of your mind no matter what you do.

"What if I want to be distracted by you the same way you want to be distracted by me?" Angela cocks her head, her eyes searching mine.

I lean back as laughter sounds from somewhere in the restaurant. It mixes with the quiet music and the clatter of silverware against plates. I've been so focused on her, I forgot there were other people around us and haven't checked my phone once.

Strange.

"I don't see it," I say, enjoying the way it feels to have her undivided attention.

"What's that supposed to mean?"

"You're not the kind of person who's looking for distractions."

"Oh, really?" Angela scoffs. "Enlighten me then, since you know me so well. What kind of person am I?"

"You believe in real love." I grab my water and eye her as I drink. "You want to be seen for who you are. You want to share important facts about yourself and to hear deep personal stories in return. You want connection."

She recoils. "And you don't?"

"I don't." Liar. I very much do, which is why I need to shut this down.

"Why?" Angela's brow furrows.

Because connection leads to pain.

To loss.

To anniversaries of terrible events that come back to haunt you year after year for the rest of your life.

"Because I'm not easy to connect with."

"That's something you could fix if you wanted to."

Angela's frown deepens. My worldview confuses her, as it does most people who don't know how easy it is to lose the people you love. Life changes with the snap of a finger…

…the blink of an eye…

…the shriek of tires on pavement and a nightmare of twisted metal…

Pushing those thoughts away, I fold my arms on the table, leaning closer. "So is your desire to have a serious relationship."

She mimics the action. "For starters, you're the one who decided that's what I want and for two, how in the world is that something that needs fixed?"

"There's nothing wrong with people coming together just for sex."

Thoughts tick away behind her eyes before she says, "Just like there's nothing wrong with someone wanting the happily-ever-after. And, you know, bonus points if the sex is on fire too. It's probably the only way the happily-ever-after will happen." Angela sits back like she's won the match and I laugh wryly.

"What's this, Angel?" I lift a condescending eyebrow. "A proposal?"

"What? Jesus, Garrett. No. I'm just saying. I don't think there's anything wrong with wanting a serious relationship, especially not if you find the right person. Not that I'm saying I want one with you. Or that you're anywhere close to the right person. I'm just...you know...talking."

She's flustered. Her cheeks pink. Her eyes wide. I shouldn't like it, but I do.

The bill arrives and I pay, like I would if this was any other business meeting. We leave the restaurant and drive to the hotel one town over, and I can't keep myself from watching her in the rearview. I need to know she's safe, she's paying attention, she's not about to make one tiny mistake that leads to a disastrous result. The compulsion annoys the fuck out of me. For all my talk about business this and business that, I'm blurring those lines in a big way.

We make it to the hotel without incident and, after circling a full parking lot in search of a spot, walk quietly into the building.

"I drove straight to the construction site from the airport. Still need to check in." Angela smiles sheepishly as she indicates the front desk with a jerk of her thumb. "Though I guess the suitcase I'm wheeling behind me probably gave that away."

"Same." I heft my own bag, then set my jaw and focus straight ahead because if I so much as look at her, I'll drag her to my room and break the promises we made on the phone. I need to be inside her and that's not helping anything at this point. Not after all my sanctimonious preaching about distractions at the restaurant.

Two clerks check us in and we stand there, side by side, like we did at Seaside Mobile. Who would have thought a simple mistake would lead to whatever this clusterfuck of attraction is between us. If we hadn't left with each other's phones that day, we wouldn't have needed to meet at the bar. I wouldn't have kissed her. Or called her. None of this would have happened.

If only that stupid kid hadn't tried to Kamikaze off his mom's suitcase. I'd be on my way back home, where I could let all things Angela Hutton drain out of my system for good.

"Oh...Mr. Cooper." The young woman checking me in glances up from her computer. "I'm so sorry. There's been a problem with your reservation." The screeching and squealing of children playing comes from somewhere in the hotel and she shakes her head in annoyance.

This does not bode well. Judging by the glazed over smile, the stupidly full parking lot, and the way this woman is fidgeting, I'm about to be righteously pissed off.

"What kind of problem...Tara?" I arch an eyebrow as I read her name tag.

The poor woman grimaces. "Unfortunately, the

guests who checked out of your room this morning left a lot of…umm…damage. I'm afraid it's not habitable."

"And won't be for some time," murmurs the woman working with Angela.

Not habitable? Are you fucking kidding me?

"Then find me a new one." This is what I get for staying in a cheap hotel. A more expensive establishment would have solved the problem before I arrived.

"Well, see—" Tara glances at the clerk beside her "—unfortunately, the hotel is completely booked. There's some sort of dance competition in town and—"

"Are you telling me I flew down to nowhere South Carolina, where you are the only hotel for miles, you don't have the room you promised me, *and* it didn't occur to you—to anyone—to call me?"

"We did, Mr. Cooper. Multiple times." Tara glances at Angela as if help waits for her there.

I dig my phone out of my pocket and open the call history, ready to unload my anger on the woman with both barrels…

Would you look at that.

Four missed calls, all from the hotel. I was so preoccupied with Angela at dinner, I didn't hear them come in. Fucking perfect. Grimacing, I slide my phone back into my pocket as a herd of little girls and their mothers filters into the lobby. They mill around like lost geese, increasing the sound level by a thousand percent.

"I'm very sorry, Mr. Cooper." Tara raises her voice to be heard over the din. "I wish there was something I could do. There's a motel about twenty miles north of here. It's not as nice as this one—"

"Not by a long shot," the clerk helping Angela says with a laugh. "Unless you intend to pay by the hour, if you know what I mean."

"You've got to be fucking kidding me," I murmur under my breath and Angela puts a hand on my arm.

"It's fine," she says with that optimistic twinkle in her eye. "You can share my room. All they had left when I made my reservation were rooms with two queen beds. So...we're good. Problem solved. Fate is looking out for us."

Fate is not looking out for us. Fate is laughing her ass off.

Two beds won't change my urge to fuck Angela senseless.

It'll only make it harder to ignore.

God help me, I'm in over my head.

CHAPTER TWENTY-ONE

Angela

What the hell did I just do?

Like, from start to finish, what went on this evening?

Garrett was so hot and cold at dinner; I couldn't tell which way was up. And now, I offer to share a room with him? Because *that* will make ignoring the swelling in my ovaries any easier?

Like it or not, I want him. And not just in an "Oh golly gee, I'd like to see him naked" way. I'm talking full on, I want to have a torrid love affair with this man. One that haunts my dreams for years. The kind they make movies about, where I'll be old and gray and still thinking back to the night of passion I spent with Garrett Cooper in a small town called Bliss.

When he looks at me, the whole world falls away. I feel safe with him. Complete. His intensity feels comfortable—when it's not making me want to strangle him. It's like his energy matches mine, yet is the opposite of mine.

Like yin and yang.

Masculine and feminine.

Two halves of a whole.

He balances me, which is so freaking annoying I don't know whether to laugh or cry.

The clerk checking me in hands over a set of keycards and Garrett and I walk down the hallway, side by side, drenched in awkwardness. He's mad. It radiates off him like heat waves off the pavement. I don't understand. There was a problem, but it's solved. And maybe, just maybe, the solution is fate looking out for us once again.

My keycard slides into the lock and we jostle our way into the room, then pull up short once we're inside. The space would feel small without him beside me but now, with Garrett's energy sucking up the oxygen, it's downright claustrophobic.

Worse, there's only one bed.

Just one giant bed and the two of us standing there, staring at it like it might bite.

"Fuck this day." Garrett pauses in front of the thing with its cheap hotel comforter and uninviting pillows, hands in pockets, looking unsure what to do with himself. A few uncomfortable seconds tick by with him just standing there.

"It's fine." I swallow hard and wheel my suitcase deeper into the room. "I'll sleep on the floor."

"Like hell you will." Garrett leans his bag against the wall. "You get the bed. I'll take the floor."

Footsteps thunder down the hallway with shrieking laughter and girlish yelling following behind.

"Not like we'll get any sleep anyway," he finishes, pinching the bridge of his nose with a sigh.

My mind immediately presents a list of ways we could entertain ourselves with one bed, while not sleeping. All of them require us to be *indisposed* and most of them have me sounding like the kids in the hallway. Shrieking. Squealing. My voice rasping its way up my throat...

"All I can think about is what I want to do to you in that bed." Garrett's eyes swim with something dark. Something needy. "That's all I've been able to think about since our phone call."

Would you look at that. We're thinking along the same lines.

And that calls for emergency tactics.

"Wow. Okay. We're gonna jump right in there." I move past him to sit in the chair near the windows with the thick, blackout curtains drawn. "Look, Garrett.

Whatever's going on between us, you're right. I'm not the kind of woman who wants to be a distraction. I feel like it's important I put that out there before things get more complicated than they are."

"Sorry. Sorry." He holds up his hands then rakes one across his mouth. "You've got me off balance, Ms. Hutton."

"Ditto, Mr. Cooper."

There has to be a way to break the tension because he's just standing there and I'm just sitting here. How is this even real? I shift in my seat and clear my throat. "What would you be doing right now, if you weren't here with me?"

"I'd probably climb into bed, turn on the TV, and wish I'd thought to bring a bottle of whiskey."

"Aha! Great minds!" I stand and cross the room, aware of every inch of Garrett's body as I pass. The desire to leap into his arms is so strong, I clasp my hands together until I'm clear. "It's not whiskey but..." I dig through my suitcase and pull out a bottle of wine. "Feel like having a drink? We can sit. Talk. And if we run out of things to say, we'll turn on the TV."

Garrett grunts, folding his arms over his chest as he considers. "Sounds harmless enough."

I can't help myself.

I laugh in his face, which shocks a quizzical smile out of him.

He physically wipes away the expression. "And that's funny because...?"

"Because the last word I'd use to describe you is 'harmless.'" I dig for the bottle opener and go to work on the wine while he strips the paper cups near the coffee pot of the protective wrapping and sets them on the dresser.

"Show me the harm I've caused you," Garrett says in such a pompous, condescending, utterly unaware of himself way, my eyebrows launch into my hairline.

"Would you like me to explain my embarrassment when I walked into a meeting with my dad and uncle, only to find the guy I'd drunkenly chewed out the night before?"

He folds his arms and looks unimpressed. "That one's not entirely on me."

"What if I said the guy totally knew who I was and chose to keep it to himself? Or perhaps I should highlight the time I invited said guy out for drinks to apologize for that behavior and he kissed me. Just out of the blue. For no reason. Or what about the night he called and told me to get naked—"

"Okay, okay." Hands up. Lips tight. "I get the point. I'm not harmless."

"We haven't even gotten into the emotional whiplash you're giving me," I say with a shake of my head. "First you hate me. Then we're friends. Then you're flirting. Then it's all just business. Then, after that, you…you stand in front of that bed and tell me you want to…to, uh…to do things to me in it."

Great. And now I sound like I'm twelve again. What happened to powerful women not lusting after bad matches?

Garrett slides the paper cups my way with a smirk. "Like I said, you've got me off balance."

"Is that why the hotel mysteriously didn't have a room for you?" I pour wine into the first cup, then hand it over. "This whole thing is a cheap ploy to get me into bed?"

He shakes his head as he accepts the drink, his eyes locking onto mine with intention. "If I'm trying to get you into bed, you'll know."

Well, shit.

If Garrett's going to be making statements like that, I need to be significantly less sober.

CHAPTER TWENTY-TWO

Angela

The conversation with Garrett needs to move away from beds and sleeping together or this night is going to take an unexpected turn. And, even though I definitely want to take that turn, the future of my family's business rides on how I handle myself tonight.

So...as much as I'd like to ride *him*...I need to get that shit under control.

"You've been significantly grumpier than usual today. What gives?"

Garrett rakes a hand through his hair as he inhales deeply, then downs his wine in one long swallow before refilling his cup. "I'm not grumpy."

I arch a brow and he lets out a long sigh.

"Tonight's the anniversary of my mother's death."

His voice is low, the admission difficult. His posture looks defeated, or embarrassed, or maybe he doesn't wear vulnerability well.

"I'm so sorry." Almost without noticing, I step closer. Reach for him but let my hand drop.

"Don't be." He turns away. "I was only nine when it happened, and my dad remarried. My adoptive mom? She's a great woman who was really good for us..." He leans on the wall, cradling his paper cup, and it sounds to me like he's reciting lines. He's rehearsed them so well he believes them himself.

I smile softly, then take a drink as the air conditioning unit near the window rattles to life. "That doesn't make the loss any easier."

Garrett glances up, surprised by my statement. "It doesn't. But admitting that makes me sound awful. Amelia...we're so close I call her Mom now. She adopted us a couple years after she and Dad got married. Mourning my mother makes me feel like a selfish prick. Why mourn that loss when someone so wonderful took her place?"

I'm out of my depth here. With my head swimming in gin and wine and *him*, I don't know what to say to alleviate Garrett's pain, but it doesn't matter. He barely pauses before continuing.

"Sometimes I wonder what she'd think of me now that I'm grown. Would she be proud? Would she like who I've become?" The words seem to surprise him, as if he didn't mean to let them into the conversation and wishes he could shove them right back into his mouth.

"Why wouldn't she? You're successful. You're intelligent."

You're drop dead gorgeous, and I keep hoping you'll call me a good girl again... I take a long drink to swallow the thought I wish I'd stop having.

"My mother married her high school sweetheart and adored him until the day she died. From what I can remember, she was warm and open and put everything she had into her family. I'm...going a different way." Garrett grimaces at the rattling AC unit, then shakes his head with derision. "Fucking cheap hotels."

"And you think she wouldn't approve? Of your different way?"

"I don't know. That's what bothers me most." He stares into his wine. "The only thing I have of her are memories, and those are faded at best. Disappearing at worst."

"You're a good guy...when you're not being an ass. You're close with your brother and sister. Any mother would be proud of her children as long as they're happy."

"Happy." Garrett's jaw clenches and he throws back the rest of his wine before refilling both our glasses. "I think the best I can hope for is 'not sad.'"

That's a strange thing for a man like him to say. A man with looks, smarts...money. He has a family. A future. He has so much more than so many people in this world, the fact that he isn't jumping for joy every second of the day tells me he's looking at things wrong.

Of course, he'll argue with me if I call him on it, but maybe the conversation will plant a seed in his subconscious. Or, maybe, we'll spend the rest of the night irritated with each other.

Either way, it'll keep us from talking about sex, and that feels like a step in the right direction. "Happiness isn't a destination. It's about enjoying the journey."

"That right there?" Garrett waggles a finger and perches on the edge of the bed. Everything about him looks expensive. He exudes quality. The juxtaposition with the sandpaper-like comforter is downright ridiculous. "That's some motivational wall art bullshit."

"Sure. If you never stop to think deeply about how to apply it," I reply with a laugh.

"Why do I get the feeling you're implying I'm shallow?"

"I prefer not to make implications. Leaves too much room for misunderstandings." I smile sweetly while he ponders whether I just hit him with another implication.

"Okay then. Teach me the depths of your motivational wall art bullshit." A hint of a smile tugs at his lips and he wears it well, like there was a time in his life where smiles came quickly and often. What happened to shut him down? To make him believe the best he can look forward to is "not sad?" Was it just the death of his mother? Or is there more lurking under that scowly, growly exterior?

"Think about it," I say. "How many times have you told yourself you'll be happy if only you could have…I don't know…more money? A better house? A different…distraction?" I heft my paper cup and arch a brow. I settle in, ready to blow Garrett's mind. My parents raised me on discussions like this. We debated the existential merits of happiness, the importance of joy, and the pettiness of modern life over more dinners than I can count.

Garrett huffs a sigh and rolls his hand through the air. "I hear you. Go on."

"Okay, well, when you got those things, were you happy? My guess is maybe for some time, but then it faded. Because happiness is about enjoying where you are. Appreciating the tiniest, most mundane parts of your day." I take a drink, then hold up the cup. "Like this. This cup right here."

"You're telling me *that* makes you happy. You're easier to please than I thought, Angel."

"Hold on now, Mr. Grumpy Pants. Think about how much was involved in making this insignificant little cup part of our night together. Once upon a time, it was a tree. How many people and processes were involved in turning that tree into paper? Then turning that paper into a cup? Then getting the cup to this hotel? This room? The two of us sitting here, drinking wine, involved so much of other people's time and energy, how can you not find a little appreciation for that?"

"That's some fluffy bullshit right there." Garrett takes a drink. "And a lot of excitement over a paper cup."

"But it's that excitement that leads to happiness. Take a look at your life. At all the modern miracles that create your day. You seem close with your brother and sister. You just said your adoptive mom is amazing, so I'm going to assume your dad is too. Judging by your clothes, your profession, and your attitude, money isn't a problem for you. Unless there's something I'm not seeing, I'd guess you need to rearrange the way you look at things and you'll be so much better than 'not sad.'"

Garrett shakes his head. "There's a lot you don't know about me."

"It doesn't have to stay that way." My voice is low, almost a purr, almost like I'm flirting.

Maybe I've had too much to drink.

"I'd rather know more about you."

Okay...maybe Garrett has, too.

"All right. Fine. Ask away." I flare my hands. "I'm an open book."

"Why are you single?"

The question takes me by surprise. I puff my cheeks and exhale. "I don't have time for a relationship. The hotel is my priority."

Garrett crosses his ankle over his knee. "Spoken like a true romantic."

"Hey." The air blasting out of the AC is frosty, so I relocate, perching on the edge of the dresser. "You're the one who decreed I'm a romantic. Not me."

"So...what? You judge me for dealing in distractions but when it comes down to it, you agree with me?"

"I didn't...okay...I guess I did roll my eyes pretty hard at the whole Future Mrs. Cooper thing."

"Exactly." He lifts an eyebrow then sips his wine.

"In my mind there's a difference between recognizing I don't have time for a relationship *right now* and decreeing I will only ever consider the opposite sex a distraction. My version is less...finite."

"Because part of you is waiting for that princess moment," he says with a cocky smile. "For the prince to come swooping in to save you. To love and adore you."

"Ahh. See? There's a lot you don't know about me too. I'm in the business of taking care of myself,

Mr. Cooper. No one else gets to have that much control."

Garrett's jaw clenches. His nostrils flare. For a moment I'm afraid I said the wrong thing, but then he laughs lightly.

"So, you're not interested in relationships, and I'm not interested in relationships," he says, shifting his weight, "yet we keep doing this dance."

The flick of his gaze across my body is a lightning strike. My heart stutters and stammers in the aftermath.

"I wasn't aware we were dancing." I glance away to find a chance to breathe. "From where I'm sitting, it looks like you don't know what you want."

I make the mistake of looking up, curious to see how my words landed.

They landed all right. A storm is brewing between us. Electric. Powerful. Capable of destroying us both.

"You think I don't know what I want?" Garrett's eyes darken, searing mine with a heat that sends my heart pounding again. "I know exactly what I want."

"And what's that?"

There's an expectancy in the air. Something big. Something important.

I stand to meet it head on.

Garrett crosses the room, his gaze locking me in place as he advances. I take an involuntary step backwards and my back hits the wall. He invades my personal space, placing both hands on the wall, caging me in as he leans forward.

His lips are a whisper from mine. I can feel his warmth and my body answers with a surge of desire.

"I want you, Angel. I want these lips. I want this body. I want to pin you to this wall and make you beg for me."

I shouldn't want this. I shouldn't want him. Garrett and I, we're a bad match.

"I don't beg." My statement sounds like an invitation, even to me.

Make me beg, Garrett. Make me beg.

He leans in closer, his lips brushing the skin below my ear. "You will."

He's so close. Right there. I turn my head, angling my mouth to his, then close the gap because fuck it, I want this. I want him. I want to come undone. To stop worrying about ifs and shoulds and burn with him. To burn *for* him.

But he pulls back.

My chest heaves as the animalistic flare in his eyes dies down, a slow freeze that elicits a shuddering breath from my lips.

"But that can't happen. *We* can't happen." Garrett pushes off the wall and crosses the room. "And yeah. I'm all over the place because I haven't wanted someone the way I want you in a long time...and I can't do anything about it. You're driving me crazy, Angel." He slams a fist into his hand and closes his eyes.

And there it is. Just out there in the open and what am I supposed to say to that? Do I laugh it off? Do I tell him I want it too? Do I ask him to leave?

Garrett shoves his hands in his pockets and shakes his head. "I'm going to take a walk before we do something we regret. Thanks for the wine."

"Any time."

He throws back the rest of his drink and places the cup on the dresser almost reverently. With one last lingering look, he shakes his head and leaves the room.

And here I stand. Watching him leave.

Wondering what in the world just happened.

CHAPTER TWENTY-THREE

Garrett

The second the door closes behind me, I thread my fingers through my hair and growl, startling an older gentleman ambling out of his room. I try on a friendly smile, but he gives me a wide berth anyway. Why do I even try? I don't like people and they don't like me.

This whole thing with Angela...

It's just...

I growl again, then stalk down the hallway, not sure where I'm going, just that I can't be here. Not with her, in there, with that one stupid bed and all the things I want to do to her parading through my mind. I need space to breathe, to think, to get myself under control so I stop acting like an asshole every time she moves.

The lobby is filled with mothers and daughters. As

I step through, the crowd parts for me, like my energy is enough to push people away.

Story of my life, I think as I exit the hotel. Now that night has fallen, the air is cooler, almost pleasant. I follow the sound of the ocean, around the back of the building, until I find myself on the beach. The waves rush and roar, but they're not enough to drown out the mess in my head. From the moment I picked up my phone and told Angela to get naked, I've made one stupid mistake after the next, and that? In there? Just now? That was some high school stalker, creepy ass shit.

It's almost like I've lost my mind.

And damn it, that's basically true.

She's in my thoughts, driving me crazy on a daily, no...*hourly* basis. Whatever this is, whatever is going on, I can't walk around, trapping her against a wall and telling her I want to fuck her.

That's not the way these things work.

Especially because I have to walk back into that room, where there is only one bed, and spend the rest of the night with her. And after that? Sign a contract binding her business to mine. Angela will be part of my professional life for a long time and I'm putting so much at risk by acting the way I am.

I walk to the edge of the water, watching as it rolls to a stop just inches from my feet. The sky is dark, the stars bright, the moon heavy and swollen. For as beautiful as it is out here, and for as tense as it was in the room, all I want is to go back. To her.

And then what?

Assault her again? For what? The *third* time? When did I become such an asshole?

It's not like I'm making conscious decisions here. My body is acting on its own. Without my permission. Working on urges and impulses instead of common fucking sense. I've never been so unsure of what I want in my life because my desires conflict.

Do I want to treat Angela like a colleague? Yep.

Do I want to bury myself inside her so deep she screams my name? Hell yes.

Are those things mutually exclusive? You betcha.

Growling, I scrub my face and stare at my feet.

Something's gotta give.

I just don't know what.

The walk back to the hotel room might as well be a walk down death row. Am I just going to pretend nothing happened? Pretend like I didn't admit how much I want her? Like I didn't almost take what I wanted even though we both know that's a terrible decision?

Stopping in front of our room, I reach for my wallet, only to remember Angela never gave me a key. Shit.

I hang my head, knock, and am rewarded with a muffled, "Coming!" before the door cracks open and Angela peeks out. Her hair is loose, her face fresh and clean, and she's wearing a pink silk tank and shorts that could very well be the same set she wore the night we had phone sex.

Fuck.

It was hot in my mind, but in person? Her nipples are hard and the fabric clings to a pair of tits so insane I regret leaving the room to get control. It's like she's taunting me.

That has to be it.

She's taunting me.

I drag my gaze back to Angela's face, only to glance away because things aren't any better there. The sweetness in her smile. The uncertainty in her eyes. She's just as confused as I am.

"I forgot my key," I murmur, swallowing hard.

She swings the door open, and I step in. There, on the floor, is a nest of comforters and pillows, with her laptop nearby.

"I told you I'd sleep on the floor." The words come out harsher than I intend.

"Yeah, but then you left and forfeited your right to make that decision." Angela crosses the room and sits cross legged on the comforter. "I'll pretend I'm camping. No offense to the good people at this hotel, but it's not exactly the kind of place I'm used to staying. Sleeping on the floor will just add to the experience of it all."

"The experience…" I rub a hand down my face, huffing a laugh.

"Yes, Garrett. The experience. The whole being happy in the moment thing I was talking about earlier. And you know, being here, in this hotel with its crappy customer service and cheap…everything…" She waves an arm around the room, staring balefully at the hiccupping AC unit. "It just reiterates how much Bliss needs a Hutton Hotel."

"You…" I shake my head, staring down at this beautiful woman wearing not enough clothing. "You are something else, you know that?"

"I've heard that before. Got a problem with that?"

"The only problem I have is with you sleeping on the floor. Get in bed."

She folds her arms over her chest. "I am in bed."

"Get in *the* bed." I stab a finger at the thing.

"Garrett…I'm fine where I am."

"Could you please, just for once, not argue with me about something?"

"Same could be said for you."

"You know what? You're..." I shake my head.

"I'm what?" She cocks a brow, daring me to say what I'm thinking.

"You're insufferable and this disagreement is over."

"Says who?"

"Says me." I bend down and scoop Angela into my arms, her skin like satin, her scent irresistible. She shrieks, kicking her legs in surprise.

"Garrett! What are you...? Garrett! Stop!"

I place her on the bed, my face inches from hers, her nipples pebbled and begging me to tease, to taste, to torture.

I lick my lips as her chest heaves.

I pull back.

"I'm gonna..." I jerk my thumb toward the bathroom. "I'm gonna get changed."

Angela nods, her eyes wide, lips parted. "Okay."

Her voice is low. Sweet.

I wipe a hand over my mouth and retreat to the bathroom before I do something I regret.

CHAPTER TWENTY-FOUR

Angela

While Garrett's in the bathroom, I retrieve my laptop and curl into bed but there's no way I can concentrate on work. My head is swimming. Drunk on wine, on him, on being pushed against a wall and carried to bed. On the swollen erection pressing against my hip before he left the room.

If fate has anything to do with Garrett and me being here together, then she has a twisted sense of humor.

He finishes in the bathroom, stepping into the room wearing a pair of plaid pajama pants and a t-shirt with the words Cheers 'n Beers on his chest. His feet are bare and his guard is down and oh, for fuck's sake, I'm not going to make it through the night.

"Jesus. It's freezing in here." He beelines for the AC unit and messes with the settings. "Are you cold?"

I nod, appreciating the way the tee stretches across his back, the cotton adhering to muscles that beg my fingers to feel, to explore. After several minutes, he steps back, shaking his head. "I can't get it to turn off."

"That's gonna suck. Especially with only one of us having access to the blanket."

Garrett gathers the comforter from the floor and yanks the sheet off the bed. "You take the blanket. I'm good with the sheet."

"I can't let you sleep on the floor with nothing soft to sleep on..."

"You don't have to *let* me do anything. This is what's happening, Angel. I'm fine." He arranges the sheet on the floor, then stretches out, wrapping one edge of the thin material around him.

"Wanna watch some TV?" I ask, rolling my eyes at his stubbornness.

"I'm good to turn off the lights and try to get some sleep." Garrett squishes his pillows into submission, barely glancing my way.

"Yeah. Sure. That's good too." I close my laptop and flip off the light, but sleep won't come. Not with him, right there, just a few feet away. My body is aware of his presence, every nerve, every cell, lit up, electrified.

The way he looked when he pushed me against the wall...

It unlocked something in me. Something real. Something deep. Some primal part of me that wants to be claimed and taken and protected...

But then he ran out of the room like I'd slapped him and has barely been able to look at me since he came back. It's a good thing we're leaving Bliss tomorrow. He'll go back to his life, and I'll go back to mine. We'll communicate about work via text and email and this whole thing between us can die down.

I can't take this tension, this back and forth. How many times can he make me feel like he wants me only to reject me before I lose my mind?

"Are you asleep, Angel?" Garrett's voice is so low, I wonder if I dreamed it.

"No. Are you?"

"Not even for one minute."

The words grit into the room with an undercurrent of desire, and I can't. I just can't. I divert the conversation.

"Is it because you're uncomfortable?" I ask. "I feel terrible, up here while you're down there."

"I'm fine."

"You're not. This mattress has to be better than the floor and I'm freezing *with* the blanket. You've got to be miserable. Come on, this thing is huge. You could take that whole other side and it'll still be like we have two separate beds." I sit up and flick on the light, then gesture at the space beside me like a game show model. "We can even put pillows between us, if that'll make you feel any better."

"It's not necessary." Garrett rolls over, tugging the sheet even tighter around his shoulders and back.

"I swear to God, your lips are blue." I stare him down, unimpressed with his obstinance. "Sharing a bed doesn't mean anything. I'd do the same for anyone else in this situation."

"Fine."

Garrett grabs the sheet and pillows off the floor, then stalks around the bed to climb into the other side. For as much as I pretended this was no big deal, it feels like a huge freaking deal once he's stretched out on the sliver of mattress he allowed himself.

"See?" I say, as nonchalant as I've ever been in my life. "Isn't that better?"

He grunts in response, so I flick off the light and curl up.

We might as well be sharing a twin bed, as far as my body's concerned. There is no way I'll be sleeping tonight.

"Angel?"

His voice sends a shiver of expectation down my spine. Is this it? Are we about to make a terrible mistake I'll remember for the rest of my life? Will he roll over, trapping me beneath him? Will we finally succumb to the wildfire blazing between us?

"Yes?" The word slips into the room on a whisper, heavy with expectation.

"Thank you."

I wait for more. For movement. For Garrett's lips on mine, but he lays still, so I exhale a quiet breath and settle in for a restless night.

CHAPTER TWENTY-FIVE

Garrett

The scent of coconut pulls me from sleep. My eyes blink open, then fall shut again. There's warmth and softness curled against me. I wrap my arms tighter around her and pull her close...

Oh, shit.

I lift my head to find Angela curled into me, one arm thrown over my chest, a leg tossed over mine. Her hair fans over my shoulder and I'm holding her ass like it was made for me. I drop my hand, then try to ease out from underneath her, but she moans, somehow managing to roll even closer. Fucking hell, it's like she wants to be on top of me.

The thought sends an explosion of images through

my mind. Her, riding my cock. Breasts bouncing. Head tossed back. Lips parted. Chest heaving.

My dick swells against her thigh.

Fuck, fuck, fuck.

This is not good.

Angela mumbles something, shifting even closer, then freezes. Her eyes spring open. Her head lifts. She meets my gaze with a look of shock slackening her jaw. "I am so sorry." She pulls away, her thigh crushing my cock and her eyes go even wider. "Oh my God. Yep. Super sorry." She scoots as far away as humanly possible, sits up, and swings her legs off the bed.

"Nothing to apologize for. Just, you know, it happens in the morning."

"Right. Yeah." She glances over her shoulder. "Morning wood. Everyone knows about that. Totally, one hundred percent natural and normal."

Her jaw drops. She slaps a hand over her face, laughing as she shakes her head. "Yep. I just said that. Welcome to first thing in the morning with a filter-less Angela Hutton."

We spend the next hour pretending she didn't accidentally squeeze my dick with her thigh. Rinsing our paper cups to reuse for coffee. Moving around the small space, careful not to touch. Or stand too close. Or hold eye contact too long. You'd think we'd been caught having sex in the boardroom and were trying to pretend no one saw.

"What are your plans for today?" I ask as I come out of the bathroom, making space for her to use the mirror and brush her teeth. A whisper of coconut breezes by as she passes and fuck if I don't pause to breathe it in.

"My flight leaves at two." She leans against the door and scrubs her face. "I was gonna sleep in and fly home. Now, you know, I'll skip the sleeping in part because it's early and we're awake."

I press my lips together and bob my head. I had the same plan but now, after sharing a room with her, I don't want to follow it. The thought of going back to our respective corners of the world just doesn't do it for me. But she does.

She really fucking does it for me.

And what does that mean about the deal? About work? Angela is not just the daughter of a client; she *is* a client.

My gaze wanders her face, lingering on luscious lips, clear blue eyes, and I come to a decision I didn't know I was making.

"Stay. With me. We'll go to the beach. Get to know Bliss better. Get to know each other better. Grab some dinner and fly home tomorrow."

Angela narrows her eyes. "Why?"

Because I'm tired of this back and forth. I want to focus on the journey instead of the destination and that means acknowledging I feel better when I'm with you. I want to know you and I want to stop giving a shit if it'll end in disaster.

I stare while those thoughts run through my mind and Angela squirms.

"Because you're distracting me," I finally grit out, looking away and clearing my throat.

"I thought you liked distractions."

My attention slams back into hers. "Not like this." The words grind up my throat. "I can't think. I can't sleep. I can't work. I need to know what this is."

"What do you think it is?" Her cool stare dares me to say what neither of us are brave enough to admit.

"Damn it, Angel. I don't know." I laugh as my fists clench, holding back the desire to grab her shoulders and kiss her until I remember who I am. "But I want to. Don't you?"

Her soft blues blink up at me, wide and wondering as she nods. "I want to know."

Her admission feels like triumph. I wipe a hand across my mouth to hide my smile. "Good. Change your flight. I'll let the hotel know we're staying another night. Then we'll get ready and hit the road around noon."

"There you go, being bossy again."

"Be a good girl and follow directions." I wink and shove my hands in my pockets, stepping back as I let my eyes wander her curves, drinking her in like the fucking masterpiece she is. Her jaw drops and the corner of her mouth lifts in a smile, before she laughs, shakes her head, and closes the bathroom door.

Nerves flip and flutter in my stomach. Fucking nerves. It's been a long time since I cared what someone thought and the last time I did, it ended in disaster. Since then, I've changed the way I look at people.

If I have fun with someone, great. If I don't, that'll be the end of that.

But Angela?

I want today to be special. If that isn't a problem, I don't know what is.

I lean on the doorframe, folding my arms across my chest while I wait. My Angel's hair is swept back into a ponytail. Her eyes sparkle with a smile. A white sundress glistens against silky skin and her ass looks so amazing, I want to sink my teeth into it, to squeeze it, to leave my mark on a luscious hip...

"Sorry to make you wait," she says. "I didn't exactly pack with a day at the beach in mind..." She flares her hands at her body. "I hope this'll do."

"It'll do." Holy fuck will it do. I push off the wall. "You look beautiful."

"And you look brooding and intense as usual." Angela's smile brightens as she steps into the room. "And not at all prepared for the beach." Her eyes sweep along my dress slacks and polo. "Are you sure this is what you want to do?"

"I'm dead set on it." I smooth the front of my shirt, glad I at least thought to pack something with short sleeves, then meet her worried gaze. Oh shit. Here I thought she was questioning our day together because of my clothes.

But maybe...

"Are you having second thoughts?"

"A little. I don't know. It's just..." A shrug. Broken eye contact. "What if this is a mistake? What about the deal? Your boss? My dad?"

I don't have answers to those questions, even though I've been asking them myself. All I know is that I can't ignore what I want any longer. And what I want is her.

"Here's what we're going to do. For the rest of the time we're in Bliss, we forget that you're Angela Hutton, representing the Hutton Hotel, and I'm

Garrett Cooper, from Vision Enterprise. The rest of our time here is..." How can I explain what I'm thinking without sounding like an idiot? "It's a bubble of stolen time."

Angela's hand coming up to cover her smile says I shouldn't congratulate myself on my word choice. Why does nothing feel normal with her? I'm a man who knows what he wants and takes action to get it. I know what to say and when to say it. With her, I bumble and blunder like someone handed me the wrong set of rules.

I swipe a hand over my face. "While we're here, we're just a man and a woman who like being together."

"But do we?" Angela bites her bottom lip. "Like being together?"

Another question I keep asking myself.

"We'll have the answer to that after today, won't we?"

"I guess we will." She smiles shyly. "So, what do you want to do while we're in our bubble of stolen time together?"

With anyone else, I'd be done with this conversation. I hate feeling like an idiot and the way she grins after saying "bubble of stolen time" makes me feel like she's laughing at me. But, for her, it seems I've been given a bigger dose of patience.

"According to my sister, I don't know how to have fun. We're going to prove her wrong."

The AC unit rattles, hisses, then falls silent as I reach for the door. If I didn't know better, I'd say the thing had a sick sense of humor. Switching to the Arctic Freeze setting long enough for me to know what Angela's breasts feel like pressed against my chest, then back to Desert Heat as soon as we leave.

"Ahh, yes," Angela says with a laugh. "The very definition of a good time. Showing loved ones they don't know as much as they think they do."

The door slams closed behind us as a family emerges from the room next to ours. The little girl's hair is slicked into a bun and she's wearing too much makeup, a warm up suit, and a pair of fuzzy slippers. Her mom has her nose buried in her phone and her dad's gaze detours to my Angel's ass. I arch a brow and he looks away.

Damn straight.

"I don't see the problem here," I say to her, still eyeing the dad who has no right to look at her like that. "Winning is very entertaining."

"It is. Very. But, I don't know, maybe you should have fun for the sake of it, rather than trying to prove a point?" Angela takes off down the hallway, glancing over her shoulder with that damn sparkle in her eyes. "Are you coming or what?"

Grumbling, I lengthen my stride to catch her. The idea of chasing after a woman is...well...it's not very Garrett Cooper. We step outside together and I groan at the heat as I squint into the sun. Damn these tropical locales. I thought a New England summer was bad, but this? This is intolerable. A bead of sweat trails down my spine after a two-minute walk to my rental.

As we drive into Bliss, we chat about pleasantries, everything and nothing. It's the kind of chitchat I usually excel at, a little flirt, a dash of charm, no depth whatsoever. But today I'm aware it's empty. Pointless. I don't want to laugh about pop culture or comment on the weather. I want to know what makes this beautiful woman tick, and I want to learn these things while tracing a finger along the delicate skin of her thigh, up...under her skirt...and up some more until I find out if she's still wearing white lace.

"This place reminds me a lot of the town I grew up in. Wildrose Landing," I say as I make the turn into Bliss.

"I never pegged you for a small town guy."

"Like I said last night, there's a lot you don't know about me." I point at a cafe called Good Beginnings. "I bet the person who owns that place knows the names of all her customers and has their orders memorized. My mom's store is next to a coffee shop just like it."

"Your mom's...?" Angela cocks her head and I chuckle. My family structure is confusing.

"Amelia. My adoptive mom," I clarify, glancing at my Angel. "When we were little, we started calling her Mom-Amelia, which eventually became Momma, and then switched to plain old Mom."

Angela's soft smile says she approves of the story. "What kind of store does your mom have?"

"You'll laugh."

"I won't."

"I bet you will."

"I'll take that bet," she says with a challenge in her eyes. "If I win, I get to pick what we're doing today."

"And if I win?"

"Then you pick."

I lift an eyebrow. There's no way she's gonna win this one. I love Mom to death, but she's not conventional. Growing up, I accepted her outlook on life as fact, but all too often people see her as a joke. A punchline. A cliché. Younger me got in a fair amount of trouble defending her until she sat me down to explain she doesn't care what people think of her and I shouldn't either.

I've tried to take on that perspective, but my protective streak runs too deep.

"Mom owns a store called Woo-woo Wildrose. It's focused on essential oils, healing crystals, positivity, and spirituality." I watch Angela's reaction out of the corner of my eye.

Her eyes widen and she purses her lips, but there isn't a hint of laughter. "I have to admit, that is not what I was expecting from someone like you."

I frown as I slow to allow an elderly couple more time in the crosswalk. They pause to wave and Angela returns the gesture, her eyes sparkling like a true romantic as she takes in their clasped hands.

"From someone like me?"

"You aren't exactly the free flowing, gentle spirit with jewelry and long hair. And you told me my outlook on happiness sounds like motivational wall art instead of the very good advice it is."

I grunt a response because I hate being judged. She doesn't know me well enough to decide who I am.

"Oh, come on Garrett." Angela shoves my shoulder with an exasperated sigh. "I've been around long enough to know that frown and that pulsing jaw muscle right there means I've managed to irritate you."

"I'm not irritated."

"And I'm not buying it."

"You don't know if I'm easygoing or not."

"I'm sorry but look at you." Angela shifts in her seat as we turn off Main. "You're wearing dress pants to the beach. Does that say free spirit to you?"

I huff a laugh, cutting a glance her way. "I'm wearing what I packed. Like you."

"Fine." She throws up her hands. "I take it back. You are the most easygoing person I've ever met. Now…about that bet I won… This day is mine, Bucko." Angela looks so proud of herself; I concede without a fight.

Almost.

"Bucko? Did you really just call me Bucko?" I tighten my grip on the steering wheel to stop myself from putting a hand on her knee.

"Why yes sir, I did. Got a problem with that? *Bucko?*"

"Would it change anything if I said yes?"

"You know it wouldn't."

"That's what I thought." I roll my eyes and shake my head. "What's first on the agenda?"

Angela bites her bottom lip. Her eyes shift away as she thinks, then she turns to me with a wicked grin. "Have you ever been boogie boarding?"

I grimace. "Not since I was a kid."

"See! Same! That's what we're going to do today."

Boogie boarding. She's got to be kidding.

Right?

"We're here, negotiating a multimillion-dollar deal and you want to play in the ocean on pieces of Styrofoam."

"Oh no. We're in a time bubble, remember? You're just a man and I'm just a woman and we're trying to decide if we even like being together. What better way to do that than playing in the ocean?"

I laugh at the absurdity of the idea. "I'm not exactly dressed for that."

"We passed a shop." She spins to point behind us. "That's what made me think of it. We'll buy some cheap suits. Grab boogie boards. Hit the beach."

Fuck.

Angela won the bet fair and square, but that doesn't mean I have to like it. I set my jaw and search for a place to turn around.

"Now don't look so upset, Captain Grumpy Pants. This is your chance to prove how free flowing and easygoing you are. As a bonus, I bet your sister will never believe how much fun you had when you tell her."

I park and we head into the store. Angela makes a beeline for the swim trunks and I follow, shaking my head. She's buzzing with excitement, smiling like she's won the world. It's cute, in a "just released from the psych ward" kind of way.

"The women's section is over there." I point toward the mannequins in bikinis lining the back wall.

"Right. But if I let you pick out what you're wearing, you'll come out with something boring like these."

She flicks through the hangers and stops at a plain black pair of swim trunks.

"Maybe you know me better than I thought." I reach for them, and she jerks them away. "Those are perfect. Hand 'em over."

"But where's the fun in that?" Angela arches an eyebrow and continues searching until she finds a light blue pair covered in bright yellow rubber duckies. "Now these. These are fun."

"Those are ridiculous."

"I'm glad you agree."

I fold my arms over my chest. "I'm not wearing those."

"Are you backing out of our agreement?" She puts a hand to her chest. "Garrett. I'm shocked."

"Fine." I snatch the garment. "And for the record, *this* is the only thing shocking about this situation."

"Don't you worry. I plan to join in the fun." With that, Angela bounds towards the back to dig through bikinis. Fifteen minutes later, we leave the shop with new swimsuits, boogie boards, and a bag full of sunscreen, towels, and flip flops. After finding a beach with changing booths, she gleefully hands me my bag with the swim trunks inside and dashes off to change.

I glare at the things. I'll play her game. For now.

But only because she'll be playing my game later.

CHAPTER TWENTY-SIX

Angela

I don't know what I expected when Garrett stepped out of the changing booth in his rubber ducky swimsuit, but reality doesn't sync up. Not only are the trunks a tad too small, affording me a tantalizing view of a body I am not prepared for—*in any way*—but the wicked gleam in his eyes and stubborn set of his jaw warns that revenge is incoming.

I can't wait.

Bring it on, Bucko. Challenge me. I'll rise to it. I promise.

The glimpses I've caught of the man beneath the grump are tantalizing.

While Garrett tugs at the too small trunks, I hold

back a laugh, waiting for him to catch on to what I'm wearing. "You look amazing."

"Amazing is the word I'd choose as well. Though I don't think we're using the same definition." Garrett freezes, his eyes widening while a hint of a smile brightens his scowl. "Is that pizza? Are you wearing a pizza bikini?"

I turn in a slow circle, letting him in on the magnificence that is the pizza bikini. It's hideous. Four triangle slices of fabric held together with string, each of them displaying a greasy pepperoni pizza and barely covering my naughty bits. It's ridiculous. And embarrassing. And I'm sure to end up *indisposed* while boogie boarding, but I couldn't let Garrett be the only one making a fool of himself today.

A low laugh has him shaking his head as his gaze travels my body. "I keep saying it, and I keep meaning it. You are something else."

"Personally, I think we make quite the pair."

Garrett's jaw tightens as he processes my statement. There's a long moment of eye contact and what I wouldn't give to read his mind. Or just have a hint of what he's thinking. By the looks of it, there's a lot going on in there and I can't tell if it's good, bad, or indifferent.

"Let's get this over with." He sighs heavily as if to prove how much he's not looking forward to boogie boarding, but he's more excited than he wants to let on. I can see it in the gleam of his eyes. In the teeny-tiny almost smile lifting his lips.

Without waiting to see if I'm following, Garrett takes off toward the water, his flip flops flicking sand behind him.

"Hold on now, Bucko," I say, as I catch up. "I need some sunscreen first. Redheads weren't made for the sun." I pull a bottle out of one of the plastic bags. "The spray always gets in my eyes and mouth, so I go for the old-fashioned stuff. Want some?" I jiggle the bottle his way.

Garrett shakes his head. "It's all yours."

I squirt some into my hands and rub the lotion into first one arm, then the other. His eyes follow the movement as I rub my belly and breasts and I like the way he looks when he's looking at me.

I see him want me. The flare of heat in those icy blues. The pulse in his jaw. The jut of his chin. Watching him stare at me like that turns me on, so I drop my gaze to hide my grin.

"Can you get my back?" I ask, my voice low, almost embarrassed.

"Sure." Garrett seems hesitant as I hand the bottle over. Like the mere thought of touching me is problematic.

I lift my hair and his warm hands pass over my

shoulders, rubbing the lotion into my skin. Delicately at first and then with more confidence.

He was right to hesitate. This is problematic.

This is really fucking problematic.

As his hands work down my back toward my waist, his touch grows insistent and my body throbs with want. With desire. With a flare of heat, a pulse in my jaw, and a jut of my chin.

I close my eyes and am greeted with an image of Garrett backing me against the wall last night. His gaze hooded...dark with lust and good God...

...what the hell am I doing?

Clearing my throat, I open my eyes and blink furiously. The stupid swimsuits. The boogie boards. They were all part of my grand plan to focus on fun and not the chemistry that sizzles between us when we're together. How has it backfired this early in the day?

Garrett's thumbs graze the skin so low on my back, they brush the inconsequential triangle of fabric covering my ass. I shiver as he steps away.

"All done." His voice is low, vibrating with tension as he removes his hands and shakes his head. "You are sufficiently protected from the sun."

If only there was a way to protect me from my hormones hijacking my common sense.

"All right, then." I pluck the sunscreen from his hand and drop it into my bag. "You ready for this?"

"As I'll ever be."

We grab our boogie boards and jog towards the water. After a few false starts, my body remembers the years I spent running into the waves with Nick and I manage to ride a few like a pro. Garrett shakes his head while I laugh in delight. Finally, he joins in and watching his muscles bunch and twist while he churns through the water is a different kind of delight. He is power and strength. His body is beautiful. Long, lean muscles tightening in his thighs and hamstrings. His abs flex, highlighting the delicious V that disappears into his shorts. Broad shoulders glisten with droplets of water.

This is nothing like playing with Nick after all.

This is something else altogether.

CHAPTER TWENTY-SEVEN

Garrett

Angela's pizza bikini leaves nothing to the imagination, but mine is in overdrive anyway. Droplets of water gleam on her shoulders, her tits, her ass. My hands itch to touch her again, and these stupid rubber ducky trunks cup my junk so hard, the surge of blood in that direction is more unfortunate than usual. Every moment I spend with this woman makes me want her more than I did before. Which is saying a lot.

"Excuse me, Mister?" A young man with sun-bleached hair and skin the color of a nut taps me on the shoulder. "It looks like your girl is caught in a riptide." He nods towards Angela who has drifted far from shore but appears clueless about her situation.

"Fuck." I wipe my hands through my hair and

wade into the surf, calling a curt "Thank you!" over my shoulder.

I dive in, my arms slicing the water, pulling through the waves, my focus locked on Angela as she drifts further and further away. The current is strong, pushing me towards her but not fast enough.

Not fast enough.

She doesn't know she's in danger. Doesn't know she's caught in a riptide. Doesn't know she's being pulled out to sea. I kick harder, desperate to get to her sooner, faster, *now*. My lungs burn and my muscles ache. Salt stings my eyes and I shake water out of my hair as I come to a stop beside her.

She's surprised by my arrival. "What are you—"

"You're in a riptide. Hug your board and swim this way." I wrap an arm around her slick body, aiming us parallel to shore.

"Garrett..." Her voice is light. Amused. She never takes anything seriously. But this? This is fucking serious. This is how drownings happen and I won't, I can't, let that happen.

Not to her.

Not on my watch.

"Don't argue, Angel. Swim." I kick my legs and she follows suit, the two of us slicing through the water like our bodies were made to work together. As we exit the current, I aim us for shore, holding her even though she's safe now. She has her board to keep her afloat and the waves are guiding us to the beach instead of dragging us away.

Water pours out of my shorts as we emerge from the ocean. I blow air past pursed lips, fighting to catch my breath. "Are you okay?"

I straighten, looking her over for any signs of injury. She's barely winded, staring at me like I'm the butt of a joke while my lungs burn.

"Garrett, I'm fine." Angela swipes her hair back from her face then pulls it over her shoulder to wring it out. The nonchalant shake of her head says she's oblivious to what just happened.

"You were caught in a rip current." I suck in air, revved up on adrenaline and exertion. "They're dangerous..."

She puts a hand on my arm. "I grew up in the Keys, with the ocean as my backyard. I know how to swim out of a riptide."

I bark an embarrassed laugh, hands on knees, still catching my breath. "Right. Obviously."

"But thank you, for swimming out there to save my life. It's nice to know I have a prince waiting to save me, even if I'm no damsel in distress."

Straightening, I shake my head as I swipe my hair off my forehead. "I feel like you're making fun of me."

"I'm not making fun. Why would you think that?"

Angela rolls her eyes skyward, popping her fists on her hips. "Silly me. The answer to that is obvious. You see the worst in everything."

If that's true, I think, *then why do I see the best in you?*

I scrub my mouth to keep the thought inside, where it belongs.

"Garrett." A hand on my arm. A sweet smile. "Thank you. Truly. You were swimming like your life depended on it."

I was swimming like *her* life depended on it. When did I start caring about her enough to react first and ask questions later?

I scowl as Angela's lips quirk into a crooked smile.

"See, now I feel like you're laughing at me again."

"I'm not." She holds up her hands. "I promise. It was really sweet. And now I know you'll keep me safe from assholes named Tank armed with cheap pickup lines and rip currents dragging me out to sea."

"Both things you can handle on your own, apparently."

"But now I don't need to. Because I've got you."

Angela smiles up at me, her hand on my arm. Her touch lingers, like she's hesitant to let go, and I get that, I do. I've had her in my arms twice now and in my head for days.

"I wouldn't go that far," I say, as a man and his dog amble past. "I'm no prince."

"You can drop the tough guy act, Bucko. We both know you'll come charging to the rescue the moment you think I'm in trouble." Her smile grows. Her eyes sparkle. She looks so fucking perfect it makes my head hurt.

I turn away. "See, now I know you're laughing at me."

"I'm laughing, but not *at* you..."

"Jesus." Disappointment sinks my heart into my stomach before I look to her. "If you say you're laughing with me..."

"Obviously I'm not laughing with you, because you're not laughing. I'm just...having some fun." Angela drops her hands from her hips, her smile fading.

"At my expense."

"No, Garrett! Not at your expense. I'm having fun, in the sun, at the beach, *with you*." She stabs a finger into my chest in time with her last two words. Her gaze drops to my pec. She bites her bottom lip, then drags her eyes back to mine, hopeful I saw nothing.

I see everything, Angel. The sooner you realize that, the better.

I saw the way she shivered while I rubbed sunscreen into her skin. I saw the way she couldn't stop staring at my junk when I walked out of the changing room. I see the way she wants me, almost as much as I want her.

I wipe a hand over my face to hide a smile. "Why do I feel like you still managed to sneak in an 'I'm laughing with you?'"

"I don't know," she says, sighing deeply, "maybe because you're clinically cynical?"

"Clinically cynical." I snort and shake my head while Angela's eyes go wide.

"*That* makes you laugh? Not the rubber ducky shorts? Not the pizza bikini? Not rescuing me when I didn't need rescued? But 'clinically cynical' does it for you."

"What can I say? I'm a complex guy."

Truth be told, she does it for me.

And I'm tired of pretending she doesn't.

CHAPTER TWENTY-EIGHT

Angela

"I actually didn't think this would be as fun as it is. I like being in a time bubble with you," I say later, as Garrett and I sit on the sand, the waves lapping our ankles before retreating, only to return again and again.

"Same, actually." He focuses on the water, and I admire his chiseled jawline before he meets my eyes. A knowing smile graces his lips, then he smirks and looks away.

I dig my toes into the sand, watching the water fill the holes left behind. "You think Charlie would approve?"

"I'll have to bring the shorts as proof, but yeah, she'd approve."

There's more to what he's saying. It's humming through the undercurrent of his tone, the charged look in his eyes, but I don't know what it is. This man, with his grunts and frowns, his wild mood swings, I can't read him. I don't know what he wants. What he's thinking.

It drives me crazy.

Because even though I know I shouldn't care, I do. I don't just want to know what he wants. I want to know if *I'm* what he wants.

We leave the beach and get dressed, then stop for dinner at the café he pointed out earlier. Good Beginnings. Part of me whispers the name is prophetic. That today was a good beginning to whatever is growing between Garrett and me. The rest of me screams that nothing good can come out of the two of us together. Not when there are so many reasons to keep us apart.

Unfortunately, the café is only open for breakfast and lunch, so we walk the streets until we find a bar called Fisherman Jack's that serves food and has a musician setting up on a small stage. The meal is simple and delicious, and Garrett and I sit quietly while an older man plays his guitar, singing in a husky baritone, deep and rolling, just like the sea. At the end of his set, a woman who must be his wife pulls him into her arms and kisses him like her life depends on it. Something in the way she looks at him reminds me of the way my mom looks at my dad. That makes me smile until I glance at Garrett and find him scowling in my direction.

Hot and cold.

Push and pull.

He's a freaking enigma.

As the night comes to a close, he drives us back to the hotel. We walk quietly down the hall towards our room, pausing in front of the door like we're afraid of what comes next.

"I had a lovely time," I say, feeling ridiculous at how childlike I sound.

"I had a nice time too." Garrett smiles, his eyes locked onto mine with intent. "Such a nice time that I feel like I can do this..."

He threads his hands into my hair, cupping my face as he leans close, his lips brushing mine, softly, insistently. His fingers tighten into a fist, tilting my head back as his kiss deepens, our tongues sweeping together like the waves licking our skin. He advances and my back presses against the door, the thick length of his erection digging into my stomach.

This is bad.

This is wrong.

This puts everything I've been working for in jeopardy.

But we're in a time bubble and I'm past caring

about right and wrong because good things happen to good people. And Garrett and me? We're good people.

And we're even better together.

His push and pull, hot and cold, it lights me on fire and everything feels *more. Better*.

I like being with him.

"Should we... Do you want to go inside now?" I ask, breathless between kisses.

He nods, capturing my bottom lip with his teeth. "Open the door, Angel."

Fumbling in my purse, I dig for my keycard while Garrett slides his hands down my waist, around the curve of my hips, and grabs my ass. His growl of approval puts my body on alert. Nipples pebbled. Thighs clenching. Desire pooling in my lower belly. I turn to slip the keycard into the lock and Garrett brushes my hair aside, kissing the delicate skin at my neck, then nibbling at my ear.

His touch is fire. Destructive yet necessary for existence.

My life will cease to exist without it from this point forward.

The door opens and we stumble in. His hands. His skin. His voice. The low groan rolling through his chest. It blends with the throbbing in my core. I drop my bag and fumble at his shirt because after a day of looking and not touching, I need my hands on his body.

He catches my wrists, stopping me from pulling the hemline from his pants. "I want you to beg for it, Angel."

I laugh, reaching for his belt, but he tightens his grip. "The day was yours, but this? This is mine." He traces a finger down my cheek as I drop my gaze.

Why do I like it so much when he talks like that?

Garrett pinches my chin and lifts my face. "Beg."

"Beg?" I scoff, looking away. Embarrassed that he'd ask it of me.

"We won't go any further until you do."

My voice catches in my throat. I've never begged for anything in my life. I've never needed to. Whatever I wanted, I either had it already, or found a way to get it for myself. I'm a strong, proud woman.

I don't beg.

I meet Garrett's eyes and soften against the strength I see there. He is unlike anyone I've ever met. His energy clicks with mine, unlocking a part of me I didn't know existed. A part that needs someone stronger than me to relax into.

My gaze falls to the floor.

I lick my lips and find my voice.

"Please."

"Please what?" he growls.

My gaze crawls up his torso, along his chest, past his full lips and chiseled jaw until I meet his eyes.

"Please let me see you."

"Good girl, my Angel. I like it when you do what I say."

Sweet Jesus what is happening? I'm grinning—though I don't know why—and quivering with need for him.

For this.

For us.

I reach for his pants again, but he steps away.

"I want to see you first."

With one delicate finger, he slips the strap of my sundress off my shoulder, then stalks behind me to draw the zipper down, his fingers grazing the delicate skin along my spine. With another flick of his finger, the dress drops to the floor, a puddle of fabric at my feet. He growls in approval of the white lace bra and panties.

"It fucking killed me to have my hands on you today." Garrett grips my waist, his thumbs caressing the line of silk against my skin.

I glance over my shoulder. "And why is that?"

"Because I can't touch you without wanting to own you, Angel. I need to be inside you. I want your moans, your screams, your pleasure."

I shiver at his words. "Jesus, Garrett. Who talks like that?"

"I talk like that." His fingers work the clasp of my

bra and that, too, falls to the floor. He caresses my shoulders, kissing my neck, coming to stand in front of me as his fingers trail goosebumps across my skin. "So fucking beautiful."

He bends, sucking a nipple into his mouth and I gasp at the sudden warmth, the bite of pain. A hand presses to my back and he kisses the tender flesh of my breast, sucking until I'm sure he left his mark. I ease into his embrace, melting with his attention. His touch leaves me trembling.

"Please, Garrett..." I don't even know what I'm begging for, I just want more, more, more.

He backs me up, kissing and sucking, his hands and mouth sending shivers of energy through me as my inner muscles throb with want. The back of my knees hit the bed. I drop to the mattress, staring up at him as he pulls his shirt from his pants and shrugs out of it. The smattering of hair above his belt catches the light and I drag my gaze up his muscled torso to meet blue eyes as deep as the ocean.

"Scoot your hips to the edge and lay back."

I do as he says, lifting my hips to slip my underwear down my thighs, my ankles, and toss them to the floor. His eyes meet mine as he kneels in front of me, strong hands spreading my legs while he gives me a wicked smile.

It's filled with promise. With lust. With want...*for*

me. This man, this grumpy, inscrutable man wants me. He touches me like I'm precious, kneeling before me like I'm a queen, yet I'm beholden to his every word. His every command.

The gentle pressure of Garrett's tongue dancing across my clit calls up a moan from somewhere deep inside of me. A place I didn't know existed. A version of me I haven't met. My head drops back as my eyes slip closed. "Fuck, Garrett."

"Look at me, Angel. Watch what I do to you." He lowers his mouth to me, teasing this new part of me to life. My hips buck and my body writhes and pleasure wings through me like seabirds swooping and diving. Like the ocean rolling and contracting. I press up on my elbows to get a better view of Garrett's head between my thighs driving me toward the edge of pleasure and pain. He meets my eyes and smiles, pulling his head away to slowly, oh, so fucking slowly, slip a finger inside.

"You like to watch, Angel?"

"I like to watch you."

His finger caresses my inner walls, and the heat begins to build again. Garrett sucks my clit into his mouth, pushing another finger inside, then, holy shit, *another*...stretching me, testing me. The teasing is over and oh my God here we are.

It's him, it's us, it's this.

I cry out, panting and bucking as he drives a pounding rhythm and yes, yes yes! Starshine and sunbursts and fucking yes, sir! Yes, more! Let me be your good girl!

While I'm still riding the waves of pleasure, Garrett stands, wiping his face with the back of his hand, smiling down at me while I spiral back to awareness. "Did that feel good, my Angel?"

I nod, my arms flung over my head as I stare hungrily at the erection straining against his pants.

"You taste so sweet, I could do that all day, but I want to watch you come like that on my cock." His deft fingers slide the belt from his pants, a wicked glint in his eyes catching my attention. Instead of dropping it to the floor, he drapes it around his neck, then pulls a condom from his wallet and steps out of his pants. His dick is long and proud. My eyes go wide as I process his girth.

"The fingers are a warmup." Garrett climbs onto the bed. "But I'll go slow until you're used to me."

He pulls the belt off, slowly wrapping it around my wrists, then pinning them over my head.

I've never been bound before.

I like it.

Sitting up, he slides the condom into place, then presses himself against me. "Look at me, Angel. I want your eyes on mine as you take all of me."

My lips part as he presses inside. I gasp as he inches forward and lift my head off the pillow, pressing my forehead to his as he tightens his hold on the belt.

"That's my good girl. You take me so well."

My chest heaves. I'm full. So fucking full. How am I not combusting?

And then Garrett's hips touch mine and the tap on my clit has me shivering in anticipation.

He smiles. "Fuck, Angel. You feel so good. So tight. You're like silk."

His words barely register before he's moving again and I'm over the edge, beyond feeling, beyond meaning, beyond words. This is a slow fall through oblivion as he reduces me to sensation, a keening cry slipping past my lips.

This is beauty.

This is grace.

This is the thin line between pain and pleasure and he keeps me on it with the precision of an expert, the belt tight around my wrists, my hands begging to clutch his muscled back.

His thrusts gain speed. His body rocking and rolling into me, his eyes holding mine hostage. His breath hitches. His jaw grinds closed, and then he finishes with a spasm, lowering his forehead to mine as we pant together in the aftermath.

FATE

CHAPTER TWENTY-NINE

Garrett

Fuck me.

Okay then.

That was...

I don't know what that was.

I collapse beside my Angel, staring at the ceiling as I catch my breath. One arm above my head. The other on my chest. Mind racing. Heart thundering. Breath roaring.

She's...

I'll never get her out of my system.

That's the only thought in my head.

I thought that was all I needed. To get her out of my system. I've said it so many times, I actually believed it. But she's in there forever now. Swimming through my bloodstream. Rooted into my cells. I will always want her. Always want more of that. After a day spent laughing, feeling more at ease than I have since—

—feeling more at ease than I have in years, she does *that*. Responding to me like her body was made for mine. So sweet, so pliant. So embarrassed to beg but so eager for more.

Beside me, she lays on her back, wrists still trapped in my belt. I push up on an elbow, brush a strand of hair from her face.

"You okay, Angel?"

Her eyes focus on mine and a smile quirks her lips. "Is that what they call this? Okay? Because I am so much more than okay."

Carefully, I unwrap the belt from her wrists, kissing each finger and rubbing the indents on her skin. Seeing her like this, so open, so vulnerable, so...fuck. What? There's a knot of emotion twisting in my chest, my belly, and I can't make sense of it.

Can't think through it.

I kiss her forehead. Her eyelids. The tip of her nose. The corners of her lips. Then stretch out on my back, opening my arms for her to curl in. She rests her head on my chest, one shapely leg draping over mine while her fingers trace lazy circles on my abdomen. I run a hand through her hair, breathing in the scent of her shampoo.

Coconut. Lime. I've never smelled something so sweet.

If I could hold her like this forever, I'd...

I'd what?

What are those thoughts? Why can't I finish them?

"Are you mad at me?" Angela's voice is almost a whisper.

"Mad?" I lift my head from the pillow to seek out her gaze. "Why would I be mad?"

"You're super quiet and it's weirding me out."

"No, no, no my Angel. I'm not mad. I'm..." I sigh because what am I?

Awed?

Confused?

Smitten?

Off-balance?

"I'm enjoying what we did," I finally reply, running a hand through her silken locks.

"That was definitely something." Angela shifts, pushing up on an elbow, hair cascading over shoulders. "I must say, you lived up to all the fantasies I've had about you." She gasps in shock, then laughs. "Look what you've done to me. I'm still spiraling somewhere above the earth and apparently have no control of my mouth."

"Sex makes you spill your secrets. Good to know."

Angela drops her head onto my chest with a groan. "Promise you'll only use that knowledge for good?"

"I make no such promise." This feels easy. Natural. I smile. "I will use that knowledge to my advantage like any businessman worth his salt. Now spill. Fantasies?"

"Mmhmm. Ever since you kissed me at The Pact... well, no...before that..." A crooked smile twists her lips as she watches me process the timeline.

"Before that? Ms. Hutton. Are you saying you started fantasizing about me right after we met?"

I think back to her that night, a little drunk, a lot mad, giving me hell for showing up late. I thought she hated me.

"See, it's all perfectly understandable and explainable..." Sitting up, Angela runs a finger down my chest. Her smile brightens as her eyes shift to the side. "The first text I got, before I realized I had the wrong phone, was a pic of you, in bed, and the way you stared at the camera, at whoever was taking the picture, it was..." She bites her bottom lip as her cheeks go pink. "Never mind. It's kind of embarrassing."

I know what picture she's talking about, and I remember when Melinda took it, though why she chose to send it to me the same day she outed herself for cheating is beyond me.

"Oh, no," I say with a low chuckle. "You started the story. You're obligated to finish it."

Angela's eyes meet mine and the vulnerability I see there surprises me. "It was a super sexy picture okay? You looked at the camera like you were...raw and manly. Like you'd...I don't know...do all the dirty things we just did and somehow there was this...this primal *something*. This claiming." She sighs in exasperation. "It was very sexy and your shirt was off and I liked it, okay?"

Her embarrassment is sweet. It makes her seem so young and inexperienced. Surely that can't be true though. A woman like this...?

"Did I live up to the fantasy?"

"Did you...? Yes, Garrett," she says with a laugh, her cheeks darkening from pink to red. "You didn't just live up to it, you obliterated it. You blew it out of the water."

I sit up, narrowing my eyes as a thought strikes me. "What's the hottest experience you've ever had?"

"You." Angela's answer comes quickly, without a hint of deception or manipulation. "Before tonight, it was the phone sex. After tonight? That belt might take the lead. I'm...I'm not sure. Either way, it's you."

Blinking, I sit up straighter. "Don't take this the wrong way, but...have you been dating assholes?"

She slaps my chest. "Play nice."

"I am. Believe me, I am. If a woman with a body like yours...if no one's shown you what it's capable of, then..."

"Then what?"

"Then you and I are going to have a lot of fun together." God, the things I could do to her. The things I *want* to do to her. She'd blush if I voiced them, but slowly, surely, she'll beg for it all in time.

"If that means doing more of what we just did, then I'm in." Angela curls into me and I run my fingers through her hair.

"Now I'm curious," I say, distracted by thoughts of what I want to do with her next. "What's your sex life been like?"

"Garrett!" She covers her face with both hands. "You don't just ask someone stuff like that."

"Humor me, Angel. I want to know you."

She presses up on her elbow, staring in shock. "You're not...are you...? Garrett Cooper...are we *connecting?*"

I laugh despite myself and mimic her posture. "No. You're avoiding my question."

Angela's brows furrow and she captures her bottom lip between her teeth. She's considering the implications of answering while I chew over my deep desire for this piece of her. Connection isn't my thing. Not since Elizabeth. I've purposefully avoided it, but there's no denying that's what's happening. I've shared parts of myself and want parts of her in return.

"Apparently," Angela finally says, "my sex life has been underwhelming. I mean, I'm not inexperienced, but I haven't ever done anything like—" she waves a hand over my body "—this."

Pride swells my chest. I like being a new experience, a good experience, for her.

"Has it only been missionary sex and the occasional bouquet of flowers, then?" I mean the question as a joke, but the way her eyes cut away and her cheeks grow pink tell me I hit the nail on the head.

"Jesus, Angel. That's not right."

"It's fine. It's not like I'm suffering or anything." She quirks her head, suddenly shy. "What about for you? Was that…? Did I…? Did you…?"

"Did I what?"

"Did you ever think about me? Like that?"

Me in the shower, dick in hand, pumping hard while I imagined her on her knees in front of me…

I nod. "I fantasized a little."

"A little?"

"I jacked off, thinking about you in red heels, down on your knees, begging for my cock. So yeah. A little."

A blush warms her cheeks, and a smile brightens her eyes. "Is it wrong that I like that?"

"Is it wrong...? Good God woman, why would that be wrong?"

"I don't know. Shouldn't I be indignant or something?"

I shrug. "Are you indignant?"

"I kind of like it."

"Well, there you go. That's what you should feel."

"That's it?" Angela huffs a laugh. "That's what I'm feeling, so that's what I should feel?"

"My therapist says all emotions are valid. That we shouldn't try to control *what* we feel, only how we choose to react to those feelings."

I blink.

Fuck.

Therapist.

Did I really say that?

How the hell did I let that slip? The only people who know about that are my family, and even them knowing makes me uncomfortable.

Angela shakes her head and I recognize the glint in her eyes. She thinks she's gonna prove me wrong. I know because I look the same way when I dig in my heels. "So you're saying if I get super pissed at some guy who cuts me off on the road, that's valid. Road rage is a-okay."

"The emotion is valid. You can't control that. In fact, you probably need to listen to what it's telling you because it's a symptom of a greater problem. What's not valid is giving into that rage and letting it dictate your behavior. Take a deep breath, let the emotion exist, and then choose a course of action you can be proud of. Forgive yourself. Forgive the guy. Then take some time to understand why that rage was there in the first place, waiting for an outlet."

"Sounds easy enough." She smiles and I push into a sitting position.

"It's not. Believe me. I've been working on it for years and my anger issues still run deep."

I swallow hard, disbelief clamping my jaw shut.

What the hell am I doing? Talking about my fucking issues? Really?

Angela turns her focus to me. "Now see, there's something we should take some time to understand. Why are you so angry, Mr. Cooper?"

I don't want to talk about this. Not now. Not with her.

Never with her.

She doesn't know the rage filled me. The red-faced me. The choking on spite and venom me.

And if I have my way, she never will.

Time to redirect the dialogue.

I wrap an arm around Angela's waist and flip her onto her back, covering her body with mine. She squeals, laughing in delight. "How can I be angry when there's a beautiful woman, naked in my bed?"

"Your bed? I thought you gave it to me."

"Oh." I look around, feigning confusion. "Are you suggesting you want me to leave?"

"No way." Angela slides her hands up my arms, around my shoulders, and pulls me close. "I want you to continue my romantic education." She shifts her gaze to the ceiling, thinking, searching, then turns to me with a smile. "Feed me strawberries while we drink champagne until morning."

"What if I have a better idea?"

"Better than strawberries and champagne? Do tell."

"I think it's better if I show you," I say, then silence her retort with a kiss.

CHAPTER THIRTY

Garrett

We never order room service. Instead, we spend the night wrapped in each other's arms, talking, kissing, petting. At some point, we find sleep because I wake to sunlight searing through the slim crack in the blackout curtains. Angela is curled up on her side, her hair fanned out on the pillow behind her. I press a kiss to her shoulder before sitting up, my bare feet making contact with cheap carpet as I lean my elbows on my knees and rest my head in my hands.

Last night...

It changes everything.

Or maybe it changes nothing at all because in a matter of hours, she's flying home to the Keys while I hop a plane to Wildrose Landing. It doesn't matter if she's in my system, out of my system, or a figment of my imagination...

This won't work.

Assuming I even want it to work in the first place. I'm not...I'm not a relationship kind of guy. There's too much at stake, especially when people are so good at letting everyone else down.

Angela shifts, rolling onto her back with a sigh, tossing an arm overhead as her face turns my way. Her blue eyes crack open and a crooked, sleepy smile closes them again.

"Are you watching me sleep?"

"You got a problem with that?" I swing my legs back onto the bed and stretch out beside her.

"Yeah. I think I do." Her eyes open and her smile deepens. "It's creepy."

"So, learning I masturbate in the shower to you before we knew each other is fine, but me looking at you while you sleep after we spent several *very* intimate hours together is an issue." I cock my head. "Is it me? Or does that seem off?"

"That's definitely a you thing."

She laughs and makes her way back into my arms. Her head on my chest, my fingers in her hair.

"Let's stay right here, all day. We don't even have to get dressed." I pull her closer. "We never did order that room service."

"Isn't it too early for strawberries and champagne?"

"It's never too early for strawberries and champagne."

The moment we walk out of this room, this thing between us is over. It's untenable. Our lives are too set. Too complete. My head knows it's time to call it before things get more complicated than they already are, but my body…

…my body loves having her breasts pressed against me, her leg thrown over mine, her soft skin dancing along my hard edges.

"What if I said I wanted a little of this…?" Angela slides her hand up my thigh, drawing her fingernails against the skin, then wraps her delicate fingers around my swelling cock. Her eyes light up. "It looks like I'm not the only one who's fond of the idea."

I press up on my elbow and cup her cheek, slipping my fingers into her hair to draw her in for a kiss. "I'm not just fond of it," I say, my lips brushing hers. "I'm a huge fucking fan."

"And I'm a huge fan of fucking," she replies, pumping her hand along my dick. "I don't know why we're still talking about it. Let's get to it, Bucko."

In one swift movement, I roll on top of her, my hands on either side of her head as I position myself between her thighs. "Easy now, my Angel. I'm the one who gives the orders around here."

FATE

While Angela's in the shower, I call room service to order a fresh fruit platter and a bottle of Prosecco—they don't offer champagne. I one hundred percent will hand-feed this woman fruit just to see her smile. I consider hopping into the shower with her but pull on a pair of pants instead. After all, checkout is only a few hours away.

My phone vibrates with a text, and I swipe it off the nightstand, grinning like a fucking idiot. What's it say about Angela that I'm smiling so damn much? It says she's magic, that's what. Mom would tell me to take that feeling and roll with it. That it's a sign I'm finally on my path. And I'm in such a good mood, I might even believe her.

My smile falters when I see who the message is from. The Future Mrs. Cooper. I was so done with Melinda after everything went down, I didn't change her contact info.

A morbid sense of curiosity has me clicking on the text. I know better. There's nothing good waiting for me there. Nothing at all. Melinda is toxic layered upon greedy layered upon selfish and if she's texting me, she's working an angle.

> THE FUTURE MRS. COOPER
>
> Hey Bear. Hope everything's okay with you. Any chance you want to meet up? Have some fun? I know everything got weird with the whole Gustavo thing but you and me? We're not built for commitment. You know that. I know that. Everyone knows that. So we're good, right? Let's go back to the way things were. I miss your dick.

I scoff and read the text three times, my jaw getting tighter with each pass. My hands clench. My brows furrow.

She has no right to say I'm not built for commitment. Once upon a time, I was a "forever" kind of guy, and that didn't work out well for me. At all.

So I've been dealing in distractions ever since.

It's a conscious choice. Not how I'm built.

Though Melinda has no knowledge of who I am or what I've been through, so her jumping to that conclusion shouldn't piss me off.

So why am I ready to punch a wall?

The shower turns off and I drop the phone onto the bed beside me. That reason to be angry? It's the shittiness surrounding Melinda. The cheapness she brings to everything. I'm mad at myself for not seeing it sooner. It's the only thing that makes sense. Although, as Angela hums to herself in the bathroom, there's a part of me that isn't convinced. There's something else at the root of the rage growing inside me.

A knock and a call of, "Room service!" derails my thoughts. I stand, grabbing a shirt out of my bag and pulling it over my head before opening the door. The guy barely looks at me until I tip him and even then, he's sizing me up, not expressing gratitude. People and their greed. I can't fucking stand it. Inhaling deeply and exhaling slowly, I choose not to focus on Melinda or the sad state of humanity.

If I only have a few more hours with Angela, I'm going to enjoy them.

When she comes out of the bathroom, I'm waiting for her in bed with a plate of fruit in front of me, and a glass of Prosecco in one hand while I beckon her over with the other.

"You didn't," she says, a smile transforming her face.

"You bet your sweet ass I did." I run a loving hand over the mattress. "Now come here and let me play with that mouth."

CHAPTER THIRTY-ONE

Angela

Stretched out on a king-sized bed in a small town in South Carolina, I allow Garrett to hand feed me bits of fruit. The way he looks at me when I suck his fingers into my mouth and lick them clean jostles for position as the Hottest Thing I've Ever Done. This man...

This silly, grumpy, sweetly crazy man.

We should have left for our respective homes yesterday. We should have signed contracts, said our goodbyes, and then had the odd email every now and then. Maybe a phone call. A text.

But now...

...*now*...

What will happen now?

I hesitate to bring up work while we're naked in bed, teasing each other into another round of Hottest Thing I've Ever Done. That would cheapen everything, and I one hundred percent did not sleep with Garrett to influence our business dealings.

They're influenced anyway.

Obviously.

You don't have a night like last night and a morning like this morning and not have the aftershocks trace their fingers along all areas of our lives.

It's not possible.

Garrett plucks a strawberry off the plate and angles it towards my mouth. When I move to bite it, he draws back. I give chase, right into his trap as he cups my head and kisses me. Our tongues glide together. He tastes of Prosecco and feels like…like…

…a promise.

A promise that will shake up my life. He's the catalyst of change and I want to believe it's positive. Otherwise, I took one mistake and rolled it right into another, bigger mistake. Instead of harnessing rocket fuel to launch me to success, I may have just dumped it all over me and lit a match. And I don't want to be that person. I've made it through my entire life without any serious mishaps and it can't happen now. It just can't.

I won't let it.

When Garrett releases the kiss, I smile, pressing my forehead to his for a few lovely seconds before I sit back and reach for my Prosecco.

"Can I ask a personal question?"

"You can ask." He graces me with a rare smile. "There's no guarantee I'll answer."

"You mentioned a therapist last night..."

His jaw tightens. His eyes harden with distrust, the way Fluff and Orange used to look whenever I stepped onto the porch. "I did. Is that a problem?"

"No, no. God no. With the way the world's going, all of us could do with a little professional help and I respect the hell out of someone who seeks it. It's just... you don't seem like the type..."

"I didn't realize there's a 'therapist type.'"

"I mean, you go around, all growly and grumbly, talking about never needing a relationship and that sounds very, well, emotionally closed off, if you know what I mean. But then, last night, you said some really emotionally intelligent stuff and I don't know what to do with that."

I'm trying to read him. To see if he's worth risking everything for, or if that's even an option...and it's impossible to tell what this inexplicable man is thinking. With the edge of our bubble approaching, I want to gobble up as much information as he'll give me. This will either be the weekend of passion I daydream about well into my old age, or it's the start of something real…

Either way, I want to hold onto this moment for as long as possible. Before the real world with work and responsibilities jerks us away from each other.

Garrett shifts as he drinks his Prosecco. "I guess you could say I'm an emotionally closed off guy who's learning to change."

"I respect that. I do." A half-smile tugs at my mouth and I run a finger along his arm. "I'm not sure it's working all that well…"

He scoffs, shaking his head. "You sound like Charlie."

"Is that a bad thing?"

"I don't know yet."

Silence hovers between us. Not the kind of silence you want to run from, but the kind you want to pause with, to drink in, to expand through.

"I don't talk about it. The therapy." Garrett rests his glass on the bed, his thumb running along the stem. "With anyone."

"Then why me?"

"It didn't happen on purpose." He shrugs. "I was surprised when it came out and relieved you didn't say anything." Darkness settles over Garrett's face as he glares at the rumpled bedsheets.

What is that? What's happening in that head that makes him look so unhappy all the time?

I crane my neck to meet his gaze. "I was...indisposed," I finish with a grin. "Definitely preoccupied with other matters."

"I see." His eyes meet mine as he plucks a strawberry off the plate and sinks his teeth into the juicy flesh. "And you're not now?"

I am, I think. *So incredibly preoccupied. Afraid I'm in the middle of risking everything and I'm looking for anything to prove I'm safe. Information. Connection. Anything at all to put me at ease.*

"I mean, watching you eat that strawberry is preoccupying."

Garrett grins as he pulls it from his mouth and traces the tip with his tongue before biting down and sucking, his gaze strong. Blistering with desire. It's everything I saw in that picture his ex-girlfriend sent...

And it's aimed right at me.

"*Really* preoccupying," I say, laughing lightly.

Garrett chews and swallows, then sips his Prosecco and sets the glass on the table. Thoughts tick away behind his eyes, and he worries the inside of his lip. The scowling, growly veneer falls away and I see a vulnerability.

A sensitivity.

The man behind the mask.

This. This is what I'm looking for. I sit up, expectation propelling me closer.

"I had a hard time after my mom died." Garrett rakes a hand through his hair. "It was so sudden, a car wreck, so, you know, no warning. I took it really hard. Started acting out. Getting in fights. That kind of stuff. Instead of supporting me, the entire town decided I was broken. Can you imagine that? An entire town against one little kid. They actually called me a monster. My dad couldn't get anyone to babysit us. It was hard. It hurt. I was young and needed help processing my grief. All I got was judgment. When Mom—Amelia—came into the picture, she was amazing, but I still had a lot of shit to deal with. I stopped being able to remember my mother's face and that kinda fucked me up."

"I can't even imagine. I'm sorry you went through that." The idea of losing my mom settles a lump into my throat. The thought of having to do it when I was just a kid, so entirely dependent on her for so much…it breaks me.

"But Mom was good for me. For Dad. For Charlie and Connor. The rest of my childhood was pretty idyllic. I got this job. Made some solid investment choices that set my life on a different path. Moved to Boston. Met Eliz—" His voice cracks and he clears his throat. "Elizabeth."

Speaking the name almost kills him. His voice tightens. Lowers. He has to force it into the conversation. He doesn't sound like someone who isn't interested in love. He says her name like someone who's loved deeply.

And lost.

I wait for him. Sitting quietly, like I did with the kittens, letting him see that I'm not here to take more than he's ready to give.

"Elizabeth, she...uh...she died too." Garrett's eyes meet mine. "Car accident. I...uh...we had a fight. About...uh..." He swipes a hand over his mouth. "And...she left. Angry, you know. It was late. Weather was bad. And she...she, uh, she never came back."

He sighs.

Eyes closed.

A complete exhalation that fails to release everything he's carrying. I see it, heavy on his shoulders, darkness in his eyes, a hollowness settling into his chest. Two tragedies. Two women he loved, dying the same way. Taken from him. Stolen long before he was ready to let go.

I see now why he's so closed off. Why he pushes people away. He's afraid to let people in because he's already loved and lost.

Garrett traces a finger along my shoulder. "And ever

since then, since that, since...*her*...I, well, I see life differently. I get mad at things that don't bother other people. I don't trust everyone to be who they pretend to be. And I see a therapist who congratulates me for simple stuff like getting through a day without losing my shit." He clears his throat and forces a smile. "So, there it is. Garrett Cooper in a nutshell. Do with it what you will."

"Thank you for sharing that with me." I cup his cheek. Press my forehead to his. There's more to the story, but I won't push for it. He'll tell me when he's ready. I'm just grateful he was willing to connect that much.

Garrett clears his throat. Clenches his jaw. The vulnerability leaves his eyes and is replaced by something...uncomfortable.

It's nearly time to leave for the airport. This magical moment outside of time is almost over and we'll never be together like this again. I can feel it in my bones. I need to ask Garrett about the contracts. I need to refocus on why we're here in the first place, but I don't want to bring this whole thing crashing down around me.

"Come back to the Keys with me." The words are out before I knew what I wanted to say.

Garrett looks surprised, then frowns. "Angel..."

He's going to turn me down. I can see it.

I hurry ahead before he can. "You can stay at The Hut, or you can stay with me. But...don't go home."

This is the man who admitted from the start he's not interested in relationships. He just told me he struggles to trust people. I'm already afraid I've pushed him too far and yet, *and yet*, I can't help myself. I'm not ready for this to be over and after we make our way back to our respective homes, that's it. Whatever this is? Done.

Maybe I'm being greedy, but I've never done something just for me. Never. Not once in my life. Every choice I've made has been about what's best for the family. What's best for the business. And Garrett? He feels like what's best for me. It's time to accept that.

"Okay." He nods, looking as surprised by his response as I was by my question.

I sit up straighter. "Okay?"

"Yeah. Okay. I'll...I'll look into switching flights."

A reprieve.

That's what this is. A reprieve. We don't have to say goodbye. Not yet. Not now.

"That makes me so happy!" I'm up and moving, propelled off the bed by excitement, then stop, cup his face, and kiss him deeply. "I'll call The Hut and get you a room. It's probably better if you stay there instead of with me. You know. Optics." I shrug. "I'll tell Dad we're working out some details or...or something."

My dad's a smart man and if he's paying attention at all, he'll know something is off, but that's a risk I'm willing to take. Dad won't like it. Not at first. But he'll understand. He always does.

And if he doesn't?

That's a bridge we'll cross *if* we get there.

CHAPTER THIRTY-TWO

GARRETT

Angela's flight is sold out, so I buy a ticket for a plane leaving a few hours after hers. With time to kill, I grab a coffee and sit at the airport, my thoughts growing darker with each minute that passes. I committed the cardinal sin of connection, of vulnerability, of sharing parts of myself best left in the dark.

I can't shake the feeling I'll pay for it sooner or later. The deal is in jeopardy. My reputation is in jeopardy. My heart is in jeopardy.

I scoff. This is why I told Charlie work's my priority. Making money is a straight give and take. You get out what you put in. But people? They're fickle. Unpredictable.

While Angela feels like she's different from anyone I've known before, I can't forget this is a brand-new friendship. Relationship. Whatever this is. There are parts of her I haven't met yet, just like she's yet to meet the worst of me.

Uncomfortable, I distract myself by watching people come and go, making up stories for them as they pass.

That guy with the strange limp and the goofy grin? He spent a week with his mistress, suffered a sex-related injury, and is going home to tell his wife all about his golf trip where he mysteriously pulled a muscle in his groin.

That woman glaring at her phone as she cuts off an elderly couple? She's running from authorities after embezzling millions of dollars into an offshore account. She's one flight away from pulling it off.

I amuse myself with the stories, making them more and more outlandish until I'm surrounded by double agents, murderers, and super spies. Anything to distract myself from what I told Angel. The only people who know the whole story about Elizabeth are my therapist, my family, and Jordan Clement...and that bastard only knows because he was there. It's the single worst thing that's ever happened to me, but I almost told Angela everything.

All of it.

The whole filthy debacle almost spilled right out of my mouth.

Thank fuck I stopped myself before I told her what really happened that night.

What the hell was I thinking?

I wasn't. That's the problem. My Angel does something to me. Something that disarms my defenses. Something that makes me fly to Florida on a whim...for an indeterminate amount of time...knowing this will only end in disaster.

A call yanks my attention to reality. Shit. Branson Masters.

My boss.

He's going to want an update on the deal and the only one I have is that I slept with Angela instead of finalizing things.

Grimacing, I accept the call and put the phone to my ear.

"Cooper," he barks. "What the fuck is going on down there?"

"Things are good." I rub a hand over my face and sit back. "Locked, loaded, and ready to go."

"As in you've signed contracts and we just took on a solid long-term investment? Or more like you're blowing smoke up my ass and I need to send Clement down there to clean up?"

My fist tightens around my coffee, obliterating the

cup. Hot liquid sloshes onto my hand. I swallow a curse.

Jordan fucking Clement.

That asshole can stay right where he is.

He doesn't belong within a thousand miles of this deal and if he so much as whispers my Angel's name, I'll murder him in his sleep.

I'll button this whole thing up as soon as I land in the Keys, and I'll make sure the deal is fair for everyone involved. Clement will screw the Huttons without thinking twice. It's kind of his thing. He'd excel at the type of company that took advantage of Angela the first time. It's all about the money for him, and he doesn't care the slightest about who gets hurt in the crossfire.

Friends. Colleagues...

They're all collateral damage as far as that asshole is concerned.

"Everything's on track." I pinch the phone between my ear and shoulder, wiping coffee off my hand with a napkin that disintegrates before the mess is clean. "This deal's lookin' good. Yeah. Very good."

"It'll look *very good* once signatures have happened and your ass is back home. I've got a potential client who's looking for a line of credit. This could be a good deal for us, and I want you on it."

"Put Jordan on that one. I've got the hotel under control."

"These people requested you specifically. They heard about your work with Wayfair Resorts and have made it clear you're their guy."

"Then I'll be their guy after I'm done here." My jaw clenches so tight my teeth ache. The idea of Jordan's smarmy ass down here, his greasy smile aimed at Angela…

"I want to know why this is taking so long. What's getting in the way of the deal, Cooper?"

My Angel's body, stretched out on the bed beneath me. Her hair fanned on the pillows. Lips parted. Chest heaving. Moaning in ecstasy as I bury myself inside—

"We, uh…" I rake a hand through my hair. Get it together, fucker! "I went through their projections and actuals with a fine-tooth comb, then flew to South Carolina to poke around the new site and make sure they're not hiding a time bomb in the details. They're not. Everything about this deal looks solid."

Everything except for me sleeping with Angela Hutton. There's nothing solid about that.

"Ms. Hutton has verbally confirmed and I'm flying back to the Keys to get the signatures of everyone involved."

"Good." Masters clears his throat. "Because I *will* send Clement down there."

"Jordan Clement will ruin everything that's good about The Hutton Hotel."

"He'll also close the deal."

"*I'll* close the damn deal!" I lean forward and scrub a hand over my face. "I don't want him anywhere near this. Give me forty-eight hours and this thing is done. I'm on it."

"You better be. Because if you're not? Jordan is. Forty-eight hours, Garrett."

The line goes dead. I put my phone on the table and glare at the screen. My brows furrow. Anger twists and bites, an angry dog straining against his chain.

Jordan fucking Clement is a dirty move and Branson knows it. I don't want him so much as whispering Angela's name, let alone shaking her hand. Sitting across from her. Leering. Plotting.

I can't sit still. I'm up and moving. No destination. My fists clench and I push past a group of twenty-somethings clogging the walkway.

"Watch it, dick weasel!" squawks a douchebag in a neon tank top, his floofy hair screaming, "Daddy never gives me attention, so I'll steal it from you!"

Every cell in my body wants to channel my anger into his face. That would give him the attention he's looking for. But I keep walking because I'm not that guy. Not anymore.

Your anger isn't proportionate to the situation.

I repeat the mantra over and over but it's not helping. It only makes me madder because it's not fucking true. My anger is proportionate. It's so damn proportionate I find myself growling as I detour into the restroom.

I pace the space.

Trapped.

I fucking...opened up to Angela. I lay in bed with her, feeding her strawberries while I shared my sad little story. And now she has that part of me, and I don't know how I feel about that.

I like her, and I don't know how to feel about that either.

And the thought of Jordan coming anywhere near her?

I grip a sink and glare into the mirror.

Our signatures need to hit the bottom line of a contract that skews in favor of Vision Enterprise. But I don't want to fuck her over. Am I really going to put my job at risk for someone I barely know? For someone who doesn't even live in the same state as me?

I don't know.

I don't know what to do on this one.

Angela's smile. Her laugh. The way she tosses her hair. She listened to me. She listened to me and didn't judge, and I'm not supposed to like the way that feels.

But I do.

Fuck.

I slap a hand against the porcelain and push off, wandering the airport until they board my flight.

Standing at baggage claim after a tense couple hours, I shoot a text to my family.

> Hey. In case you're worried, I'm alive. Back in the Keys, finishing up this deal.

CHARLIE

> Was just thinking about you. Things good?

> Things are…complicated. But good. I think.

CHARLIE

> This wouldn't have anything to do with that woman, would it?

MOM

> I had a feeling good things were happening for you, Gare. You just open yourself up to it and enjoy the ride.

I laugh, shaking my head. Mom and Charlie's perpetual optimism never ceases to amaze me. Even if I explained all the ways this ride is doomed to fail, they'd point out the one way that might lead to success. They are amazing women.

So is Angela.

I refocus on the baggage carousel. The last time I was here, my phone met its untimely end, squashed by a precocious toddler. What if I hadn't seen him climbing on that suitcase? He would have fallen. Maybe smashed his head on the tile. His mother never would have forgiven herself. My phone wouldn't have been broken and I wouldn't have met Angela Hutton until I walked into the meeting the next day.

I'd have closed the deal and been back in Wildrose Landing days ago.

Would things be easier that way?

That version of me would have missed out on all of this. He wouldn't have remembered how it felt to look down at a woman and want to protect her. To claim her. To open to her.

Fear tightens my lips.

I have no fucking clue what to do. I'm not equipped to deal with emotions like this.

"You're overthinking," I murmur to myself as I study the baggage carousel.

"I'm sorry. Did you say something?" A young man pauses as he passes.

I meet his confused eyes with a self-deprecating laugh. "Just muttering to myself."

"I do that all the time," he says with a grin. "Hope you figure everything out." He lifts a hand as he heads off on his way again. "You have a good one."

Huh. Whadaya know. Decency still exists in this world after all.

CHAPTER THIRTY-THREE

Angela

I lean against a wall, watching the airport doors like a hawk. Despite the merciless sun, a breeze cools the sweat at my temples, and I close my eyes, sighing in appreciation of small mercies. Any minute now, Garrett will step through those doors. It's only been a few hours since we've seen each other, but I crave his touch. His smell. The comfort of being near him. My heart doesn't understand time or distance. The only thing it knows is "with him" and "not with him" and even a second spent apart is—

Oh shit.

I put a hand to my mouth.

What's this nonsense I'm spewing? *My heart doesn't understand time or distance?*

Am I...?

Am I developing *feelings* for Garrett Cooper? I mean, lust is one thing and that's definitely there. He lived up to every single dirty fantasy I've ever had, and I can't wait for more.

But feelings?

That's a different story altogether. Like, record scratch. Stop the presses. What the hell is going on, you foolish woman? This is the worst case scenario for me.

How long ago was I standing at the new site, congratulating myself on having a casual sexual encounter and not letting it turn into A Thing? I count the days on my fingers and shake my head.

I don't know Garrett well enough to feel anything more than "dang that's a sexy hunk of man who can feed me strawberries in bed any time." And even if I'd known him longer, he's grumpy and closed off and oscillates from pushing me away to pushing me against a wall while telling me how much he wants to sleep with me.

What happened to step one, assume everything that comes out of Garrett Cooper's mouth is a lie? And step two? Remembering he is not my friend, no matter what he says? Yeah, that one's pretty much blown all to hell at this point.

What the hell is wrong with me?

I've known from the get-go that this relationship is my one chance at saving The Hut. The phone sex was bad enough. Falling for the time bubble nonsense was worse.

But feelings?

How did I end up with feelings for a man I wasn't even sure I liked a week ago?

The pushing me against a wall thing is a major perk. Just thinking about it has my body on alert, even more eager for Garrett's arrival than I already was.

So yeah. That's lust. Not feelings.

Which means everything's okay.

I'm in the clear.

He's hot. He's good in bed. He's got that whole "intense and growly" thing going on, which for some reason really does it for me. Anyone with eyes would fall into lust with Garrett Cooper.

As if summoned by my thoughts, the airport doors slide open and out he steps. My entire body lights up with too many sensations to name.

Lust is there, holding hands with desire.

Excitement, too. Totally natural when you're in the middle of an illicit tryst that puts your whole life at risk.

But what's that? The tingling sensation running along my skin? The swelling of my heart as I take an involuntary step forward? The smile growing on my face just seeing him?

Shit.

Those are feelings.

I have stupid, sick in the heart *feelings* for Garrett Cooper.

He must never know.

This is the man who managed to mention, at least once a day—if not once an hour—that he doesn't do relationships. That he's not an "emotional connection" kind of guy. And I've promptly declared *every single time* that I'm fine with that. That I'm in the market for a distraction too.

Neither of us signed up for feelings!

As my heart performs backflips at the sight of him, I do what any sane woman would in this situation. I shove all that nonsense into a shame box in the back of my mind. Maybe if I ignore them, they'll go away.

Garrett zeroes in on me, a smile brightening his face, then strides over, draws me close, and presses a kiss into my hair. "How did you get even more beautiful?"

Do. Not. Swoon.

"It's the Keys," I reply as casually as possible. "They look good on everyone."

When I meet his eyes, there's something there.

Something...unpleasant. Like maybe the Keys don't look so good on him.

Although, that could be Garrett's natural grumpy setting on display.

And it disappears so quickly I wonder if I imagined it.

We walk to the car.

...feelings...?

I pop the trunk for Garrett's bags, then climb into the driver's seat.

...how can I have feelings...?

His fingers twine through mine as I pull out of the parking space and he brings my hand to his lips, kissing me once, twice, a third time.

...are you sure...?

...feelings...?

My heart clasps its hands and sighs dreamily, so I do the only rational thing: toss a conversational bomb into the mix.

"Apparently there's a thing at my parents' house." I glance Garrett's way, chewing my bottom lip. "The whole crew will be there. All my aunts, uncles, cousins, and their significant others. I was so...uhh...*preoccupied* earlier that I forgot it was tonight. Wanna come?"

That's right, I invited Captain Noncommittal himself to meet my parents. That should do...something. What? I haven't a clue, but I doubt it'll go over without a hitch.

Garret lifts his brows and gives an uneasy laugh. "You want me to come to a family thing?"

"Yeah." I flip a hand as if it's no big deal. "We're all super easygoing."

"So easygoing that no one will think it's strange you brought a business connection?" His expression says *yeah, I don't think so.* And for some reason, my heart finds that so cute, it starts practicing writing my first name with his last name.

So not cool.

I clear my throat and mentally put down the pen. "We'll have to go easy with the touchy-feely stuff, but yeah. Huttons are all about welcoming others. We'll say we had some contract stuff to go over or something, and you coming with was the best way to get it all done."

"Speaking of contract stuff." Garrett's entire demeanor changes. He sits taller in his seat, letting go of my hand. "It's time to finalize."

A tremor of worry zips through me. Something seems off, but I don't know what—

I laugh to myself. His change in demeanor couldn't have anything to do with the conversational bomb I knew I was dropping, could it?

"Yeah. Okay." I run a hand through my hair and order myself to chill already. "It definitely is."

Only, as soon as I sign that contract, which I totally should have signed days ago, Garrett leaves. His business in the Keys will be done and that's the end of that. We'll go back to our respective corners of the world, and he'll take his bossy self and his "good girls" with him. And me? I'll be left here to deal with these stupid feelings all by my lonesome...not to mention my brand spankin' new praise kink.

Mmmm... spanking...? What if I like being a bad girl, too?

Focus, Angela!

How does any of this make sense? I was supposed to be the smart one. The driven one. The first of the next generation to carry on the family business. Instead, anyone watching from the outside would swear I'm trying to burn it to the ground.

Garrett's waiting for an answer. Tense. Guarded. My lawyers gave the all clear on the contracts, so there's no reason to delay pulling the trigger on those.

At least, no reason that is business related.

"How about we stop at the Hut after the party and you and I can sign then? You'll still need Dad and Wyatt's signatures, but we'll take care of that tomorrow." I flick on an indicator and check my mirrors, distracting myself with driving so I don't freak out over every micro-expression that crosses Garrett's face.

"Sounds like a solid plan. It even provides a reason for me being at a family party."

The shift in him is subtle. So subtle I'm not sure I'm seeing it properly. He takes my hand again, but it feels forced. Meets my eyes, but that unpleasant something is a giant wall between us.

Was this whole thing between us part of a bigger plan?

Did he ask me to stay in Bliss for an extra day as some part of a twisted negotiation tactic? Get me to let down my guard then swoop in for the kill?

Jesus.

That's...

Is that even possible?

I shove those thoughts into the same box I shoved my feelings, fully aware how freaking stupid that makes me. I'm falling for a guy I worry might have slept with me for nefarious reasons.

Way to go, Angel. Way to go.

On the other side of the windshield, white clouds dot a sapphire sky. Palms blur by, bending lazily in the breeze, offering glimpses of the ocean. It's hard to be tense in a tropical paradise, but the atmosphere in this car is creeping toward arctic.

But then, the wall slips from Garrett's eyes and his

touch is warm and his smile is real and maybe, *maybe*, lack of sleep due to too much sexy times is taking its toll.

"You think your family will like me?" The question is so simple, so genuine, so...not Garrett, I can't help but smile.

"They're gonna love you. We're all about wildly intense people who go after what they want. My dad, my uncles...hell, the only Hutton who isn't intense is my Uncle Caleb, but he's so easygoing, even that is kicked up to eleven if you get my drift. They're gonna be massive Garrett fans."

And what then, Angela? What then? They love him, which will only make your feelings harder to ignore. He flies home. The end. I let out a nervous breath and inwardly shake myself away from that thought pattern.

Worrying will get me nowhere. It'll eat up the time we have left together, souring the experience. What will be, will be. Maybe I should just sit back and enjoy the ride for once.

I take the turn that leads me home instead of to The Hut and Garrett shifts, watching through the window as we leave the road we were just on.

"Now granted, I don't know my way around here all that well, but are we going the right way?"

"We are." I glance over with a mischievous smile.

"I could have sworn the hotel was down that way." He points behind us.

"We're not going to the hotel. We're going to my house. I want you where no one else can see us for a little while."

A glimmer in his eyes. A devious grin. A shift in his seat. "I like the sound of that."

When I pull to a stop in front of my house, an odd sense of homecoming washes through me as Garrett gets out of the car. Seeing him here, in my space, it solidifies everything. The feelings I shoved into a box in the back of my brain start creeping out.

I *like* having him here.

Shit. That's not going to help matters. Not at all.

A flash of fur disappears off the steps as we climb to the porch.

"Do you have a cat?"

"Two. Kind of." I shrug as I unlock the house. "We're...working it out." I toss my keys into the bowl near the door and grab the cat food before stepping back outside. "They may not come out with you here, but maybe, if we're really quiet, you'll get to see them."

"That sounds ominous," Garrett replies, leaning on the doorframe with his arms crossed. He's wearing his standard dress slack and button-down uniform. But his sleeves are rolled up and his face is more relaxed and the humidity has added some curl to his hair. Maybe the Keys look good on everyone, after all.

I grin, then scoop food into the bowls. Fluff appears, leaping onto the porch in a flash of white and brown. Instead of dashing away, he cautiously walks over to me, rubbing against my thigh on his way to the food bowl. My face lights up as I turn to Garrett. "He's never done that before," I whisper-yell so as not to scare my furry friend.

He pushes off the wall and shakes his head. "This seems a lot like you have a cat."

I share the story of them appearing, of the weeks of feeding them and watching behind my screen door as they hungrily crunched kibble. "I called the Humane Society, and they won't come get them. I can trap them, take them to the shelter to have them neutered, and then release them back to the wild, which is my fallback plan. My happy path is I desensitize them to human contact and adopt them myself."

Orange hops onto the porch and eyes me while his brother eats.

Garrett crouches, holding out his hand and clicking his tongue, which sends Orange right back into the bushes.

"He's always been a little more shy than his brother."

I give Fluff one last pet before straightening and

heading inside the house. Garrett follows, looking uncomfortable as he crosses the threshold. His energy takes up space, making my home reverberate with tension.

"How long until we need to be at your parents?"

"Couple hours? Why?"

He takes my hand and pulls me close. "Because if I have to share you tonight, I need you to myself for a while."

This is a bad idea.

I'm in over my head.

I need to put a stop to this before things get out of control.

But as Garrett's lips claim mine, I realize they're already out of control. I couldn't stop if I tried.

CHAPTER THIRTY-FOUR

Garrett

Watching Angela light up as she feeds a pair of stray kittens unlocks emotions I'm not prepared for. Emotions I never wanted to experience again. And being in her house, surrounded by her style, her personality, it feels so intimate, makes this so real, I can't deal with the implications.

I don't want to deal with the implications.

I have forty-eight hours to close a deal I should have finalized days ago. Giving into whatever this is between Angela and me, it's a distraction from what really matters. Doing my job. By focusing on intimacy, on the glimmer of feelings I promised to avoid for the rest of my life, I'm letting myself down.

So, I shift things back to the physical, where everything makes sense. Where there's touch and sensation and all you have to do when you want it to stop is walk the fuck away. These other feelings, they linger. They torture. They twist and turn into something ugly and I just...

I can't.

Angela lifts her face, smiling into mine, and I slide my fingers through that silken hair before pressing my lips to hers. She tastes sweet and feels like sin. My dick throbs with want.

"What was it you told me this morning?" She slides her hands up my arms, around my shoulders, then trails a finger along the back of my neck. "You jerked off, thinking about me on my knees?"

Her voice is low, sensual. It obliterates any thoughts about emotions or things I don't want to process and it's just her. That's all I see. All I know.

Her.

My Angel.

I run my hands down her back and cup her ass, pushing her hips to mine. "You did a lot more than get on your knees."

"Why don't you describe it to me." Angela kisses the corner of my mouth, slips her fingers into my hair. "I'll make your dreams come true."

"Red lips," I murmur. "Red heels. The skirt you wore to our first meeting."

Her eyes light up and she steps out of my arms. "The living room is in there. Make yourself comfortable and I'll be back in a minute."

She strolls away, disappearing down a hallway, leaving me to burn in her wake. I step into her living room, taking in the pictures, the dark blue wall with a painting done in whites and golds. Large shelves frame a television, with knickknacks and flowers artfully accompanying an array of books. All of this, this is her. The colors. The warmth. The comfort. The fact that I feel immediately welcome here is a flashing neon sign I can't ignore.

We're good together in more than one way. Our connection goes beyond sex, and I can't continue to lie to myself about it. Like it or not, Angela means something to me.

She's good for me.

And that's some scary shit.

The click of heels catches my attention and I turn to find her lingering in the doorway. A black skirt clings to her hips. Sky high heels make her legs look so fucking delicious, I want to skip the foreplay and get straight to the main event. To turn her around, bend her over, and spread her legs wide. I want her begging for more as my hips crash against her ass and I tighten my grip on her hair.

Angela leans against the wall, a lazy finger tracing her bottom lip. Her breasts spill out of a white button down, so tight the buttons strain to keep it together. Her hair is pulled up off her neck and her lips...

...those fucking lips...

...are painted a vibrant red.

"Fuck, Angel."

Her eyes travel the length of my body, gleaming with want. With heat. With...Jesus I don't even know anymore.

She pushes off the wall, hips swaying as she advances. "Now what?" Her hands are on my chest. Her gaze, wide and trusting, locked on mine.

"Kneel."

That's all I have. One word. One fucking word.

And damn if she doesn't comply.

With a sultry smile, she lowers herself to the ground in front of me, her delicate fingers working my belt, the light clink of the metal filling the quiet space. Then the button. The zipper.

Her hands reaching for my cock.

Stroking. A brush of her thumb over the tip and I shudder with desire.

Those red lips, open for me, wrapping around my

dick and fuck...I watch, one hand in her hair, guiding her. Faster. Deeper. I hit the back of her throat. Again. *Again.*

She pulls back, panting, those blue eyes locked on mine. Mouth open. Tongue out. Begging for more.

"Good girl. Good fucking girl." I reach for her hair, my fist in those red locks, and press past her lips again. Desperate. Needy.

This is everything I wanted.

She is everything I wanted.

And I need more than her mouth. I need all of her. I pull back, a string of spittle drooping between us.

My Angel looks worried.

"Did I do something wrong?"

"Not a damn thing." I reach for her, helping her off the floor. "You're driving me fucking crazy."

My lips crash into hers. My hands knead those perfect tits, her shirt an unwelcome barrier. I tear the thing open and dip my head to her breasts, her gasp lighting me on fire as buttons scatter across the floor.

"Shit, Garrett..." My Angel stares up at me.

"I'll buy you a new one."

And then she's tugging at my shirt and me at her skirt, stripping each other bare in the middle of this room that feels so much like home. She moves to kick off her heels and I pull back, shaking my head, licking my lips, panting like a fucking dog.

"Leave them."

Her eyes light up with a crooked smile and she beckons me forward.

And that's the last coherent thought I have for a while.

CHAPTER THIRTY-FIVE

Angela

"Are you sure this isn't going to come off wrong?" Garrett meets my eyes in the mirror and swipes a hand through his hair. "As far as your family knows, we're business partners."

Stretched out in my bed, I roll onto my stomach, propping myself on my elbows and crossing my ankles. "Business partners who do nasty things to each other in the bedroom."

After what we did, it's amazing I can move at all. I'm loose. Boneless. Utterly relaxed and completely at ease with this man in my room. All the worries that have been plaguing me have faded to whispers. I'm simply happy in the moment.

I focus on that.

Garrett laughs. "And you think *that's* a reason for them to invite me into their home?"

"Just because it happens doesn't mean they have to know about it." I shift into a sitting position and swing my legs to the floor. "Look. I like being with you and want to soak in as much Garrett time as I can before you go home. If that means you have to endure meeting my giant family, then so be it."

And the clock is ticking down to his departure so quickly, my heart can't help but fret. Here I am with my newfound feelings, trying to pretend I can pull off casual while swooning over every move he makes. Every breath. Every touch. Every word.

He calls me his angel and I want that to be true. I want to be his.

Garrett's face tightens into the unreadable mask that drives me crazy. I couldn't guess what he's thinking if my life depended on it. "If your dad finds out what's going on, it could jeopardize everything."

And just like that, I lose focus on the moment.

When Garrett says everything, does he mean what's going on between us? Or is he talking about the business deal? I want to believe it's the former, but logic says the latter must be involved at least a little.

The pleasantness sours. Sweet satisfaction turns bitter.

I don't want this, us, to be about business, but I'd be

an idiot not to recognize it is. At least on some level. We should talk about it, but now is not the time.

I love having him here and never want him to leave and he can't know that. He just can't.

Not yet. Maybe not ever.

Especially because he *will* leave. Soon.

I stand and cross the room, wrapping my arms around him and resting my cheek against his back. "My dad won't know anything's going on. I promise. Everyone's gonna love you and you'll see exactly what I mean when I say my family is insane. It's a win-win."

Garrett grunts, grasping my hands, his thumb caressing my wrist. "If it's such a win-win, why do I feel like I'm losing? I think you dropped this family event in my lap on purpose."

"I did no such thing."

"Do you really expect me to just take your word for it?" He spins in my arms, brushing my hair out of my face. "That's not how this works."

"That might not be how it *used* to work. But with me? Yes, you take my word." I slap him on the ass. "Grumpy grump."

He captures my wrist and pulls me close. "That's Mr. Grumpy Grump to you. And if anyone is smacking an ass, it's me." Heat builds in his eyes as he leans in for a kiss. "What is it about you?" he murmurs. "Have you cast some sort of spell on me?"

It's no spell. It's serendipity. The more we're together, the more I know it's true. Fate brought Mom and Dad together in the strangest of ways, but it was right for them from the start—even if they didn't see it until it was almost too late. I'm starting to think the same is true for Garrett and me. He...us...this is right. I see through his grumpy exterior to the amazing man underneath.

If only he didn't have to leave.

Running my hands through his hair, I press my forehead to his. "The only spell I'm aware of is the one you're working right now."

With that, I tip my head back and let Garrett do what he does best, play my body like it was made for him.

We're the last to arrive at my parents' house, which means we park at the end of a long line of cars, spilling out of the driveway and onto the street.

Garrett's eyes go wide. "How many people did you say were gonna be here tonight?"

"If everyone shows up, there's what? Twenty-seven, twenty-eight of us Huttons? That's counting

Uncle Joe, Aunt Kennedy, and their kids, who aren't blood related but that doesn't matter. Plus, there might be wives, husbands, girlfriends, and boyfriends. It'll be crowded."

"Twenty-seven or twenty—" He scrubs a hand over his face. "That's a lot of people."

"A lot of people who are plain amazing." I lead him up the lantern-lined walk, towards the door. "We'll hang out with Nathan and Micah if that makes you more comfortable."

Garrett rubs his jaw, eyeing the house like it might bite. "You and I weren't exactly on friendly terms the day I met those two. Hanging out with them might make me less comfortable."

It's a glorious evening, with a breeze that flutters my sundress around my thighs and my parents' house looks stately and welcoming, with the splattering of palms in front and the ocean stretching out forever behind. The first floor is an enclosed outdoor living area with a bar, a pool, hot tub, and boat dock. The home's two bedrooms, kitchen, and living area were built on the second floor to minimize damage from flooding.

"Did you grow up here?"

I shake my head. "We had a much smaller place when I was a kid. They bought this after I went to college. Our old home was, I don't know, comfortable?

Is that the word? It's not quite right, but it'll do. Anyway, I was sad at first, when they bought this one because it's more like a piece of art than a home and I couldn't imagine it would ever feel as welcoming as the one I grew up in. But, go figure, Mom and Dad managed to—"

Garrett puts a hand on my arm. "Breathe, my Angel. There's no need to be nervous."

"Who me?" I squeak. "I'm cool as a cucumber."

"You ramble when you're nervous."

I blink, surprised by how intimate his statement feels…and by how much I like it. "I just…got excited about the house."

Garrett drops his hand with an understanding smile. "It's an amazing house."

"It is. And now, thanks to you and all the wonderful things we can do with the Bliss location together, they'll get to keep it." The words were meant as a joke, but they strike a sour note. I hate that Garrett and I came together because of business. It cheapens everything we've done.

The feeling dissipates as we step inside, walking in on a heated conversation between Nathan and his girlfriend.

"Hey! There you are." My cousin straightens and plasters on a smile when he sees us. "We were starting to think Miss Always Early was gonna pull a no show."

"Are you kidding? And miss a chance to see the whole family in one place?" I give Nathan a quick hug. "This is Garrett Cooper. You've met before—"

"Oh, I remember. I'm surprised you're giving her the time of day after the talking to she gave you at the bar." Nathan extends his hand. "Nice to meet ya, man. This is Blossom, my girlfriend. Her girls Cathlynn and Carabell are out by the pool."

Freaking Cathlynn, and Carabell. The names conjure images of toddlers forced into beauty pageants before they can walk—which is exactly what happened with these two. And, you know, that's fine...kind of. Though to listen to Blossom talk, the pageant thing has more to do with her ego than anything the girls get out of the experience.

"Good to see you again," I say to Blossom while Garrett shakes her hand. She murmurs a response and rolls her eyes while I turn to my cousin. "Thank you so much for feeding the kittens while I was gone."

"Are you kidding me? It was the best part of the day." Nathan turns to Garrett. "You hear about this? Feeding kittens just because they showed up on her doorstep. She really is the angel of the family."

Blossom steps between the men before Garret can respond. "We were in the middle of a discussion more important than some stupid feral cats," she says, then drags Nathan away, chewing his ear off the entire time.

Garrett huffs his disapproval. "She seems pleasant."

"That's not the word I'd choose, but sure."

"Angel!" Micah appears out of nowhere and wraps me in a giant hug before turning to Garrett. "And friend?" He gives me a crooked smile, jerking a thumb Garrett's way. "You stole his phone, right?"

"I didn't steal—"

"Whatever." He dismisses my explanation with a chuckle. "That's the story I'm telling."

"No one's gonna believe that." I roll my eyes. "I'm the angel of the family, remember?"

"You and I both know Nathan's the only one who believes that. Besides, I can be very convincing, especially if this guy backs me up." Micah offers Garrett his hand. "Whadaya say? Wanna tell everyone she stole your phone, then bitched you out when you showed up to get it back? I guarantee that'll get you points with the Hutton clan. Everyone knows what it's like to go head-to-head with our Angel here."

Before Garrett can respond, Micah whisks him away, leading him into the fray.

Garrett glances over his shoulder, eyes wide as he mouths, "Help."

I flare my hands because this was out of my control the moment he didn't correct Micah about the phone mix up. We talk to Uncle Eli and Aunt Hope before moving on to the bar where I introduce Garrett to Uncle Caleb, Aunt Maisie, and their three girls. We wave at Uncle Joe and Uncle Collin, deep in conversation with Aunt Kennedy and Aunt Harlow.

Garrett frowns, cocking his head as he studies the group. "Is that—?"

"Collin West? Award-winning musician who happens to be my uncle?" Micah says with a twinkle in his eyes. "That'd be him. Nathan's dad. And that man right there is the reason Nate is the way he is. Just all-around good energy. You need a thing? If Nathan can't, Collin will." Micah turns to me, his brown eyes dancing the way they do when he has gossip to spread. "Did you see him, by the way? Nate? He's having drama with the single mama. Again."

I clamp my jaw shut to keep from spewing a few choice words. "She was chewing his ear off when we came in."

"Collin West," Garrett murmurs, almost in awe. "My mom loved him when I was a kid."

"I don't know what Nathan sees in that woman," Micah continues, giving Garrett a knowing grin. "He's too young to tie himself down with kids, especially when the kids are so...I don't know. Cathlynn and Carabell. Ugh. The whole thing leaves a bad taste in my mouth."

"Like you're so wise in the relationship department." I turn to Garrett, ready to explain that my cousin shares his opinion about dating, but Micha butts in.

"I am very wise in the relationship department. I've been in love, unlike others who shall remain nameless around here." He jabs a finger my way as if his point wasn't obvious already. "Ivy Cole. High school sweetheart. Man. I'll never find someone like her again. She was...she was something." Micah's face transforms into what we've dubbed his Ivy face. This weird combination of serene and wistful. They were inseparable in high school, until out of the blue, she broke it off. Moved away. And Micah? He's never been the same about women since.

"You haven't dated anyone since high school?" Garrett doesn't sound like he believes the story for one second.

"I mean, sure. I've been with women." Micah rubs a hand over his mouth. "I'm only human. But nothing, no one, will live up to Ivy Cole. She was it for me." He stares into the distance, his Ivy face taking over before he visibly shakes thoughts of her away.

I roll my eyes, laughing as I fold my arms over my chest. "You say that like you're this great romantic, but you're not the type to stay celibate your whole life—"

"Now hold on a second. I didn't say anything about staying celibate." Micah laughs, elbowing Garrett in the ribs. "She doesn't know jack shit about men. It's all about the commitment and the connection for her."

"Micah!"

"I'm just saying. She dragged you to a family event and you're not even dating. If that doesn't scream commitment crazy, I don't know what does." The twinkle in my cousin's eyes says he thinks he's hilarious, but I want to Kung Fu chop him in the balls. He catches my gaze, notices my murderous intent, and quickly switches tracks. "I'm kidding, man. Angel is great. A total slut. No commitment anywhere. You're gonna love her."

"I swear to God, Micah Hutton, I'm going to kill you. No. I'm going to call Ivy Cole and tell her you're still single because you only have eyes for her."

"Do it. I dare you. Oh wait, what's that I hear? I think there's a more interesting conversation happening over there. Toodlepip, people." With a laugh, he wanders off towards the pool where Cathlynn and Carabelle are screeching at each other over who gets to use the diving board first.

"So that's Micah," I say to Garrett, widening my eyes as I await his judgment. "He thinks he's very hilarious."

"I can see that." Garrett shakes his head, watching Nathan deescalate the disagreement between Blossom's girls. He's faraway again. That giant wall of something lowered between us while Micah was talking. It sets my heart pounding.

"He was joking about that commitment thing. And the slut thing. I didn't drag you here to trap you into anything." Jesus. I can't believe those are words actually coming out of my mouth. What kind of insane situation have I gotten myself into?

"I know, Angel. That's not the way you work."

And yet, Garrett's smile seems tight, and his eyes seem off. For the love of everything holy, I am so tired of worrying about where I stand with him.

Maybe I really will Kung Fu chop Micah in the balls.

CHAPTER THIRTY-SIX

GARRETT

As Micah strolls away, Lucas Hutton's gaze locks with mine. Angela's father. An ex-Marine who clearly adores his only daughter and doesn't take shit from anyone. The look that crosses his face isn't the easygoing, instantly-accepting-of-me bullshit Angela tried to feed me earlier. This is a man who understands business, a father who would go to war for his daughter, his family and the hotel they built from the ground up, and he doesn't trust my presence here. He watches us with an intensity I respect before catching the attention of an older woman who has to be my Angel's mother.

They have the same smile.

The same hair.

The same breath-of-fresh-air energy.

"Just a heads up." I create a professional amount of space between Angela and me. "Your parents are heading this way."

She glances over her shoulder. Her wide smile says she senses no danger whatsoever. She's just...happy.

"Oh, good." Angela clasps her hands under her chin. "I've been wanting you to meet my mom. You're gonna love her. She's strong, and sweet, and always knows the right thing to say, and before you know it, she's taking care of you in exactly the way you didn't know you needed."

"Mr. Cooper." Lucas extends a hand as he arrives. "I didn't expect to see you here tonight."

I translate his polite tone and watchful eyes as a warning. I don't belong here. He knows it. I know it.

"Garrett and I spent an extra day in Bliss, looking over the new site," Angela says, and her dad definitely notices her use of my first name. The way her eyes light up when she glances my way. The way she leans closer, obliterating that professional amount of space I so carefully created.

"We flew in today and came straight here to talk about getting those contracts signed. This deal is good. I feel it." She puts a hand on my arm while her father frowns. "Oh. Right. Silly me. Mom, I'd like you to meet Garrett Cooper. Garrett, this my mother, Catherine Hutton. I've been excited for you two to meet because you guys are just gonna love each other."

The smile I force has to look suspicious. I know I wouldn't trust me. Between Angela practically broadcasting that we slept together and Branson's clock ticking over the entire evening, my nerves are cranked. The first rule of business negotiations? Never trust the nervous guy. And tonight, I'm the nervous guy.

Fuck my life.

"Please, call me Cat." Angela's mother takes my hand and for some weird reason, it feels like she's welcoming me home. She's the polar opposite of her husband, warm instead of intense. Open rather than prickly. And yet, the love they share might as well be tattooed on their foreheads. "It's a pleasure to meet you, Mr. Cooper."

"If you're Cat, I'm Garrett," I respond. "And the pleasure is mine."

"Garrett it is." Cat turns to her husband, and her grin falters when she sees the way he's looking at me.

"You two have a lovely home. I'm...well I'm honored to be here." I force yet another smile.

Damn it, I feel so fucking awkward.

I want to impress the Huttons, which leaves me feeling sleazy. I stopped worrying what anyone thought about me the day I realized people only cared about themselves. This world runs on greed and narcissism and I'm tired of participating.

But the Huttons are good. I can feel it radiating out of everyone—

The shriek of those horrible little girls fighting over the last cupcake interrupts my thoughts. Their mother dashes over to yell at *Nathan*—because somehow, it's his fault her offspring don't know how to share.

Okay...goodness radiates out of *almost* everyone here.

Regardless. I like the Huttons. And I want them to like me. Yes, part of it is because the deal will be more successful if we all get along, but there's more. I want them to like me because I like their daughter. I don't just want to fuck her; I want to be with her.

My Angel isn't a distraction, she's the answer to questions I didn't know I was asking.

She *elevates* me. I am *more* with her. I am *better* with her.

And that leaves me standing here, salivating over her parents' acceptance.

I'm a grown ass man. I should barely care what *my* parents think, let alone someone else's.

But I do care. Jesus. When did that happen?

As if that wasn't confusing enough, I'm supposed to get them to sign a contract within the next few days that, while I'll do my best to make fair, also needs to land a lot of money into Vision Enterprise's pockets over the next several years. How could anyone believe I *didn't* sleep with Angela to entice her into the deal?

I feel slimy. Which isn't the way I operate.

And everyone's just standing here, watching me frown.

Instead of smiling, laughing, and turning on the charm, I let out a long sigh and admit at least one truth. "Forgive me if I seem tense. My boss gave me forty-eight hours to close this deal or he's sending another man down. And that guy? He doesn't have your best interest at heart. I promise you."

"And you do?" Lucas lifts a brow. "Have our best interest at heart?"

I glance at Angela, then back to her father. "I do."

"He does." She beams at Lucas. "I trust him."

The words send a spike into my chest. How did we get here? Me, feeling like this, and her, saying things like that. I'm not supposed to want to be with someone, especially when I met that someone through business. Nothing but trouble waits at the end of this road. I've been there once and promised myself never again.

I realize I'm just glaring at Angela as these thoughts batter my brain. With a laugh, I shake my head to reorient myself. "Again, I apologize. I'm not myself tonight. All the travel and..." I sigh, refreshing my smile like the good businessman I am. "I just need a good night's sleep."

Lucas glances over my shoulder at someone behind me, then meets my eyes and it feels like he can see right through me. He probably can.

"I bet you'll feel even better once things are settled between us," he says. "Signatures. Dates. Agreements."

"That wouldn't hurt."

Lucas nods, his gaze slipping over my shoulder again as he gestures someone over. "You remember my brother Wyatt," Lucas says to me. "And this is his wife, Kara."

Hands are shaken. Introductions made. We chat briefly before Wyatt claps a hand on my shoulder.

"I'm hearing good things, Cooper."

Angela beams. "That's because Garrett and I make a good team. With us working together, the future of the Hutton Hotel is set in stone."

The brothers exchange a look before Wyatt shoves his hands in his pocket. "I like to hear that."

"Let's meet tomorrow," Lucas says with a nod. "First thing in the morning. Angela said our lawyers approved the contracts. We'll go over everything one more time. Sign some papers. Get this show on the road."

"Well now hold on a minute." Cat looks at her

husband like he's lost his mind. "You just heard the man say he's worn down."

And I'll be less worn down the second I tell Branson everything's taken care of here.

"I'm fine, Mrs.—"

"Cat." She puts a hand on my arm. "You call me Cat. And 'fine' is a great place to start, but you'll be even better after experiencing The Hut at its finest. He has a room with us?" she asks Angela, who nods.

"I put him in one of the bungalows with private beach access."

"Good. Good. Now, set him up with our deluxe package. Massages. Meals. Meditation. Drinks by the pool. You spend a day letting us take care of you," Cat says to me before turning to her husband. "*Then* you guys can meet to sign those contracts and afterwards? We'll have dinner to celebrate. We'll dress up and have the kitchen prepare something special. Make a whole thing out of it."

All I hear is another delay I don't need. A delay that'll bring Branson one step closer to sending Jordan down. A delay that'll keep me out of my Angel's bed all day.

I hold up my hands. "That's completely unnecessary. You don't have to make a big deal out of me being here."

"You let me decide what is and isn't necessary. If

we don't stop to celebrate every now and then, life grows tiresome." Cat arches a brow, looking both firm and sweet at the same time. She reminds me of my mom. Of my mother.

"I wouldn't argue with her if I were you." Lucas takes her hand and kisses each finger. "My wife comes across as gentle, but she's been married to me for decades now. She's made of stern stuff, this one."

"And we all know how hard it is to live with you, you glowery, Robocop, son of a bitch." Wyatt guffaws, his eyes twinkling with the same look Charlie gives me when she lands a zinger. "Cat's the real head of the family," he finishes with a wink.

"We all know that's not true," she begins, but no one seems to agree with her.

Lucas cups her face, his thumb grazing her cheekbone. "You came into my life and set all this in motion. This wouldn't exist if it wasn't for a journal tucked into a booth at a coffee shop." He indicates the family with a sweep of his arm. "We'll have to tell you the story at dinner tomorrow," he says to me.

"I'd like that." His love for his wife reminds me of the love my dad has for Mom, and before that, for my mother. I never thought love like that was in the cards for me, but now, standing next to my Angel and her family, I wonder if I was wrong.

My jaw clamps shut.

Of course I wasn't wrong. Love is fickle, especially when business is involved.

"Now," Cat says to her daughter, "you take this man back to the hotel so he can get some shut eye. Stop in the office and set him up with the deluxe package, throw in any extras you see fit, and we'll all see each other again tomorrow."

Angela hugs her family goodbye and I shake hands with too many people to remember, then we're finally alone. Silence wraps around us as we walk to her car. Me lost in thoughts about her. About this. About what fucking happens next.

That was a shitshow in there. I fumbled and bumbled like an intern eager to prove himself. Lucas and Wyatt clearly don't trust my relationship with Angela. And Cat? She may have the best of intentions, but I don't have time for massages. For drinks by the pool. And meditation? That's not my deal. Mom tried to build it into me when I was a kid and if she couldn't get it to stick, no one will.

Angela glances at me, looking so hopeful, so beautiful, my heart hurts. "I think that went well."

"Your dad knows there's something going on between us," I respond with a laugh.

"What?" She scoffs. "No way. We played that off to perfection."

I turn to her, certain she's joking, but she's not. My

Angel is so bad at being dishonest, she genuinely thinks her family didn't notice the way she looked at me. The way she touched me. The way she hung on my every word. She may have the smarts for business, but I see now how the schmoes before me took advantage. She's naïve. Trusting. Genuine.

She's low hanging fruit for someone like Jordan.

She needs someone to stand between her and the bad guys, the prince she swears she doesn't want.

The prince I definitely am not.

"Is something wrong?" she asks.

"I'm just tired," I say.

The silence that follows feels too heavy. Too filled with meaning. So I lean down to whisper, "and it's taking everything I have not to touch you right now."

Angela beams and practically skips to her car. I hold her hand during the drive to the hotel, kissing it lightly as we pull into the parking lot. Stars shine over the water, the moon hanging low and full. It's been a while since I stopped to appreciate the sky. I should probably do that more.

"Promise me something," I say as I grab my suitcase out of the trunk.

"Anything."

"Be careful on the drive home. Please. And text me when you get there. So I know you're safe." The request feels like an admission. *I care about what happens to you. You matter to me.*

Did she take it that way?

A gentle smile lifts full lips. "I'll be careful, and safe, and I'll text you when I leave and then again when I get home."

"Thank you, Angel."

And in that moment, I'm filled with gratitude for her smile, her laughter, her naivete, her ridiculous can-do attitude.

"Don't thank me yet. Wait until you've experienced our deluxe package. I'm hitting you with everything we've got, Garrett Cooper." Walking backwards, she blows air off a pair of finger guns, her eyes twinkling with humor. "Prepare yourself. You're not going to know what hit you."

"I think that's already true," I murmur as Angela skips up the steps to the main entrance. I watch a moment before following.

I'll grab my key. Fall into bed. And tomorrow, business will be taken care of.

After that? I can worry about whatever the fuck is happening between us.

CHAPTER THIRTY-SEVEN

Angela

The coffee won't come out of the machine fast enough. Yawning, I lean on the counter, put my head in my hands, and beg the hiss and gurgle of boiling water to come to an end. To say I slept poorly would be overselling the situation. I'm not sure I slept at all. To make matters worse, the sky offshore is dark and dangerous. The mood is ominous. Sunshine over my head, but doom heading my way.

A check of my weather app confirms my suspicions. While I was preoccupied with Garrett, a tropical storm spun up in the Atlantic and set the Keys in her sights. The prognosis looks scary but survivable, though lord knows the weather can change on a dime.

The good news is Garrett might be trapped on this

island with me a few days longer. The storm might give me some extra time with him, but then what? I groan at the thought, so like the ones that kept me awake last night.

What now, Angela?

What now?

We sign on the dotted line tonight. We have dinner with my family and then...what?

Surely, Garrett has a life to get back to, but what about me? About us? Is this the end?

I scoff. The end of what, exactly?

The relationship he was super clear he didn't want?

A part of me dreads what's coming. The meeting. The dinner. Garrett leaving.

I'm not ready to give him up.

A better person would have talked to him about it last night. Explained what I was thinking. How I've been feeling. But no. Not me. I ran away faster than you can say, "So where do we go from here?"

Ugh!

Who am I right now? Angela Hutton doesn't run away from difficulty. She puts her head down and does what needs done.

The end.

After pouring myself a cup of coffee, I pace into the living room, which instantly brings Garrett to mind. His hand on my head as I took him deep into my mouth. The silky warmth of his dick against my tongue. The way it felt when he pulled me to my feet, bent me over the couch and—

Nope. The living room is not the place to be.

I about face and head to the deck. I'll watch the storm stir the ocean, the palms lash in the wind. I'll count flashes of lightning and wonder how long until I hear thunder.

Being with Garrett is doing something to me. I'm... weaker. More vulnerable. I'm thinking with my hormones instead of my head and if I'm right...if I actually have feelings for him, then I need to talk to him about it. He deserves to know what's going on and I deserve a chance to speak my truth and see what happens.

I fight an urge to call Nick. Not only does the time zone thing always mess me up—I have no idea if he's at work or fast asleep right now—but I don't want to admit to him how awful I'm being. He's so good. So genuine. So...

...he's one of the best people I know and if I tell him this story, he'll be disappointed in me. He'll tell me to stop being an idiot, put all things Garrett Cooper out of my mind, and get my head on straight. He'll tell me to forget the craziness between us and focus on the job at hand.

And he'd be right.

I just don't think I can do it.

After talking myself out of a rare bad mood, I grab the kitten food and head outside. Fluff hops onto the porch while Orange dashes away, only to think better of it and slink back. "The weather's going to be bad for the next couple days," I say as kibble clatters into bowls.

Surely, they have a place to go. They're basically wild animals, and therefore better equipped to handle this kind of stuff than I'll ever be.

But the thought of them out in the storm...wet, cold, scared...it breaks me. I'm going to have to figure something out.

Maybe Garrett knows—

His name brings a boatload of stress...excitement...anticipation...

It blends together and washes through my system. I growl in frustration, scaring the shit out of Orange, who disappears into the bushes probably never to be seen again. Fluff jumps off the porch, then right back up again, cocking his head as if to say, "Are you *trying* to give me a heart attack?"

"Sorry," I say. "I'm driving myself a little crazy here."

The wind picks up, blasting my hair into my face as Fluff makes his way to the food bowl. I have to figure out some kind of shelter for them.

This storm looks like it's going to be a doozy.

By the time I've showered, the weather forecast has worsened. A line of dark clouds marches in from the ocean. The palms whip back and forth while the waves crash and roll, attacking and retreating again and again, abusing the beach with their rage.

I'm so nervous I can't sit still, and the weather is the least of my concerns.

With tonight's meeting at The Hut being the only thing on my agenda, I'll worry myself into oblivion if I don't find a distraction. So, I do the only rational thing in this situation. I drive to the pet store, grab a litter box, a scratching post, and more toys than any animal needs, then head home. The kittens are on the porch when I pull to a stop and don't scurry away as quickly as they normally do. Maybe they know I'm a place of safety. That I mean them no harm. Maybe they want me as much as I want them. Maybe I wasn't stupid to cultivate this relationship.

Or maybe I'm losing my mind and spinning the story to make myself feel better about the mistakes I've made with Garrett.

After unloading the bags of cat gear, I stand with my hands on my hips and stare at the door. What now?

...What now, Angela? What now...?

It's not like I can so much as touch them...

After some internet searches, I choose the easiest option and cross my fingers. Propping the door open, I leave a trail of treats from their favorite bush right through the house and into the guest bathroom. Then, with nothing better to do, I camp out in my living room and wait.

But not for long.

Fluff appears first, always the brave one, with Orange skittering along behind, too afraid to be without his brother. They follow the line of treats right into the guest bathroom, where I have two bowls of food and a litter box waiting. While they chow down, I quietly close the door, then stare in shock.

I laugh lightly, happiness warming my heart as a roll of thunder sounds outside. "I think I just adopted a pair of feral kittens."

A teeny tiny mew sounds in agreement.

The reading I've done suggests getting them used to the house one room at a time. I'll let them acclimate to this one while I choose an outfit for the meeting, then check on them before I leave.

I'll wear the red heels tonight.

CHAPTER THIRTY-EIGHT

G̲arrett

Catherine Hutton might be the most business savvy human being on the planet. *Maybe* she suggested I spend a day relaxing at her hotel out of the goodness of her heart, but she knew my experience would affect my view of the place. After a day of enjoying locally sourced, nutritionally balanced meals, followed by a Reiki massage on the beach watching a storm gather over the water, I'm more determined than ever to ensure their success.

I'm feeling good. Easy. Relaxed. More like myself than I have since I found Elizabeth with—

I rake a hand through my hair, staring down at the ridiculous rubber ducky trunks I bought with Angela.

A laugh chases away the terrible memories. Fucking rubber duckies.

Charlie would fall over if she saw me like this.

She'd fall over just knowing I allowed myself to be *seen* like this.

But here? For some reason it doesn't matter.

Everyone at the hotel seems nice. Genuine. Little carbon copies of my Angel. The guests. The employees. No one cares how much money I have or how big a tip I might give them. They seem sincerely interested in my wellbeing. Am I enjoying the food? The massage? The fresh air? They laugh with me about my rubber ducky trunks instead of judging me because they're cheap and tacky. For the first time in a long time, I have hope for the world at large.

Just a sliver.

A glimmer.

But it's there.

That means something. Shit, five hours at the Hutton Hotel has done more for me than how many years of therapy? Though maybe, Angela started the process that led to me feeling like the real Garrett Cooper and not the cold and uncaring jerk who's been occupying my body.

She's good for me. I'm better with her. And I can't believe I haven't so much as spoken to her today, let alone seen her, touched her.

"Excuse me." I hold up a hand to catch the attention of a passing employee. "What time is it? I left my phone in my room."

"It's three o'clock, sir." The man clasps his hands behind his back as a gust of wind sends wispy hair dancing. "Is there anything I can bring you? Refresh your drink, perhaps?"

"I'm good. Thanks."

Two hours. Just two measly hours until I'm supposed to meet the Huttons. We'll do our thing, eat some dinner, and then I'll have Angela to myself. I'll have to leave the Keys soon, and it'll suck, but we're only a flight away from seeing each other again. When your bank accounts look like mine, who the fuck cares?

I shake my head.

I care. I don't want to be states away from Angela. I don't want to hop a plane in order to see her. I want her in my bed. My arms. All the time.

Look at that. I've lost my Zen.

A low roll of thunder confirms what I already know. It's time to get inside before the storm breaks.

I'm up and moving before I know where I'm going, my flip flops in one hand while my feet slip and slide through the beach. I brush off the sand as I climb onto the back patio of the hotel, then pull on my sandals and step inside.

A familiar laugh sets my teeth on edge. My fists

clench. Lightning ignites the sky the way adrenaline lights up my body. A jagged flash. A surge of energy.

I round the corner and there he is.

Jordan fucking Clement. Standing too close to Angela. His hand on her arm. Her smile is sweet while his is criminal and I can't stand the way he looks at her. She's wearing the red heels, the lipstick. I know they're for me, but he's the one enjoying them. Her hair is wild and her eyes light up when she sees me, only to falter when she processes my expression.

"What the hell are you doing here?" I growl at the asshole who won't stop ogling my Angel.

Jordan turns with a smirk, his retort dying on his lips as he scans down my body and back to my face. "What in the world are you wearing?" He snorts a laugh. "This is a side of Garrett Cooper I didn't know existed. That's..." He shakes his head, still laughing, as he turns to Angela like she's in on the joke. "This is priceless, isn't it?"

Jordan's dressed impeccably, as usual. His shirt is crisp, expensive. His pants pressed, the hem sitting at just the right height to show off shoes that cost my dad's monthly income. His blond hair falls into his eyes, and he gives it a shake. Fucker spends a fortune on products and stylists and swears it's his secret weapon with women. *They never see you coming when you've got great hair.*

I used to laugh when he said it.

Angela's gaze flicks from Jordan's to mine. "I like his shorts. The duckies are fun."

Her voice is sweet. Placating. Like she can get us back on track with little more than a smile and polite words.

If only she knew.

"Why are you here, Jordan?"

"Same reason you are." His gaze flickers to Angela's breasts and back again.

It's like he knows. It's like he knows and he's doing it on purpose and—

I step between them. "Branson gave me forty-eight hours and last I checked there's twenty-four to go."

Jordan grimaces. "Aww. See. That's where you're wrong. After you two had your little chat, he and I put our heads together, looked at the contract drafts and you know—" he turns to Angela, his grin sliding into the predatory range "—things seem a little...*off*."

"Off." My jaw crunches the word. Thunder rolls.

"Yeah. Off." His eyes meet mine. A challenge. "He sent me here to check things out. Of course, I assured him Garrett Cooper would have everything under control, but—" a deep sigh and light shrug "—he insisted."

I arch a suspicious brow as Jordan continues.

"I didn't think it was possible, but Branson was

right. What do I find but you lounging at the pool, in the middle of a tropical storm, in cheap swim trunks." His gaze drops to the floor, and he rubs a hand across the back of his neck. "Look, I know you've been off your game since Elizabeth—"

"Don't."

Jordan's not allowed to look like he misses her. He's not allowed to pretend he cares. He hasn't earned the right to look at me like he's sorry.

He lifts his gaze, his dark eyes cool. Emotionless. "You've been off your game since Elizabeth passed," he finishes without a hint of remorse. "And I'm broken hearted about it too—"

"Not another fucking syllable about her comes out of your mouth." I clench my fists, my jaw, my entire body. "Ever." I growl the word. A threat.

No.

A promise.

Angela steps forward, putting herself between us with a nervous smile. "Why don't we move this conversation into the office?" She puts one hand on my arm and another on his. "Where things are more private."

Jordan's gaze starts at her face and caresses her body before a casual smile says he's being perfectly reasonable.

That's it.

That's fucking it. All the anger I've been burying

and mantra-ing and letting eat me up boils out of my stomach and into my fists. I need to hit the guy.

He deserves to be hit.

He was supposed to be my best fucking friend and now he's just an evil asshole and if he looks at Angela like a piece of meat one more time…

"I can't be here." I pace the lobby, staring down a couple after they gave up pretending not to eavesdrop. I stalk back to Angela and stab an angry finger at Jordan's chest. "Not with him. Not without making a scene."

"Garrett." He says my name like he's sorry for me. "Don't you think it's time we moved past this?" His gaze darts to Angela and I'm in his face. Nose to fucking nose. His breath huffs out. His eyes dilate. He's had this coming, and he knows it.

He knows it.

"Garrett!" Angela puts her hand on my arm, and I shake it off.

She gasps. Steps back.

I suck my teeth and shake my head.

"I gotta go…I can't…"

Her heels click after me as I head for the exit. I step outside. Humidity blasts me in the face. The sky is black and boiling. I pause, growling as Angela catches up to me.

"Garrett. Talk to me. Please. What's going on?"

I can't. I'm seconds away from losing my mind and she can't see me like that. I need to get out of here. Now. Ten minutes ago. Two weeks ago.

"I don't have a car," I growl. "And I'm wearing these stupid trunks and flipflops."

Her eyes hit mine and I brace for the barrage of questions I don't want to answer. Instead, she nods. "Get some clothes. I'll drive you to my house."

CHAPTER THIRTY-NINE

Garrett

I've never felt more ridiculous in my life. To be so furious, with rage churning my gut...while flip flops smack my feet and too-small rubber ducky swim trunks cup my junk. My fists are hammers, desperate for a nail, for anything to channel my fury into, but there is none. Not here. Not now.

I need to leave.

To move.

To be anywhere but here.

My anger is one hundred percent in proportion to the situation, and if Jordan so much as comes near me, I won't be able to hold it in any longer.

I'll ruin the way Angela sees me.

I used to think Jordan had a shred of human

decency hiding under all that greed but now I know the truth. He's a villain. An asshole. He's everything the world doesn't need.

Who acts like that? After everything we've been through and everything he's done, he has the balls to look me in the eyes, man to man, and act like I'm the one in the wrong.

I push through the door into my room in time to see a notification light up my phone. I swipe it off the bedside table. Five texts and two missed calls, all from Branson. I scan them and bark laughter.

The last message? Branson telling me he was right to send Jordan down, seeing as I spent my day sitting by the pool instead of answering calls and working the deal. Is Jordan feeding him minute by minute updates? Fucker talked our boss out of trusting me and weaseled his way down here. But why? Hasn't he fucked with my head enough?

I toss the phone onto my bed. Pace to the bathroom and back to the door. What now? What fucking now?

Thunder rumbles. Closer now. The storm will be here any minute.

"I should have punched the guy. I should have punched him years ago and I should have punched him again today." I strip out of my trunks and yank on some clothes—something better suited to going to war—then grab my phone, pull up Branson's info, and stab the call button.

"What the hell?" I grit out when he answers.

"I could ask you the same thing."

"No. You can't. You gave me forty-eight hours. It's been twenty-four. I have a meeting in two hours with the family and signatures *will* hit the line."

"Jordan will take that meeting."

I pause in front of the full-length mirror and glare at my reflection. "Like hell he will."

"You'd do well to remember who you're talking to."

"Branson. You have to listen—"

"No, you. *You* listen, Garrett. I've done nothing but accommodate you since your girlfriend died. You wanted to move out of the city? Work remotely? I didn't like it. I wouldn't do it for anyone else. But I did it for you. Your track record is strong enough that I thought, hey. This guy's going through a difficult time and he's great at what he does so I'll bend for him. But it's been years now and you're still living in some shitty small town. Rarely in the office—"

"Being in the office doesn't make me more effective."

"Is this deal closed?"

"Yes." I pinch the bridge of my nose.

"I don't have a signed copy of the contract." Branson speaks as if reprimanding a child.

"It's as good as closed. I just fucking told you we're meeting tonight to finalize."

"You mean Jordan's meeting tonight to finalize."

"No. No way. I brought the deal this far and I'll be the one to bring it home."

Branson scoffs. "This deal should have been over in a couple days. Max. You've been flitting around down there for how long now and all you can say is you're meeting tonight. I've been as patient with you as I'm willing to be. You're done, Cooper. Effective immediately. Anything dealing with Vision Enterprise and the Hutton Hotel belongs to Jordan."

I pound a fist into the wall. "He'll gut the hotel."

"Good! Great!" Branson laughs. "He can turn it into a theme park for all I care. But let me reiterate. Anything dealing with that hotel and Vision Enterprise will go through Jordan. If I hear you're anywhere near that meeting, you're fired. Are we clear?"

I close my eyes and rub my temples. "Crystal."

The line goes dead, and I hurl my phone onto the bed. Fucking money. It all comes down to money. Branson doesn't care about saving the hotel. He never has. He's no better than anyone else, skewing, twisting, manipulating things to increase his earnings. To improve *his* life. Nothing is about what's best for society anymore. About what's best for other people. Everyone's out for themselves. Right now. Short term.

It's a race to the bottom and I want off this fucking ride.

A knock at the door. Cursing, I cross the room and haul it open.

Angela stands there, hair whipping around her face as the wind howls. "Everything okay in here?" she asks, gathering her red locks into her fist. "I waited, but then got worried…"

Her eyes are tight. Her face pinched. She's never seen me like this, and I hate that she's looking at me like a feral animal.

Jordan's hand on her arm…

His eyes on her body…

I turn and pace toward the bed, shaking with rage. "No. Nothing is okay."

Angela steps inside, shutting out the wind as she closes the door. "Wanna talk about it?"

"Nope." I glare at the floor. I don't want her to see me like this and there's no way I can talk about it without letting my emotions fly. If she'd just stayed by the car like I told her to, I'd have gotten myself under control before I came back out. She wouldn't know this version of me.

This angry, snappy asshole who needs an outlet for his fury.

"Okay, well, if you still want to leave, the weather's getting bad, and we should probably—"

"What, Angel?" I bark. "We should probably...what?"

She jumps. Frowns. Lets a long breath out through her nose. "Don't do that, Garrett. Don't push me away because you're mad at someone else."

She's right. Of course she is. I know that. I feel it. But I'm so fucking upset I can only grunt a response. I care about her, and I swore that would never happen again. With anyone. Especially someone connected to work.

"What's going on, Bucko?" My Angel's voice is soft, concerned. It juxtaposes the ridiculous nickname she gave me, and I let out a long, slow sigh.

"They took me off the deal. I dragged my fucking feet, messing around with you and now *he's* down here." I stab a finger at the wall, face screwed up, red, tight. "If I step foot in the meeting *I set up*, I lose my job."

Not that I need the money, but work is all I have. Who am I if I'm not sealing a deal?

"Garrett. Come on." Angela's still soft. Soothing. "It's not that big of a deal for Mr. Clement to finish this up."

I whirl. "Not that big of a deal? *Not that big of a deal?*" My voice rises and I set my jaw to keep from launching a double-barrel shotgun of animosity her way. That assault is aimed at Jordan, and she doesn't deserve to get caught in the crossfire.

She doesn't.

But I'm losing my ability to control it.

My anger *is* proportionate to the situation.

Angela steps closer, holding out her hands. "The deal is still gonna happen, and that's good, right? You're the one who got us this far and I'll make sure your company knows you're the only reason this is happening."

I scoff, shaking my head and chewing my lip. Getting credit doesn't even register on my give-a-fuck radar.

"And," Angela continues, as wind rattles the window, "if this other guy is connected to the hotel instead of you, maybe that's a good thing. You know, for *us*."

Harsh laughter barks up my throat. "You are so sweet and naïve, my Angel. There's nothing good about Jordan being anywhere near here. Near *you*." I turn away, rubbing a hand over my mouth to physically shut myself up. "Those 'issues with the contract' he mentioned? They will not work out in your favor. He will screw you worse than the guys before us." I rattle off all the ways Jordan could ruin her life. Buried clauses that list the hotel as leverage or give too many shares to Vision Enterprise, leaving them in control of her family's future.

"We won't sign until we've gone through everything and the lawyers have had a look."

She sounds so confident, so sure I'm overreacting. I shove my hands in my pockets and press my lips together. I should tell her. I should share the whole fucking story of what happened between Jordan and Elizabeth. As much as I hate talking about it, as much as the very idea of opening that massive wound scares the shit out of me, I should tell her—

"Garrett." Angela puts a hand on my arm. "I care about you. I...I think..." She takes a deep breath, her eyes bouncing across my face. "No. I don't think; I know. I'm developing feelings for you—"

"Now?" The word drops into the conversation like a stone. "You're going to start this conversation *now*. In your mind, *this* is the best time to talk about...about feelings?"

Can't she see the water's rising around me? It's at my fucking throat and it's still pouring in? How am I supposed to have this conversation when I can barely think?

Angela's brows furrow. "If not now, when? After you've gone home?"

"Any other time would be better than now." I stalk away, images of her laughing with Jordan blurring with memories of Elizabeth doing the same. "*Never* would be better than now."

My Angel's face falls. "Okay. Wow. There it is then."

"Shit." I drag a hand down my face. "I didn't mean it like that. I'm just...I'm... Can we get out of here? I have too much energy to stay in one place."

She nods, confusion swimming in those beautiful blues. "Come on, then," she says, opening the door with a sad smile. "Let's get out of here."

Wind slashes at our clothing. Thick drops of rain splatter on the pavement. Lightning streaks and thunder rumbles and the sky is black, black, black.

This is a bad time to be on the road.

We stop in front of her car and she heads for the driver's door, but I catch her wrist. "Let me drive."

"Garrett...I'm perfectly capable..."

"I know. But the weather's bad and I..." Twisted metal. Broken glass. The squeal of tires. "I'd feel better if I was in control."

With a shake of her head, Angela hands over the keys, then crosses in front of the car and lowers herself into the passenger seat. Her jaw is tense. Her face drawn. I'm being an absolute asshole and she's so understanding...

I don't deserve her.

Or rather, she doesn't deserve me.

I scoot back the driver's seat and adjust the mirrors, then let out a long breath as round after round of lightning illuminates the sky.

"I didn't mean anything bad. Back there." My throat tightens, but I force the words out anyway. "When you brought up your feelings…"

"It's fine." Angela chews her lip. Won't look at me. "You're right. It was a bad time to talk about it."

I nod, struggling with more emotion than I can name, then bring the car to life and back out of the spot.

CHAPTER FORTY

Garrett

Wind blasts the car, rocking it back and forth as I hurtle across Overseas Highway. Never in my life have I felt as small as I do speeding down a bridge with miles of ocean stretching out beside me, behind me, in front of me. Rain buffets the windshield. The wipers thunk back and forth, but I can't see shit. Just raindrops blasting through headlights, and the blur of tail lights ahead.

It fits.

"Garrett?" My Angel clears her throat. "You should slow down. These conditions are rough..."

The streaks of lightning are the anger blasting through me. They're my clenched jaw. My knuckles white with rage. I can't believe I let myself hope things would work out. I'd close the deal. Get the girl. And what? Live happily ever after? That's Angela's dream. Not mine. Not anymore.

"Fuck." I slap the steering wheel, then readjust my grip when a blast of wind pushes me over the double yellow line.

"Garrett..." Angela peeks at me from the passenger seat and I purposefully exhale, looking for the calm she deserves.

"I'm fine."

I channel my anger into the gas pedal. Faster. Like I can outrun my past. Outrun my present. Skip to the future where all of this is over, and I never have to see Jordan leering at my Angel again.

My hands flex as lightning flashes and the ocean churns.

Rain pelts the car. A cacophony of percussion drowning out the roar of the engine.

Faster. We go faster.

"Garrett..." Angela presses a hand to the dash, eyes wide. "Slow down. Please..."

Thunder adds its low rumble to the orchestra of chaos and a tight smile twists my lips.

Fucking Jordan.

Fucking Elizabeth.

Fucking Jordan *fucking* Elizabeth...

And there he was, flirting with my Angel.

"Garrett!" Her voice barely registers.

Red.

I see red.

Fuck...! I see...

Tires squeal. Red smears...

....*Taillights!*

Taillights smear into focus. Too close.

"Shit, shit, shit!"

I slam the brakes but it's too late. Too late!

Angela screams.

The wheels lock, skidding on the slick pavement. I swerve. We miss the car in front of us but careen onto the shoulder, grinding into the guardrail.

The car jolts to a stop, jerking me against my seatbelt and there's a sickening thump and soft gasp from the passenger seat.

I rake a shaking hand through my hair.

"Fucking hell," I murmur before every cell in my body focuses on my Angel.

Her hand is on her temple. She pulls it away, shocked by the streak of blood on her palm.

My heart battles the cage of my ribs as another roar of thunder rattles my bones. "No, no, no. Oh, goddammit Angel."

I can't do this again. Not with her. I can't lose another woman I love.

...can't lose another...

…another woman I love…

The thoughts barely register as I struggle to see in the low light. "Oh my God. Oh fuck. How bad is it? Oh, shit, shit shit…"

I'll never forgive myself for hurting her.

I free myself from my seat belt, fumbling, cursing, frantic. Grip her face

There's a cut above her eye. Bleeding. She's bleeding and it's my fault…

Fuck.

Fuck!

"I'm fine, Garrett." Angela cups my cheek and meets my eyes, blinking as blood drips down her temple. "I'm fine. Everything's okay. It's just a little cut."

Her words barely exist under the roar of the rain.

"You're hurt. You're not fine." I need to stop the bleeding. Need to do something. I yank open the glovebox and am rewarded with a pile of napkins. I wad them up and gently press them to her temple.

She winces.

"I'm so sorry. God, I'm so fucking stupid!" I dab away the blood to reveal a gash that isn't as bad as it could have been.

My breathing slows.

…could have been so much worse…

"I'm fine, Garrett. I promise." Her blues meet

mine, guiding me back from panic. "It's okay. Everything's okay."

I flip on the emergency lights and let out a shuddering breath, losing myself to the thunk, thunk, thunk of the wipers. The hard splatter of the rain. The blur of taillights and the slashes of lightning illuminating the world every few seconds. All that matters is right here. Right now.

Where we *didn't* hit the car in front of us and my Angel is okay.

"Hey. You with me?" Angela grips my hand. "You good?"

Her voice comes from far away.

I nod. "I'm good."

"Because you don't look good."

But I'm not the one bleeding, so I look better than her.

"That was...that was so bad." I rake a hand over my face. "I thought...for a second...I thought I was gonna lose you."

"You didn't. I'm right here." Angela leans down to catch my attention, leading me back from the edge. "I'm not going anywhere until you tell me you're done with me."

She's smiling, laughing lightly, warm and inviting, but her words strike a wound that never healed.

"Elizabeth used to say that." I drag myself from the

brink of panic and refocus on the woman beside me. "She was lying."

Sympathy softens Angel's face. She takes my hand, eyes searching mine as if to see inside my soul and understand how I ended up so broken. "I can't imagine how hard it was to lose her like that, but accidents... they happen."

It's time.

It's time she knows the truth.

The thought is so clear, so pure, I speak before I can second-guess.

"I lost Elizabeth before the accident." I lick my lips, as if wetting them will make telling this story easier. "I told you how she died. You should know how she ended up behind the wheel."

I expected to choke on the words, but they whisper into the conversation instead.

"I loved her." I glance at Angela. "I loved her so much; I was thinking about proposing."

Her gaze is gentle. Soft. So willing to take my pain and hold it for me. *With me.*

"She was the daughter of a client. Like you, but not like you at all. The only reason she cared about her father's business was because she'd inherit a lot of money one day." Rain pours down the windshield as I stare through it to my past. "Elizabeth...she could make you feel like you were the only thing that mattered in her world. She had this way about her, you know?"

Angela smiles sadly. "Sounds like the best kind of person."

I thought that, too. At first. Funny, how much a person can hide.

"Jordan...he was my best friend. I didn't...I hadn't seen him for who he is yet. We were working with this client—Elizabeth's dad—together. I trusted him. I trusted her. I thought they were exactly who and what they said they were."

Just like I trust Angela to be exactly who and what she says she is.

I stare hard at the thought, studying it, accepting it. The differences between Elizabeth and my Angel are vast. If I'd been paying attention, I would have seen them from the start.

"And then, you know, I found out she was sleeping with Jordan."

There it is. Out in the open.

Angela's jaw drops. Her eyes glimmer with understanding, with sympathy. Her hand tightens around mine. "Oh my God..."

"She started seeing him the day after we went on our first date. And she had me twisted around her little finger and he...he knew. He watched me fall in love and make a fool of myself, all while he was fucking her on the side, because he didn't want to jeopardize the business relationship. He actually said he'd fuck his way to rich if he had to." It's such a bitter truth, my lip curls and my nostrils flare. I can't stand the taste of it.

"Shit, Garrett." Angela covers her mouth with a slim hand.

"I found them together. There was this big confrontation and...uh...I said some things I regret. And she started crying. Told me she never loved me. That the whole thing was just about money. Hers, mine, his. There was this big fight and uh...she got behind the wheel. It was late. Raining. And she ran off the road. She was trapped there for, uh...for several hours before anyone found her. She died the next day."

"I can't even imagine." Angela rubs her thumb along my knuckle, her touch soothing the ache in my heart. "I don't have words…"

"Elizabeth taught me to be careful who I trust because the only thing that matters to other people is money. Everyone's only in it for themselves."

She also taught me not to think about forever, because no one is who they want you to think they are.

Angela shakes her head. "You can't let one person change how you see the world."

"You can when it keeps happening to you. When my mother died, an entire town turned against me. They didn't see a child hurting, in need of help, they saw a monster. A scapegoat. So I became that, until Mom changed the course of our lives. But then...Elizabeth."

"Is that how you see me?" Angela asks, carefully, quietly, as if she's afraid of my answer. "Do you think I only care about myself?"

"No, my Angel." I shake my head. "You care about making this world a better place for others. You feed feral kittens and take the time to see past the defenses of a broken asshole like me. I think your whole family is that way."

"They are," she says with a smile. "It's why The Hut is so important to me. It's our way to give back to the world."

"I know. My family started coming here in the summers when I was a teenager. The year the adoption went through, we celebrated at The Hutton Hotel. I could feel it even then. As a kid. That's why *I* was the one who fought to take your account, and I'm still gonna fight even now that I'm off it. I knew I was coming down here for a reason..."

It's time for another truth, this one more terrifying than the last.

My eyes meet hers.

I take a breath.

"...I never expected that reason to be you."

Angela's lips part and her eyes soften. They trace

the lines of my face before she tilts her head, questioning. "Me?"

I stare for a long moment, wrestling with this, with us, with *myself*. "After everything happened, I swore I'd never let myself care about another person." My attention wanders to the cut above her eye. "It's too easy to lose people."

She sits back with a sigh, staring at her lap as her fingers twist together.

"Garrett...I understand. You made it clear you weren't a relationship person from the start. I'm sorry I said anything about feelings. Please don't feel obligated to acknowledge them."

She's distancing herself from me. Protecting her heart because she hasn't heard me. Not yet. She doesn't understand.

"I have to acknowledge them." I pinch her chin and turn her face to mine. "I feel it too, my Angel. I'm falling in love with you, and this feels bigger than me, bigger than Elizabeth. You're..." I shake my head, searching for something to describe the immensity of what this is. "You're *more*. You're *everything*."

CHAPTER FORTY-ONE

Angela

Of all the ways I saw my day going, sitting in my wrecked car in a tropical storm while Garrett tells me he's falling in love with me didn't make the list. I take his hand, press it to my cheek, and make a sound that's half laugh, half sigh, all relief.

This growly, grumpy man who never wanted a relationship...wants me.

His gaze bounces across my face, then drops to my lips. I cup his jaw and pull him close. His kiss is sweet. Desperate. It's a promise. A confirmation. His tongue sweeps across my lip and my heart, oh my heart. I could stay like this forever.

Garrett presses his forehead to mine. "I don't know what I would have done if I lost you."

"But you didn't. You won't." Wind rocks the car and rain pelts the glass as thunder rolls in the distance. "Our story doesn't end in tragedy. I think I was made for you."

The admission feels ridiculous. It's too soon. Too much. But it's been there from the start, this knowing. This awareness. The first day we met, standing side by side at Seaside Mobile, it felt as if Garrett could see through my bullshit to the real me. The moment I met his eyes, I felt uncomfortably alive and finally it all makes sense.

I am for him and he is for me.

We're *more*. We're *everything*.

Now that the layers have been pulled back, the boundaries between us obliterated, we can see it. Admit it. Do something about it.

Garrett threads his fingers into my hair, his energy chaotic, wild. "Jesus, Angel. I'm still...I'm sorry. So sorry." He traces the cut above my eye with a gentle finger. "I don't know what I would have done...another fucking car accident. Another woman I love...gone..."

"But none of that happened. I'm right here and when I say I'm not going anywhere until you tell me to, I mean it. I'm not Elizabeth. I want you for you. The good. The bad...I want all of it, for as long as you're willing to let me have it."

But how long can I have him when he'll be leaving

so very soon?

Garrett's sharp exhalation is an admission. He doesn't know what happens next either.

Everything feels bigger now, after what we've said, what we've done, but love doesn't change the fact that we live in different states. That the two of us coming together is temporary. The structure of our lives makes *us* impossible.

I don't know what comes next.

I avoid the future in favor of the present.

"My family will not be doing business with someone like Jordan Clement. I can tell you that much."

Standing next to the man at the hotel made me want a shower. The way he leered, hanging on my every word, the pompous toss of his hair as he expected me to hang on his. I won't have someone like that connected with the Hutton Hotel.

Especially knowing what he did to someone who called him "friend."

"Damn straight." Garrett bobs his head. "Not if I have anything to say about it."

I text Dad to let him know we were in an accident, that we're okay, but running behind.

My phone rings immediately.

"What happened? How bad is it?"

"I promise, we're fine. Some guy was driving like

an idiot, and we swerved into the guardrail." I don't mention that Garrett was the idiot and shoot him a look as he rubs his forehead.

"You're sure you're not hurt?"

"I'm fine, Dad. We'll be there as soon as possible and listen, don't start the meeting without us, no matter what Mr. Clement says."

"Angel." There's a moment of silence and I imagine him moving away from listening ears. "You know I'm going to need more information." A long peal of thunder joins forces with the wind and the rain. It devours Dad's hushed voice.

"I know and I'll give it to you, but now isn't the time. It's really loud out here and I want to focus on the road, but I promise I'll fill you in when we get to The Hut. It's just...it's important, okay? That guy isn't who he says he is."

"I'll stall, but damn it, Angela, you know better than to be out in these conditions." The fatherly concern in his voice has me shaking my head. No matter how old I get, I will always be his little girl. We say our goodbyes and I end the call.

"Some idiot, huh?" Garrett lifts a brow.

"Yeah, I kept trying to tell him to slow down, but..." Humor is easy to hide behind, when everything is up in the air, when we don't have time for the difficult conversation of what happens for us next.

The damage to the car appears mostly cosmetic and the drive back to the hotel is harrowing, though uneventful. While we drive, I steal peeks at Garrett, only to catch him stealing peeks at me.

I'm giddy. Stupid-in-the-head, jump-up-and-down, cheerleader-on-amphetamines giddy.

Love.

He used the word love.

I'm falling in love with you.

I was so afraid to tell him about my feelings, so afraid to chase him away, and then just blurted it all out there at the worst possible time. His question said it all. *Now? You're going to start this conversation now. In your mind, this is the best time to talk about...about feelings?*

He had enough on his plate without me piling on too and I was certain I'd lost him forever. But no. We're here. Together.

Whatever that means.

How can we be together when we live so far apart?

Later. We'll ask those questions later.

Right now, there's so much more at stake. My family's business. Garrett's reputation.

Our future hangs in the balance of what happens next, and it looms like a shadow as we pull into the parking lot of the hotel.

CHAPTER FORTY-TWO

Angela

Garrett and I park at The Hut and race to the porch, shaking rain out of our hair before stepping through the door. Jordan's with Dad and Uncle Wyatt, standing outside the office. His eyes narrow when he sees Garrett. I give him my best "fuck you very much" smile while Dad's face morphs from pleasant to ready to murder someone when he sees me.

"You said you weren't hurt." He crosses the room in three long strides and cups my face, inspecting the cut over my eye. "And you're soaked. Therese!" He turns, barking for our receptionist. "Call housekeeping for towels for Angel and Mr. Cooper. Blankets, too."

Her startled face pokes out of the office. "Yes, Mr. Hutton," she says before dashing off.

Dad turns to Garrett, and I know that glint in his eyes. The one that says he's decided who to murder and it's the idiot who was driving too fast in the rain.

"It looks worse than it is." I wave a hand over the cut, flashing my father a look I hope he understands. A warning that things are about to get bumpy, but to buckle up and enjoy the ride because this time, I know what I'm doing.

Dad lifts a brow and shakes his head. "I'll have to take your word on that," he says, with a heavy undercurrent of *what the hell is going on, Angela?*

I meet my father's eyes.

Trust me, says the tilt of my head, the arch of my brow.

He glowers, every bit the inscrutable Marine while Therese returns with an armload of towels and blankets, handing them over with a shocked expression.

"Remember that time when I was seventeen or eighteen?" I say to Dad, accepting a towel and dabbing at my face, my hair. "And you were having a hard time letting go? I wanted to hang out with friends, but you were doing your overprotective daddy thing..."

Dad nods, listening intently, as if a walk down memory lane is perfectly normal at this moment. I could hug him for understanding me so well.

Careful of my throbbing forehead, I dry my face. "And I sat you down and told you it was time to trust me. That I deserved more credit than you were giving me. Remember?"

"I think I remember the day you're talking about."

"Do you remember what I said? Right before I left?" I meet my father's eyes and pray he's catching everything I'm not saying.

"How could I forget?" Dad turns to Wyatt and Jordan, shaking his head and laughing lightly. "My seventeen-year-old daughter looked me in the eyes and said 'Semper fi, Daddy,' then walked out the door like the biggest badass that ever was."

Semper fidelis. The motto of the Marine Corps. *Always faithful.*

"And things turned out okay, didn't they?" I finish drying off and wrap a blanket around my shoulders while the men chuckle at the idea of seventeen-year-old me standing up to Lucas Hutton.

Trust me.

"They did." Dad's nod is almost imperceptible, but it's there. He caught my drift. I'm sure everyone else did as well, given that subtlety isn't my thing, but whatever.

"I think we should postpone the meeting one more day, don't you?" Wyatt folds his arms over his chest, leaning against the wall. "Deals like this are too important to be made while half of us are wrapped in towels and bleeding."

Jordan starts to speak, and I shoot Dad a warning look. "I'm fine," I say with a smile, "and I'm sure Garrett is, too."

"If Angela says she's fine, then she's fine. Let's get this over with." Dad walks into the office. Wyatt follows. I step through, giving Jordan another "you're such a fucking dick" grin while gesturing for Garrett to step inside.

Jordan's jaw drops. His eyes narrow. He turns to my dad, his face a mask of professional embarrassment. "I am so sorry, Mr. Hutton. I can't believe I'm in the position to have to tell you this," he says, smooth as silk, "but Mr. Cooper is no longer working on this account. It'll just be me in today's meeting."

I close the door with Garrett firmly inside the office and fight back laughter as Jordan's mask slips. He's pissed and what I'm about to say will piss him off even more.

Good.

This is gonna be fun.

CHAPTER FORTY-THREE

GARRETT

Standing in the office of the Hutton Hotel, wrapped in a blanket while water drips into my shoes, I glare at Jordan. My nemesis. The man I used to admire. When I changed into these clothes, I told myself I was dressing for war.

Well, here we are.

The trumpets are blowing and the drums are rumbling and every nerve in my body is ready. Eager.

I haven't hit the asshole yet, which is a testament to how far I've come. A month ago, the man would have been bleeding five seconds after I walked through the door.

Jordan's gaze cuts my way when he announces I'm

no longer working the account. Snide. Proud. Happy to watch me fall.

My fists tighten and my jaw clenches. There's a limit to my patience. He hasn't found it yet, but he's trying.

"We have a bit of a problem then, don't we?" Angela turns to her father, oh so innocent as she lifts her palms. She's drenched, and the cut above her eye is starting to swell, and my instinct is to wrap her up and protect her, but she's made it clear she's no damsel in distress.

"A problem?" Jordan tilts his head. "What kind of problem?"

"The Hutton Hotel will only do business with Mr. Cooper. If he's not managing the deal, we're out."

Jordan's lips tighten and Angela holds her father's gaze. There's a whole lot of silent communication going on, the kind that only comes with deep connection and a lifetime of understanding. I have it with Charlie, with Connor, with Mom and Dad and in this shitty moment, I realize I want to have it with my Angel too.

Shocked, Wyatt steps forward, but she lifts a hand.

Trust me, says the sharpness in her eyes.

"This is…this is unacceptable," Jordan sputters. He turns to her dad and uncle as if to dismiss her from the conversation. Fucking misogynistic prick. "Backing away from a deal this good over something as trivial as who's managing the account…it's ridiculous."

"It's not trivial." Angel squares her shoulders, lifts her chin. So strong. So proud. So confident. She's a force to be reckoned with as she turns to Lucas. "This man is a cheat and a liar. He'll do us dirty just like the company before. All those changes he proposed? They're not good."

I nod as she rattles off the explanation I gave her while we were in my room. Buried clauses. The hotel as leverage. Too many shares going to Vision Enterprise rather than staying in the family.

"We're better off losing the hotel than working with him."

The words send my pulse racing. She devoted her life to The Hut…and just risked it all with one little sentence.

For me.

Jordan huffs. Drops his jaw. Tosses that ludicrous hair.

"I assure you; those changes are necessary. My track record is impeccable, unlike your daughter's."

My fists tighten, ready to fix the smug look on his face. I inhale a full breath as the energy in the room transforms, Lucas and Wyatt pulling themselves to their full height, setting Jordan in their sights. He doesn't know it, but he lost ground with that statement.

When you're surrounded by people like the Huttons, the last thing you do is insult one.

This battle is no longer mine alone.

"Why don't you explain those changes, then?" Lucas's voice is too quiet. Too composed. His razor-sharp focus locks onto the outsider in the room. I recognize that stance. It's taking everything in him not to hit the asshole too.

With a smarmy smile, Jordan rattles off a well-rehearsed speech filled with enough business jargon to choke an elephant. He speaks quickly. Smoothly. But for every promise he makes, Angela has a rebuttal. I want to jump in. To take over. To fight for her. But she's doing just fine on her own.

My fucking Angel. Who knew she's been hiding a warrior's spirit under all that sweetness?

Defending himself doesn't come naturally for Jordan. He sputters and chokes before turning to Lucas. "Look, I hate to be the one to say this, but I wouldn't be surprised if your daughter and Mr. Cooper's relationship has evolved beyond professional and it's clearly skewing her judgment. He has a pattern, you see, and taking advantage of heiresses is kind of his thing."

My fists tighten. If he keeps talking like that, there's no way I'll keep my cool.

CHAPTER FORTY-FOUR

Angela

I should have known a man like Jordan would go for the throat.

With a deep breath, I meet my father's scowling face. It reminds me of being seventeen again. Me, pushing for independence, so eager to be let off my leash and him, holding on tight, unwilling to believe I'm ready.

Well, I'm ready now.

See me. See my truth. See how good this is. See the echoes of you and Mom and know, the same way I know.

"He's right," I say with a deep sigh. "My relationship with Garrett has evolved and I will not let this man make it sound like it's a bad thing." I turn to

Jordan, pointing an angry finger in his face. "I've come to understand you're the one with the pattern, Mr. Clement. Lying. Cheating. Betrayal."

My hands tremble as I meet my father's eyes.

He's glaring at me. At Garrett. He looks upset, but he always looks upset.

I can't tell what he's thinking. Is he angry with us? Does he think I've lost my mind? Or does he understand? For the millionth time in my life, I wish he wasn't so good at hiding what's going on in his head.

Uncle Wyatt runs his hands into his hair. "Can someone please tell me what in the world is going on? I'm a little lost and a lot concerned because until five minutes ago, I was under the impression we were walking into a good thing today. And this? This sounds like a whole lot of bad. Lose the hotel? Angela…"

I understand his despair, the disappointment dripping from my uncle's words, but I'm doing the right thing here. He'll understand that soon.

"Mr. Hutton…" Garrett's face is as unreadable as my father's as he steps forward. My heart races and the world swims around me.

Black spots swim through my vision.

My fingers and lips tingle.

I've finally hit my limit. From the moment construction on the Bliss site ground to a halt, I've been in water up to my throat, trying to smile through the disaster. I can't keep pushing. I'm staring at the loss of the hotel. The loss of my family's respect. The loss of the man I'm falling in love with...

"Your daughter," Garrett says, holding out his hands to my father and uncle. "Your niece. She's right. The contract I drafted is fair to you, but Vision Enterprise isn't interested in fair, not when Jordan's involved. He will bury clauses in the fine print and drag his heels until your finances are in such a dire position that you have no choice but to sign a shitty deal. He will ruin your business while he squeezes every last cent out of the name. He doesn't care about the future of this hotel or your family. He only sees a chance to make more money for our company and therefore himself."

"He's right, Dad. There's so much to this story you don't know yet."

Jordan dismisses me with a look of utter disgust. "Are you really going to take the word of a love-struck woman who already put your business in jeopardy once?"

My father scowls and Jordan takes his silence as encouragement.

"I've done some research on you family. If I were you, I'd consider Wyatt's son as heir to the proverbial throne. Or really, any of your nephews would be better than a woman willing to sleep her way out of a good deal—"

Garrett and Dad lunge forward in unison. "Shut your fucking mouth!" yells Garrett while Dad growls, "That's my daughter, asshole…"

Jordan stumbles back and Wyatt leaps into action, stopping Dad and Garrett, his hands on their chests, his calming presence the only reason Jordan isn't bleeding.

"Get out." Wyatt jerks his head toward the door.

Clement huffs. "You misunderstood—"

"Oh no…" Wyatt says mockingly, loosening his grip on the other men and pretending to falter. "I don't think I can hold them back much longer…"

"You know I'll have your job for this," Jordan says to Garrett as he heads for the door.

Garrett sneers. "Good. Take it. I have no intentions of returning to Vision after this."

My jaw drops. What could that mean for us? Do we have a future after all?

"I hope the pussy's worth it because—"

Wyatt releases his hold. Dad lurches forward. But it's Garrett's fist who connects with Jordan's face. His head rocks back. His eyes glaze over. He stumbles, then drops to the floor, blinking up at the man who hit him.

"Apologize."

Jordan coughs, dabbing at his lip and checking for blood. "When I tell Brans—"

"The next words out of your mouth had better sound different."

I always thought rage would be the primary emotion of a man willing to throw a punch, but Garrett looks so calm, sounds so composed, looks so in control. He didn't fly off the handle. He isn't a loose cannon at the mercy of his emotions. He knew what he was doing.

And he did it for me.

I blink, trembling.

Jordan sits like a sullen child and Garrett steps his way.

He glares at the man towering over him. Petulant. Unrepentant. "I'm sorry..."

"Not to me, asshole." Garrett points my way, his eyes blazing with protection, with love, with wild adrenaline.

For some strange reason, I smile.

"Apologize."

Jordan licks his lips. "Sorry..." His poisonous gaze flicks my way.

Garrett looks unimpressed. "You can do better than that."

Pulling himself off the floor, Jordan smooths his suit, testing his mouth with his tongue before delivering a tepid apology. Without waiting to see what happens next, he storms out of the room, muttering as he pulls his phone out of his pocket and jams it to his ear.

Outside, the storm rages. Rain buffets the walls as the wind-thrashed sea pulses with energy. Now what? The one chance we had at saving the hotel just walked out the door...because I chased him away.

I'm holding my breath, clenching my fists. The walls are closing in. I never wanted to be the Hutton who ruined the family legacy, but I am. That's me. It's done.

If I hadn't slept with Garrett...if we hadn't gotten so wrapped up in each other...would any of this have happened?

What now, Angela. What now?

Garrett glances my way, his face as violent as the storm, though as our eyes meet, he smiles. Gentle, almost serene. It's not a familiar look on him, but he wears it well.

Inhaling deeply, he turns to my dad. "I should probably apologize. That was incredibly unprofessional of me..."

Dad shakes his head. "If you hadn't hit him, I would've."

"And if he hadn't, it woulda been me." Wyatt folds

his arms over his chest. "Something tells me the little shit had that coming from you for a while now."

Garrett rakes his hands through his hair, huffing a laugh, shaking his head, closing his eyes. I cross the room and put my hand on his arm.

What does one say in a situation like this? Standing in a room full of men who listened to that asshole humiliate me?

A half-smile tugs at my lips as the perfect response comes to mind.

"I was handling that."

It's a callback to the night we met at the bar and my voice sounds shakier than I intended. I've never had someone talk to me, about me, the way Jordan did. Knowing I didn't have to handle it alone is a relief.

Garrett's eyes meet mine with a smile that fills my heart. "And you were doing a phenomenal job." He gently pushes a lock of still-damp hair out of my face before turning to my dad. "I care a lot about your daughter and I will not be the guy who ruins her life, I promise you that. Let me fight for you. For *her*. Not just a better deal."

Dad cocks his head. "You can't fight for anyone if you don't have a job."

"*I'll* invest in the hotel." Garrett takes my hand, smiling as his eyes meet mine. "I'll invest in Angela Hutton."

CHAPTER FORTY-FIVE

Angela

I wish I could say Vision Enterprise accepts their loss gracefully, but they do not. They threaten with lawyers and legal action. We follow suit—and our lawyers are better. Garrett receives a formal notice of termination as well as the threat of a lawsuit against him, but, after several nasty conversations and too many emails to count, we sever all ties with the company.

And good riddance.

Garrett's proposal for moving forward is simple. He wants to pool his money with ours to buy back the debt on the hotel and offer us an obscenely low interest rate in exchange for stakes in the company. He'll then help us broker a new loan to finish construction in Bliss.

It's a big risk. One I'm surprised he's willing—and able—to take.

Not only was I unaware he had that much money, but knowing he's willing to risk it all for me, for my family...it takes me back to that day in Bliss, standing at the construction site, waiting for Garrett to arrive. A feeling of inevitability, or momentum, of good beginnings saturated that moment, and now, this one as well.

There's discussion after discussion, negotiation upon negotiation, as the men in my life get to know each other. With the entirety of Garrett's fortune tied up in our future, it's important that everyone knows, trusts, and believes in each other.

"Have you ever thought about buying a boat?" Garrett asks, one night in late October. We're on my back porch, snuggled into the wicker furniture, him sipping whiskey and me with a gin and tonic. "You have this great dock, this amazing view, but no boat."

Fluff is curled on my lap, with Orange purring between us. I never intended those non-names to stick, but after using them for so long, I couldn't call my kitties anything else. Besides, the names make Garrett laugh, and I think that's therapeutic for him.

"I've thought about it," I say, leaning my head on

his shoulder, "but being out on the water alone never really called to me."

He bobs his head. Twines his fingers with mine. Presses a kiss into my hair. "I've always wanted a boat."

Later that night, we lay in bed, breathless, panting, satisfied. My head is on his chest and his hand is on my back and the thought of him leaving sours my stomach. "Do you have to go back?" I whisper.

I used to ask if he had to go home, but somewhere along the line, I realized his home is with me.

Garrett nods. "I do."

"I get so tired of missing you." My voice is low. Old Garrett would shy away from this kind of honesty. New Garrett is surprisingly sweet about it.

"Do you still sleep with my pillow when I'm gone?" There's no hint of laughter or judgment. No worry that he'll call me ridiculous for dreaming about a happily-ever-after. Just acceptance that I'm head over heels for him.

I curl my arm around his head to play with his hair, burrowing deeper into his chest. "It smells like you, so I close my eyes and pretend you're here. And then, in the mornings, I drink from your favorite mug...because I'm more of a hopeless romantic than I originally thought."

After months of Garrett living half his life with me and the other half in Wildrose, you'd think I'd be used to the pattern. But I'm not. I don't think I'll ever be. Every time I look at what lies ahead for me, he's there. Scowling, grumpy as ever, but there.

"Do you think about the future?" Garrett's voice is soft as it rumbles through his chest.

"All the time."

"Am I in it?"

I smile to myself. It's like he's reading my mind.

"In my happy daydreams, yeah. You're in it." I breathe him in, inhaling deeply as if I can store up his scent to keep with me when he's gone. "What about you? Do you see me in your future?"

"You are my future." Garrett shifts, pushing onto his elbow, sitting up just enough to meet my eyes. He stares for a long moment, his jaw clenching as he thinks.

"Everything okay, Gare?"

"So okay. Beyond okay." He pushes a lock of hair out of my face. "Hear me out on this before you say anything."

He's so charged, so tense, so typically unreadable, I get nervous.

"I'm not sure this sounds like everything's okay."

"I want to live with you." A smile quirks his lips. "I don't want to travel back and forth anymore. I don't want to miss you or know you're missing me. So...I was wondering...since most of my stuff is here already..."

"You want to move in with me?" My heart thunders in my chest, tap-dancing a happy yes, yes, YES!

"If that's okay..."

"Okay?" I sit up, beaming. "I would love that. I've been wanting that, but was trying not to push too fast. Oh my God. When? And what are you going to bring? Do we need to start talking about furniture or..." I'm out of bed, too excited to sit still. "I already made space for you in the closet, but I can—"

Garrett takes my hand and pulls me in for a kiss. "Breathe, Angel. We'll work out the specifics after I ask you this other thing."

"What other thing?"

"I want you to come to Wildrose and meet my family."

Excitement spins through my stomach and I'm grinning, pushing out of his arms to pace the bedroom because how can I be still after news like this? "Really?"

"It's Charlie's birthday and we're throwing her a giant party. I can't imagine it without you there. And we can take stock of my stuff and decide what comes and what goes."

"You want me to meet your family? And you're moving in?"

"You're my home and every day without you reminds me why I lost my faith in humanity. Besides, I met your family months ago. It's time I return the favor."

Garrett's waiting for me as I step out of the airport into a frigid November day. He leans on the wall, a black peacoat making his strong bone structure all the more striking. When his gaze lands on mine, he straightens, shoving his hands in his pockets as he grins. I huddle into the parka I bought for the occasion as a blast of wind freezes my face. Fall might be beautiful, but I am not made for it. Give me heat, humidity, and a bright sun in a blue sky any day.

Garrett wraps me in a hug, and all is right with the world again. He flew up last week to get his affairs in order and the house felt so empty without him. But the part of my life where I spend days and weeks missing him is over. We'll be flying back together.

To our home.

"You are a sight for sore eyes, my Angel."

"That's a big ditto on that one."

Laughter rumbles in his chest. "Did you just call me a big dildo?"

"No, I said ditto..." I pull back and find him smiling down at me.

"Joking, Angel. Just a joke." He takes my suitcase and throws an arm around my shoulder as we head for the car.

"I didn't realize that was something you did." I laugh, leaning into him. "I thought you were too serious to tell jokes."

"No one can believe it, but I smile now and everything. All because of you. Just don't let it go to your head."

"I might let it go to *your* head."

Garrett stops. Looks down at me. Frowns. "I don't...was that...?"

"I was trying to insinuate I'll give you a blow job later." A cold breeze slices through my coat and I shiver, burrowing into him.

"Cold?"

"How does anyone survive in this climate?"

"If you think this is bad, wait until we come back for Christmas."

I stop in my tracks. "Christmas?"

"Well, yeah. It's Mom's favorite holiday. If you think we won't be making the trip every other year, then you better think again."

How is this my life? Standing in an airport parking lot, freezing my ass off, grinning from ear to ear while we talk about holidays and family gatherings? I shiver again, though I couldn't say if it's from excitement or because the weather is a cruel beast.

"Let's get you in the car and I'll crank the heat. My family is dying to meet you." Garrett puts my bag in the trunk, then climbs into the car and takes my hand. We chat on the drive and from the warmth of the car, I can appreciate the glorious colors of autumn in New England. It's almost as beautiful here as it is in the Keys—if you don't mind living in a freezer.

Garrett turns onto a street lined with quaint shops and people hanging around on the sidewalk, talking to each other like old friends. A couple waves as we drive past and Garrett snorts a laugh.

"That's Toby and Melissa Hinkle," he explains. "I've known them since I was a kid. They're awful, just so you know. And that, right there," he says, slowing as he points out a store, "is my mom's shop. Charlie works there now and will probably take over at some point."

I turn in my seat to get a better view of Woo-Woo Wildrose. If the window display is any indicator, I'm going to love meeting Garrett's mom. "Just tell Charlie it's important to read the fine print of any contract she signs." I grin, hoping he gets the joke. "Even if she's confident she knows everything's on the up-and-up. I hear things can get pretty sticky otherwise."

"I wouldn't dare tell Charlie anything." Garrett

widens his eyes like my suggestion could lead to his death. "She's not good at being told what to do."

"Must run in the family then."

He gives me the side-eye, then turns off Main, narrating the landmarks of his life as we drive. When we finally pull to a stop in front of a stately house, he kills the engine.

Red oaks line the drive leading to a giant brick home with white columns standing guard on the porch. "Wow. This is... Did you grow up here?"

"We lived in a smaller house when I was a kid, but Mom's friend, Evie Prescott, sold her this one after she married Dad." Garrett unfastens his seatbelt, then pauses. "You know Evie met your Aunt Harlow years ago? Her husband got them together to talk about books."

I turn to him, eyes wide, jaw dropped. "You're kidding."

"Nope. It's the reason we visited The Hutton Hotel in the first place."

"Remind me to thank her husband, then. Sounds like he's the catalyst that brought you and me together."

Garrett's entire demeanor softens. A light smile tugs at his lips and he puts a hand to my cheek. There's a moment where I think he's going to say something important, but the feeling fades. "You sure you're ready for this?"

"You better believe it, Bucko. I've heard nothing but good things about these people from you."

He climbs out of the car and meets me near the hood, taking my hand in his and rubbing his thumb over the knuckle. "I'm really glad you're here," he says, bringing my hand to his lips and giving it a kiss.

"I hope you still feel that way at the end of the night." I take a deep breath and remind myself to listen more than I talk. The last thing I want tonight is for my mouth to run away with the conversation the way it so loves to do when I'm nervous.

Garrett leads me up the porch and pushes into the house. Raucous laughter greets us from deeper inside. "They're probably in the kitchen. They're always in the kitchen."

"Is that my Gare Bear?" An older woman pokes her head into the hallway with a massive smile. "Get over here and give me a hug," she says, opening her arms wide.

Garrett scowls, raking a hand through his hair. "How many times have I said you can't call a grown man Gare Bear?"

Hands on hips. Smile at maximum. She's unfazed by his grumpiness. "About as many times as I've said you're never too old for a good nickname."

"It's good to see you, Mom," he says as he pulls her close. "This is Angela Hutton. Angel, this is my mom."

Amelia Cooper's long blonde hair hangs in waves down her back. She's wearing a billowing, floor length skirt with a t-shirt that says, "Boss Mode Activated" and bracelets jingle on her arm as she turns to me. Her energy is bright and she seems so comfortable in her skin, I immediately like her. How Garrett grew up with a woman like this and ended up so serious is beyond me.

"Please," I say with a smile, "call me Angel. It's nice to finally meet you, Mrs. Cooper. I've heard so much about you."

"I'll call you Angel if you call me Amelia." She takes my hands and sighs as she studies me. "You're just the prettiest thing! And doesn't she have the best energy?" She turns to Garrett with a knowing smile. "I knew you'd find a special one when your time came. Sometimes you have to experience the bad to appreciate the good. It's the nature of duality, you know. And this one? She's your good."

With that, Amelia leads me into the kitchen where I'm greeted by a large group of people. I meet Garrett's dad Jack, his sister Charlie, and their brother Connor. After a round of hugs from them, Garrett introduces me to the Prescotts, Malones, and their children, then Austin O'Connor, all family friends. They welcome me as one of their own.

"Did Garrett ever tell you about the time he punched Toby Hinkle in the face?" Charlie asks me over dinner. She's an absolute riot. I can see why she and Garrett are so close.

"Didn't we pass a Toby Hinkle on the way here?" I scrunch up my nose as I search my memory. After hours of good conversation and laughter, the drive into Wildrose Landing seems like it happened days ago. "But please. Yes. Tell me this story. Tell me all the stories actually. I wanna hear them all."

"Oh, no." Garrett pauses with his drink halfway to his mouth. "We're not doing the whole 'embarrass Garrett in front of his girlfriend' thing. Besides," he says, lowering his glass to the table, "didn't you also punch him in the face?" He waggles a finger Charlie's way.

"Don't listen to him," she says to me. "He gets grumpy when people like him."

"That was the day Amelia yelled at all the moms in the dojo, sage sprayed the place, and stormed out, right?" Connor asks.

My jaw drops as I try to process a situation where the super sweet woman across from me would be making a scene in a dojo. "I'm sorry, what happened?"

The family explains the story in fits and starts, each one interrupting the other in a weird sense of comradery and one-upmanship. I don't know what I expected today. Garrett told me his family was as wonderful as mine, but part of me thought there'd be some darkness hiding in the corners. Something to account for his rough exterior.

There isn't.

The Coopers are loving and supportive. They've made their way through twists and turns and forged ahead when the path got dark. They remind me a lot of my family—there just aren't as many of them.

Under the table, Garrett grips my knee, gently rubbing his thumb along my inner thigh. It's a simple gesture, but it warms my heart. It brings a sense of belonging, of togetherness. There's no doubt in my mind that he's my person, and now, after meeting his family, I know we were made for each other.

I meet his eyes, those deep shades of blue and flecks of green feel like home. His smile feels like oxygen. His touch...sunlight. I bloom around him. I am more around him. I feel complete around him.

And you know, for as much as he swore he wasn't interested in a relationship, I'm almost positive he feels the same.

CHAPTER FORTY-SIX

Garrett

"I think I've met the one." I lean on the wall in my parents' kitchen, whispering conspiratorially with Charlie. The evening has been wonderful. All my people in the same spot at the same time only solidified what I already knew. I love my Angel with all that I am. "Scratch that. I know I've met the one."

I pull my phone out of my pocket and bring up Angela's contact info. The name under her smiling face? The Future Mrs. Cooper.

Charlie drops her jaw, then beams. "I hate to say I saw it coming, but I totally saw this coming."

"You just say that because you love being right." I slip my phone back into my pocket.

"I'm saying that because anyone who knows you

can see how good you guys are together." She waggles her head, her curls bouncing around her shoulders. "Plus, I like being right."

"See!" I give her arm a playful shove. "You just love poking the bear."

"Why does it sound so creepy when you say it, yet delightful when I do?" Charlie shrugs as if to say the mystery will never be solved. "Does she know yet?"

I shake my head. "Not yet. But I think I'm going to propose later tonight, when it's just the two of us."

My sister stares for a long moment, her eyes locked on mine. She's reading me, testing me, checking to make sure I'm not pulling her leg. "Oh, so you're *serious* serious," she finally says.

"The ring's been in my pocket all night. I almost asked her in the car, right before we came in but talked myself out of it."

"All ni—" Charlie's eyes go wide, and her brows hit her hairline. "What are you waiting for? An invitation? Because I don't think that's how it works..."

"I'm an asshole, not a monster." I roll my eyes. "Today's your birthday. I'm not stealing the attention by proposing here. I value my life too much to stand in Charlotte Cooper's spotlight."

"Are you kidding me? I can't think of a better birthday present than seeing you get all mushy and embarrassed in front of the family." My sister puts her hands on my back and gives me a shove. "Go on. It's my birthday. You have to give me what I want."

I twist to stare over my shoulder. "I can't tell if you're genuinely happy for me or you just like to watch me squirm."

"Both." She drops me a wink. "It's definitely both."

With that, she strolls away, smiling in that way that speaks of siblings and secrets.

I take a deep breath and let it out slowly, watching my Angel talk to my parents, her smile warm, her laugh genuine. I can't imagine my life without her in it. I thought moving in together would be enough, but it only made me want her more. I don't want a roommate. I want forever.

I lift my glass, tapping lightly with a spoon. "Can I have your attention? I want to thank you guys for being here to celebrate Charlie. There's nothing quite like spending another year with family, and we all know how much she loves it when we feed her delicious food, get her tipsy, then tell her how special she is while she demolishes cake."

Charlie puts a hand to her heart while everyone laughs. "Big Brother Bear knows me so well."

"I do. Which is why I'm going to give you that other present you asked for, even though I had a whole thing planned." I glare, then swallow hard and give her a chuckle that says, *I hope you like watching me squirm.*

"This is not how I intended to do this, so you better be happy," I say to my sister before crossing the room with my heart in my throat.

I take Angela's hands. She blinks at me, her eyes wide and trusting, shining with love and happiness.

"I didn't believe I was made for love until I met you. I believed it was for other people. For better people. I thought the only thing I was good at was making money, but then...you. You've changed everything, my Angel. You've shown me how good it feels to be whole. You've shown me that in order to make the world a better place, I can't just complain about what the world needs. I have to *be* what it needs. You've made every minute of every day feel like it has purpose and meaning beyond numbers growing in a bank account. We're making an impact on the world with your hotels, just like you're making an impact on me."

Tears well in her eyes, blue shimmering through blue. Her chest heaves. "Garrett..."

"I've been watching you with my family all night long and you belong here." I place a hand over my heart. "In the organ my sister was never sure I actually had." I cast a glance Charlie's way. "And when I told her I planned on proposing later, she insisted I do it tonight."

Mom gasps, her hands flying to her mouth while my father gives me a proud—if watery—smile. Conner whispers a quiet, "I can't believe this is actually happening," and Charlie beams happily.

"You swore you wouldn't leave until I asked you to." I pull the ring out of my pocket and lower myself to one knee. "So, I'm asking you to be my Angel forever."

I tell myself her answer is written on her face. That it's clear she'll say yes, but the silent second following my words send my heartrate into overdrive.

What if I only thought the answer was obvious?

What if I just put her on the spot in front of my entire family?

But then Angela's face lights up. Tears fall from her eyes. She drops to her knees with me. "Do you mean it? You want me to marry you?"

"I need you to marry me."

She cups my face, her thumbs grazing my cheekbones as she gives me a watery smile, then says the most beautiful word in all the world...

"Yes."

EPILOGUE

Angela

Standing on my back porch, I cup my hands to my face and call for my fiancé. He's at the end of our dock, showing off his boat to Nick like the proudest papa that ever was. He bought the thing a few months ago and has presented it to every member of my family but my cousin, who came home yesterday, on leave for our wedding.

I turn to Charlie with a roll of my eyes as Fluff twines around my legs. "You'd think he built the thing with his own hands," I say, and she laughs. "We can go out there to say hi, but it's only fair to warn you. Nick's been with Garrett for over an hour, learning enough about boats to last a lifetime." I jerk a thumb over my shoulder. "Or we can wait in the house with the rest of your family and spare you that particular pain."

Charlie crouches to pet Orange as he wanders onto the patio. "I like seeing Garrett happy, especially when it gives me ammo to mess with him later. And if he's gaga over some boat, I'll have plenty of ammo. Come on." She links arms with me, and we stroll toward the dock with Fluff and Orange trotting ahead. Their bellies swing and their tails are high. The change swells my heart after the way their life started.

"I'm glad to finally have you here," I say. "We can hang out at my uncle's bar, and you can tell me all about this guy you're seeing." Over the last several months, Charlie and I have gotten close. It weirds her brother out, but he's going to have to deal because Charlotte Cooper is quickly becoming a great friend.

Garrett frowns when he sees me. "I thought you'd already heard enough about boats to last a lifetime." He turns to Nick for support, but my cousin just gives me a knowing smile.

"Oh, I did." I stare balefully at Strawberries & Champagne as she rocks in the water. "But your sister insisted we come down anyway so she could make fun of you. The rest of your family's in the house. You know, smart enough to wait for you to come inside."

Garrett throws his arms around Charlie and pulls

her close. "I thought you guys weren't getting in until four."

"You thought right," she says with a laugh.

"What time is it?" Garrett lifts a brow and turns to Nick in shock. "How long have we been out here?"

"I'm just as surprised as you. Apparently, I love boats." Nick turns to me. "Why didn't you tell me I love boats?"

I shrug as Charlie holds her hair out of her eyes, squinting up at her brother. "How ya been, Bear?"

Garrett shoves his hands into his pockets. "Miss you guys, but living in the Keys suits me, which is another thing I never thought I'd say."

"I think being in love suits you, but whatever." Charlie holds out a hand to Nick. "I'm Charlie, by the way. Garrett's much cooler younger sister."

Nick's smile is too big. His eyes meet hers with an intensity that catches my attention.

"Nick," he says, shaking her hand almost reverently. "Angel's cousin."

Charlie blushes, her gaze darting to the ground, then right back up to his again. "It's a pleasure." Her voice is low and throaty. She bites her lip then smiles into her shoulder.

I glance at Garrett who lifts his brows in surprise. "Nick is a Marine. He's just in town for the wedding and is shipping back out soon."

I don't know if he means the info as a warning or simple conversation, but it doesn't seem to turn Charlie off. If anything, it makes my cousin all the more mysterious and enticing—if the blush to her cheeks and bat in her lashes has anything to say about it.

We head back into the house, where the rest of Garrett's family waits. He greets them with hugs all around and introduces Nick, who lifts a hand. "It's really nice to meet you all, but I'll get out of your hair and let you catch up. We'll have plenty of time to get to know each other at the party tonight."

There's a chorus of agreement and one overly loud, "I'd like that!" from Charlie, who immediately turns the color of Garrett's favorite lipstick.

The conversation makes its rounds to everyone's life. I listen as my soon-to-be husband jokes with his family. He's still my grumpy, growly guy. That will never change. But he's quicker with a joke. Easier to laugh. And anger isn't the first emotion he reaches for anymore. I'd love to think I had something to do with that, but really, Garrett's the one who's done the work.

"Construction is finished at the Bliss site," he says, his hand on my knee. "We're set to soft open next month. We're training employees, finding the weak spots, getting everything shored up."

"It's been a hell of a ride." I take his hand as Garrett's dad bobs his head in approval.

"One that's just beginning." Jack Cooper turns to his wife. "When you're sharing your life with the right person, every day is an adventure. Sometimes it's hard. Sometimes we challenge each other to grow or compromise. But always, no matter what, I know that I have my best friend in my corner. It looks like you've found someone like that, too. I'm proud of you, son."

Jack is tall like Garrett, with gray streaking through dark curls. Where my dad is strong and imposing, he's warm and inviting, though the one thing they share in common is their love of structure and order. How Jack ended up with a free spirit like Amelia is beyond me.

Garrett gives his family the tour of our space. Fluff and Orange follow, meowing like tour guides as we enter each room.

"Do you guys need to head to the hotel to clean up before the rehearsal dinner?" Garrett asks as we return to the living room. "I'd keep you here all night, being selfish, just glad to have you in our house. I've missed seeing you all."

"We've missed you too, Bear," Amelia says, gripping his arms and smiling with all the pride and pain of a mother with grown children. "But we probably should get checked in and cleaned up before we meet at Angel's parents."

The Cooper's pass out hugs once, twice, a third

time, then leave me in the quiet house with my husband to be.

"How long until we need to be at your parents'?" Garrett pulls me close, his hands sliding down to cup my ass.

"I think we have an hour or two to kill. Why?"

"Because I have an idea." His lips tease mine. "A very good idea." He guides my hand to his prominent erection.

"I like where this is going," I murmur, squeezing his dick. "Where do you want me?"

Garrett grins, a devilish glint in his eye. "The boat."

"The boat?" I huff a laugh. "I don't think—"

"Angel." He quirks a brow. "Be a good girl and get your ass on the boat."

We pull up to my parents' house, last to arrive once again. My hair is tousled, and my body is sore, and for some reason I like the Strawberries & Champagne more than I did a few hours ago. Our families mill around, laughing and talking like old friends instead of new acquaintances. Cathlynn and Carabell shriek past, one turning to hit the other before Blossom grabs them by their arms and marches them off without so much as a hello in our direction.

"There you are!" Nathan says as he trails after his girlfriend. "Miss Always Early is turning into Miss Always Late."

"That's Mrs. Always Late to you." I pop a hand on my hip. "Well, as of tomorrow."

Garrett rolls his eyes. "I'm never late, thank you very much."

"Except the day we met to exchange phones."

"I wasn't late." He taps the end of my nose. "You were early."

"I hate to break it to you," Nathan says with a cocky grin, "but you're late right now."

Blossom hisses his name, and he shoots me an apologetic glance before hurrying off to play peacemaker to a problem he didn't start.

Garrett frowns, watching him leave. "Still don't like her."

"Ditto, Bucko. Ditto."

We wander past Micah, leaning quietly against the wall, looking shell shocked as he nurses a drink. He lifts his hand, smiles weakly, then gives his attention back to the floor before the family absorbs us. We talk and laugh. Mingle and drink too much champagne.

Several hours later, Nick catches us in a rare quiet moment. "Did you hear about Micah?" he whispers.

"No. What happened? He's been weird all evening."

"Ivy's back."

"*Ivy* Ivy?" I press my hands together and put them to my lips. "She's back? As in for good?"

Nick turns up his palms. "That I can't say, but she has a kid. Micah's devastated. I think he always thought they'd end up together."

I search the crowd for my cousin but can't find him anywhere. "So, she's married?"

Nick shrugs. "No clue. You now know as much as I do." His eyes fall on someone over my shoulder and a self-conscious smile tugs at his lips. I turn to find Charlie chatting with Connor and shake my head.

"She's feisty."

Nick grins. "You say that like it's a bad thing."

"She's also my little sister," Garrett retorts.

"Now that." Nick lifts his pointer fingers. "That might be a bad thing."

Later that evening, Garrett wraps an arm around my waist, and pulls me close. "Do you think *our* family will be this..." He wobbles his head as he searches for the right word.

"This what? Kind? Caring? Wonderful?"

"Large," he says with a laugh. "Do you think our family will be this large?"

"The only thing I know for sure is that it will be filled with love, laughter, and a happily-ever-after."

"See," he says, lifting my chin with the tip of his finger, "I knew you were looking for your prince."

"No way, Bucko. I was looking for you."

Behind him, the moon hangs low and bright over the water. The stars shine, glimmering with the promise of forever. But for as beautiful as the scenery is, as happy as it makes me to be surrounded by family, the thing that matters most is him.

Garrett Cooper.

The grumpy, growly, sweetly crazy man who promised to make me happy for the rest of my life.

I hope you loved your time with Garrett and Angela!

Wanna see if Garrett's still grumpy a year into their marriage? Sign up for my newsletter and I'll send you a Fate BONUS SCENE right away!

>>Click here to sign up and get your bonus scene!<<

BONUS SCENE

Angela

Just because I love my job, doesn't make every day easy. The last several weeks have been busy stacked on busy stacked on busy. But today?

Today has been such a fucking shitshow.

Dad and Uncle Wyatt were both sick and stayed home, which wouldn't normally be a problem, but today it was. Oh my God, it was. Name a problem, I dealt with it. The Bliss location has been chugging along just fine for the last year, but not today. Oh no. The one day I'm on my own to solve everything, the entire Hutton Hotel world melts down. There were shipping issues and payroll issues and supply chain issues and I ran around like an idiot trying to solve it all from states away. At one point, I considered booking a flight to see what I could do in person, but Garrett talked me out of it, saying he'd hop on a call from home and knock some heads so I could focus on the problems here at the home hotel.

To top it off, I couldn't think straight. I haven't been thinking straight for the last several days and I've just been so freaking tired. I one hundred percent did not have the energy to deal with things as gracefully as I should have.

I barked at Therese. Growled at Martha, the head of our housekeeping department, and she's just the sweetest thing that ever was.

I don't bark. Or growl. Especially not to employees who've been with us so long they might as well be family.

I've just been…off.

I apologized and neither woman seemed all that bothered by my mood, but go figure, it's one more pebble on the pile of why I can't wait for today to be over.

It's well past eight pm before I walk out the door, and the sunset is in the middle of doing its thing. Normally, I'd pause to appreciate the beauty, but today all I can do is wonder if I've done damage to my retinas because the sun is glaring straight into my eyes. Jogging down the porch steps, the heel of my pump catches and breaks off. I totter, clutch the rail, but go down anyway, scraping a hole into a brand new pair of slacks I'd already decreed as my new favorite. I actually like the way my ass looks in them, and that's saying something.

"Great," I growl. "Just freaking great."

I am so ready to be home, where Garrett's waiting impatiently for dinner. My poor husband has to be hungry. God knows I am. My stomach growls its agreement—look at me, growling again!—as I climb into the car, toss my ruined shoes onto the passenger seat, and shoot Garrett a text, letting him know I'm on my way.

After I hit send, I take a deep, cleansing breath.

The day is over.

All will be well the minute I walk through the front door and see my darling husband.

And *that's* what I get for being optimistic.

First, the tire pressure is low, so I stop at the gas station to fill it up, but the machine takes my money and never turns on, and I step in someone's gum on my way to talk to the attendant about it. Then, an accident has me sitting in traffic for twenty tedious minutes and for some reason, none of my playlists are doing anything to lighten my mood. I text Garrett again so he won't worry and blow a puff of air past my lips.

Is this what life was like for him before we got married? Feeling like the whole world is stacked up against him? A fuse so short it doesn't take more than a flicker to set it off?

It's a wonder he got this far without murdering someone, because I swear to God, I'm definitely understanding Nick's need for a job that focuses on combat and weaponry.

What is with me today?

Finally, I pull into our driveway and climb out of the car, wincing as my bare feet come down on approximately seven thousand stones. By the time I push through the front door, I'm ready to call it a night and go to bed before I inflict my bad mood on Garrett.

Only...candles flicker on every surface. A trail of roses leads out of the foyer and hooks a left to lead toward the bedroom. Fluff rubs my pants in greeting and I bend to pet his head as Orange almost knocks me over in his enthusiasm to say hello as well.

"What did Dad do?" I ask the cats, who obviously don't answer, but trot off in the direction of the rose petals—tails high, trilling in excitement—as I stand.

"Garrett? I call, following the felines, the stress of the day melting with each step. What better way to forget about shipping issues and payroll problems then to follow my husband's orders until he calls me his good girl?

But, instead of leading to the bedroom, the petals disappear into the bathroom, where gentle music and flickering light filters out the door. Garrett sits on a chair beside a tub filled with bubbles and surrounded by candles. Rose petals float in the water.

He stands. Takes my hand and pulls me close.

"What is all this?"

My husband slow dances me in a circle, tugging my blouse out of my slacks. "It sounded like you had a bad day. I thought you could use a little stress relief."

His deft fingers undo the buttons on my shirt and he slips it off my shoulders, kissing my neck, my throat, my chest. "I thought a nice batch and a foot rub would wash away the stress of the day. Afterwards, there's some food in the kitchen and we'll have dessert on the boat."

I grab his waistband and pull him closer. "What kind of dessert are we talking here?"

"The good kind." Garrett kisses me deeply, capturing my bottom lip between his teeth. "But first, bath." He points at the clawfoot tub I love so much.

But tonight, what I really want is him.

"What if I want dessert first?"

"That's not the way it's gonna work, my Angel."

"Why not?"

"Be a good girl and follow directions." His grin is wicked because he knows he has me with that one. His praise is a siren call to my libido and I'd break myself on the rocks to get to it.

But that doesn't mean I'll make it easy on him.

Where would be the fun in that?

With a wry grin, I unhook my bra and let it slip to the floor, then trail a finger down his cheek. "Help me with my pants?"

"Fuck, Angel."

Garrett's eyes darken as he tugs at the button and lowers the zipper. My pants fall to the floor, revealing the white lace undies I knew would be his undoing. Slowly, carefully, I step out of them, then lower myself into the tub, sighing as the warm water envelopes me, then dangle a foot over the edge. "What's this I hear about a foot rub?"

Garrett chuckles. "You're not playing nice."

"I'm just doing what you told me," I reply, oh so innocent. Wide eyes. Batting eyelashes. Pouting lips.

"Is that what you're doing?" He kneels beside the tub and slips a hand into the water, caressing my thigh, then sliding a finger along my clit.

I gasp, dropping my head back, welcoming his touch. "I thought dessert came last."

"Consider this an appetizer."

***

After I've been bathed and had my 'appetite' wetted, I wrap myself in a towel as the water drains from the tub. Garrett leads me out of the bathroom to the kitchen where a charcuterie board of cheese, meat, and fruit wait. I pop a strawberry into my mouth, chewing happily as my husband pulls two champagne flutes out of the cabinet—and two bottles out of the fridge.

"Before I pour, there's one more thing I want you to do for me, Angel."

I lean on the counter, grabbing another strawberry. "Your wish is my command."

Garrett pulls a package out of his back pocket and hands it to me. I stare down at the box, frowning.

"A pregnancy test?" I laugh as I speak because really? Wouldn't I know if I was pregnant? I mean, obviously I'd know...

That's not the kind of thing that slips by a person.

"Humor me, Angel." Garrett smiles. "I have a suspicion."

"Don't you think I'd know if I was pregnant?" I scoff, but my mind is ticking back over the last few weeks. I've been so busy at work; I couldn't guess when my last period ended.

"You've been so tired lately. And your moods have been...off."

I arch an eyebrow. "Off? What do you mean off?"

Garrett holds up his hands. "Don't shoot the

messenger, my love. I did the math and I think you're late." He steps closer. "Aren't you?"

"I...I don't know. Maybe? What day is it?" But he's starting to make sense. "It's the fourteenth," I say, nodding.

My jaw drops as I process the implications.

My period is definitely late. How did I not know this? Work's been busy, but that busy?

Garrett places a hand on my cheek. "I think you should take the test." He shows me the bottles he pulled out of the fridge. One, champagne. The other? Non-alcoholic sparkling cider. "So we know which bottle to open," he says with the sweetest smile.

With a quick nod, I head back to the bathroom. After I've flushed the toilet, I call for Garrett to wait with me, though we don't wait long. He's holding my hands when two pink lines show and tears spring to my eyes.

My husband's arm wraps around my shoulder, drawing me close, but he won't look at me. He just keeps staring at those two little lines, his jaw pulsing, his expression unreadable.

You'd think after all this time, I'd be better at reading him and I am. I really am. Just not tonight, when it matters most.

We stopped using protection months ago, deciding that if a baby was meant to be, it would be. We were ready for a family but didn't want to make a big thing about it...

What if he changed his mind?

What if now that it's happened, he realized how much he didn't want to be a parent?

I need him to say something because my mind is going a million miles an hour and I think this is a really good thing but...

"Are you mad at me?" My voice sounds small, trembling into the room.

Garrett turns his attention to me. "Mad?"

And still I can't read him.

"You're so quiet and your jaw's doing that thing..."

He cups my cheeks, pressing his forehead to mine. He kisses me. Once. Twice. A third time. *A fourth.* When he pulls away, tears shimmer in his eyes. "I'm happier than I've ever been in my life." He palms my stomach, beaming down at me. "A baby, Angel. We're going to have a baby. The first of many."

"Many?"

"Many. After all, we have a legacy to continue."

***

The moon hangs low and full over the water, tracing the waves in silver as they lap against the sides of the boat. Garrett plucks a strawberry off the tray and holds it in front of my mouth. I bite into it, brushing my lips against his fingers.

The evening air is warm, soft almost as it caresses my skin and I snuggle into my husband. I never thought I'd like being out on the water, but his enthusiasm for it is contagious and it's become one of my favorite ways to spend an evening. Miles from shore, watching the sunset, or the moonrise, just...being. Together.

But tonight?

I've never been this content.

Garrett drapes an arm around my shoulder as Fluff hops onto his lap, twirls in a circle, then settles with a sigh of contentment as if to say he agreed with me.

I never thought the cats would like being on the boat, but they race us down the dock every evening.

"You know, I really like being married to you," I say.

"Yeah?"

"Definitely. And that's pretty amazing, considering I didn't like you very much when we first met."

"Wow." Garrett chuckles. "Just putting it out there."

"I thought that's how we did things in this relationship. We weren't even dating yet when you ordered me to take off my clothes for the first time. And only a few days later, you were pinning me to walls in cheap hotels…"

His laugh rumbles in his chest. "Oh, I remember. How could I forget?"

"And I think I'm really going to like raising children with you."

"I'm going to like that too, Angel." He runs a hand through my hair. "Watching them grow into little versions of you—"

"Or you."

"For their sakes, we'll hope they take after their mother. Life will be better for them that way."

I straighten to meet my husband's gaze. He's smiling, looking warm and wise and happier than I've ever seen him. "You're smart. Driven. You feel so much." I place a hand on his heart. "Our kids would be lucky to be like you."

"Right. The parent whose brother and sister repeatedly say is cold and uncaring."

"Garrett. How long has it been since they said that? You went through so much. Your mother. Elizabeth…"

He swallows and nods. "And I shut out the world because of it."

"That's not what someone does when they're cold and uncaring, that's what they do when they feel too much. The way you love me? The way you take care of me and our business? I want that for our kids."

"I want *this* for them." He brushes a hand through my hair. "What we have."

"I want this for them too." I take a sip of sparkling cider and make a silent promise that I'll do everything I can to guide our children towards health and happiness.

Garrett settles into his seat, watching the horizon as the boat rocks with the waves. His hand covers my stomach. His head leans against mine.

"And they lived happily ever after," I whisper, and he huffs a laugh.

"I thought you didn't need a prince." His voice is low, intimate without a hint of judgement.

"I thought so too." I snuggle even closer. "But fate gave me one anyway."

GARRETT AND ANGEL'S PARENTS

Did you love Garrett and Angela? You'll adore their parents' stories!

Meet Angel's parents in BEYOND WORDS.

I lost my journal. No big deal, right? It's only the most honest parts of me. Raw. Uncensored. Humiliating. It's a race against time to get it back before someone finds it.

Except someone did find it. And read it. AND COMMENTED.

Sexual boundaries aren't just crossed in his message, they're obliterated. His words drop my jaw and flush my cheeks, then piss me off. He has the audacity to demand I contact him. Not gonna happen, buddy. Except, after a tequila-fueled tirade, I do just that...

The man I find overflows with kindness and humor and depth. I don't even know his name, but I fall in love with his mind, opening up in ways I never have with anyone. I'm vulnerable. Bare. Real.

Meanwhile, I meet Lucas Hutton—a Marine with scars covering his body, heart, and soul.

The chemistry between us is a force of nature, beautiful, powerful, and impossible to ignore.

His intensity leaves me reeling. The physical attraction has me melting. I want to pull back his layers and find the man hiding under that scowling exterior.

Mind versus body.

Physical versus mental.

Kind versus passionate.

I have to choose between them.

I just don't know how I can.

Check out BEYOND WORDS now!

Meet Garrett's parents in SHAMELESS.

I'm structure. She's chaos. I'm practicality. She's spontaneity. She's off-limits. Nothing, and I mean nothing, will happen between us.

Jack Cooper's a devoted single dad, just trying to make

it through the morning without burning breakfast. His life is all about lists and rules and boundaries.

Meanwhile, I'm a shameless free spirit looking for signs from the universe.

And Jack? He's my sign all right...and he's flippin' hot. Like total package, scream-his-name-while-biting-a-pillow hot.

But he's sworn off dating. And we're total opposites. The last thing I want is to further complicate his life.

So what if I melt a little every time he smiles? Who cares if I have a thing for dark hair and blue eyes that caress my body when he looks at me?

All right, so I can't stop fantasizing about the guy and completely adore his kids. It's not like that should stop me from trying to help the guy out...right?

Check out SHAMELESS now!

FAMILY TREE

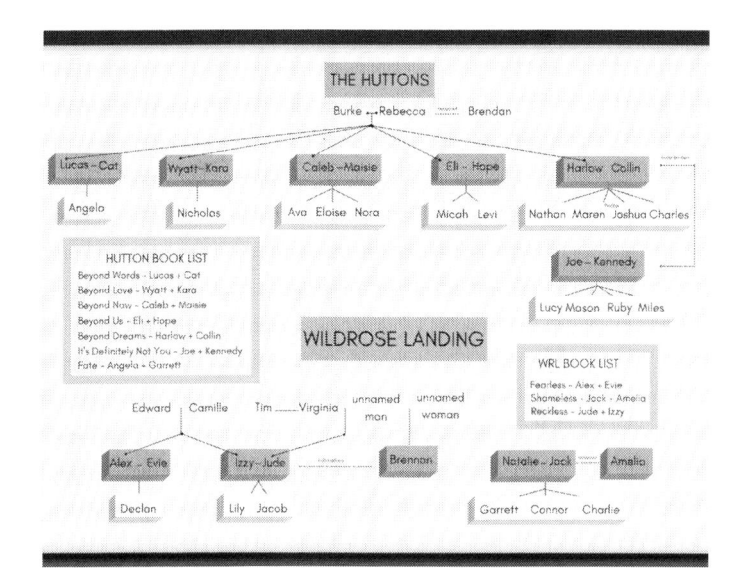

THE HUTTONS

Burke — Rebecca — Brendan

- Lucas — Cat
  - Angela
- Wyatt — Kara
  - Nicholas
- Caleb — Maisie
  - Ava, Eloise, Nora
- Eli — Hope
  - Micah, Levi
- Harlow — Collin
  - Nathan, Maren, Joshua, Charles
  - Joe — Kennedy
    - Lucy, Mason, Ruby, Miles

HUTTON BOOK LIST
- Beyond Words – Lucas + Cat
- Beyond Love – Wyatt + Kara
- Beyond Now – Caleb + Maisie
- Beyond Us – Eli + Hope
- Beyond Dreams – Harlow + Collin
- It's Definitely Not You – Joe + Kennedy
- Fate – Angela + Garrett

WILDROSE LANDING

Edward — Camille | Tim — Virginia | unnamed man | unnamed woman

- Alex — Evie
- Izzy — Jude
  - Lily, Jacob
- Declan
- Brennan
- Natalie — Jack — Amelia
  - Garrett, Connor, Charlie

WRL BOOK LIST
- Fearless – Alex + Evie
- Shameless – Jack + Amelia
- Reckless – Jude + Izzy

COMMUNITY CATS - THE STORY OF FLUFF AND ORANGE

Fluff and Orange were inspired by real life kittens who appeared on my porch last year. I woke one morning to find a mama cat stretched out on our sidewalk, nursing a litter of teeny tiny babies. We'd seen Mama around and knew her to be feral—and very afraid of humans. I immediately called the animal shelter to see if they could pick them up for adoption and this is how I first learned about community cats.

The shelter very politely told me that feral cats do not do well in captivity and are rarely adopted. (70% of cats in shelters are killed and that number raises to virtually 100% with ferals.) The woman explained that the kittens were safest with their mother. Once they were weaned, we could trap them one at a time, bring them to the shelter to be neutered, then return them to the wild.

We put out some food and water, but the little family disappeared and we assumed Mama moved on.

Two months later, I came downstairs to find two of the MOST ADORABLE kittens I'd ever seen on the porch. I watched through the window for a while—please imagine the heart-eyes emoji for reference—then went to get some food and water for them. When I opened the door, they dashed away. The next couple days proved they were just as feral as Mama, but that didn't stop me.

Every morning I put out food. Every evening too. Sometimes Mama showed up for a bite, but not always. Slowly but surely, I gained the trust of Fluff and Orange, who I intentionally didn't name so I wouldn't get attached. (Ask me if that worked.) After almost a year, I go out to feed them every morning and now, Fluff climbs into my lap for a nap and some cuddles. The best I ever got with Orange was some quick pets on the head while he ate, but he never seems to enjoy it the way his brother does.

I do love these cats with my whole heart and dream of bringing them inside the way Angela did, but I don't think they'd enjoy captivity. They are wild creatures, designed to roam. But…they will always have breakfast, dinner, and some love waiting for them on my porch if they need it.

Would you like more info on community cats and what to do if you come across them?

Click here or go to https://www.alleycat.org/resources/get-informed-discover-the-truth-about-feral-cats/

ACKNOWLEDGMENTS

Mr. Wonderful—Your love taught me how to breathe again. Thank you for supporting me on this crazy journey. I'm just gonna say "GRIDDLE TIME!!" and leave it at that.

Thank you to O, T, and C. You guys keep me laughing and looking forward to each new day. I love who you are and where you're going. So. Stinking. Proud. Thanks for loving me back.

Thank you to Linda, Nickiann, Stormi, Kieran, Elaine, Suzanne, and Cole. Your feedback and support were invaluable for this book. I appreciate all the time you spend in my worlds, with my characters, and with me. You guys are the BOMB.

And thank you to YOU, wonderful reader, for sticking with this story to the very end. I hope you enjoyed your stay in the Keys. They do look good on everyone. ;)
    Much love.

ABOUT THE AUTHOR

Abby Brooks writes contemporary romance about real people in relatable situations. With equal parts humor and heat, her books provide an emotional smorgasbord readers love. You'll laugh, cry, and cheer her characters on as they chase down their happily ever after.

Abby lives in Ohio with an amazing husband, three fabulous kids, and a stinker of a cat. In her spare time you'll find her messing around outside, dancing in the kitchen when she should be paying attention to cooking, and enjoying the company of her family.

For more books and updates:
abbybrooksfiction.com

facebook.com/abbybrooksauthor
instagram.com/xo_abbybrooks
tiktok.com/@abbybrooksauthor

Books by

ABBY BROOKS

THE HUTTON FAMILY SECOND GENERATION

Fate

WILDROSE LANDING

Fearless

Shameless

Reckless

THE HUTTON FAMILY

Beyond Words

Beyond Love

Beyond Now

Beyond Us

Beyond Dreams

It's Definitely Not You

The Hutton Family Series - Part 1

The Hutton Family Series - Part 2

A BROOKSIDE ROMANCE

Wounded

Inevitably You

This Is Why

Along Comes Trouble

Come Home To Me

A Brookside Romance - the Complete Series

WILDE BOYS WITH WILL WRIGHT

Taking What Is Mine

Claiming What Is Mine

Protecting What Is Mine

Defending What Is Mine

Wilde

THE MOORE FAMILY

Finding Bliss

Faking Bliss

Instant Bliss

Enemies-to-Bliss

THE LONDON SISTERS

Love Is Crazy (Dakota & Dominic)

Love Is Beautiful (Chelsea & Max)

Love Is Everything (Maya & Hudson)

The London Sisters - the Complete Series

IMMORTAL MEMORIES

Immortal Memories Part 1

Immortal Memories Part 2

AS WREN WILLIAMS

Bad, Bad Prince

Woodsman

Printed in Great Britain
by Amazon